FOLLOWS
with
INTENT

A HAZARDVERSE: SIDETRACKS NOVEL

GREGORY ASHE

H&B

Follows with Intent
Copyright © 2024 Gregory Ashe

Published by Hodgkin & Blount
https://www.hodgkinandblount.com/
contact@hodgkinandblount.com

Published 2024
Printed in the United States of America

Version 1.04

Trade Paperback ISBN: 978-1-63621-088-9
eBook ISBN: 978-1-63621-087-2

1

Nico

"You can drop me here," Nico said. For the fourth time.

Emery glanced out the driver-side window. Where the exit ramp merged onto Kingshighway Boulevard, a panhandler shuffled from vehicle to vehicle, carrying under one arm a crate lined with a plastic bag. He had his jeans belted below his ass, so two scrawny white cheeks poked out into the October sunlight, and the cardboard sign on a string around his neck said, VET – PLEASE HELP. A chicken poked her head up from inside the crate and glanced around, beady eyes jerking this way and that, and then bit the man. He didn't seem to notice.

"Nice try," Emery said, and then, to add insult to injury, he hit the automatic locks. Not because of the panhandler, Nico thought with dismay veering toward hysteria. To keep Nico from escaping.

"Honestly," Nico said. "You can—"

"If you say it again," Emery said, "I'm going to help you move into your dorm."

Nico managed to stop himself.

The light changed, and they drove on.

It was a beautiful October day: cool, crisp, the sunlight cut so clearly that it looked like a pane of glass. On their left, Forest Park was a mixture of harvest colors: the golden brown of prairie grass; the reds and golds of oak and maple; the slate of the creek's slow-moving waters. From living in the

Midwest all these years, Nico knew the fall could be a mixed bag—some years, the heat and humidity lingered until it was almost November, and others, the cool came quickly. And others, he thought drily, you got both, what they used to call an Indian summer. But today was perfect.

"You've got your laptop?"

"Oh shoot. Was I supposed to bring my laptop?"

Emery, of course, ignored that. "And your phone?"

"Only the one I've been playing on for the whole drive."

"What about chargers for all your devices?"

"What are chargers?"

"Keep being a smartass, Nico. I'd love to meet your dormmates."

Nico tried to imagine that. Bull-in-the-china-shop wasn't exactly right, because Emery wasn't a bull. But he could visualize, quite clearly, some degree of smashing.

"I'm sorry." They rode to the next stoplight in silence, and Nico added, "I'm nervous."

Emery grunted.

On their right, the massive complex of Barnes-Jewish Hospital slowly gave way to condo buildings, apartment buildings, and hotels. And then, in the distance, Nico spotted a limestone turret, and his heart began to beat a little faster. He began working his way through his mental list: he had his phone, he had his laptop, he had his chargers—

"What's so special about this conference, anyway?"

"Huh?"

"You've been to plenty of conferences before. They were never slumber parties. And you certainly never got nervous."

"I did, actually. I threw up. A lot."

Emery side-eyed him, and Nico recognized the look—he'd encountered it before, basically anytime someone knew he modeled (even if it was only occasionally) and heard the words *throw up*. It didn't help that

Emery was, especially for an ex-boyfriend turned friend turned boss, annoyingly perceptive.

"Not an eating disorder," Nico said. "Just nerves. And I don't need you worrying about me."

"You're too skinny."

Annoyingly perceptive, Nico amended, about some things.

"You've lost weight since we broke up."

"Because I was so devastated I couldn't eat."

"Hardy-har. You bought new clothes because the old ones don't fit anymore."

"It's a, special seminar," Nico said. "Some of the top scholars in the field are here. It's a mentorship opportunity. And a networking opportunity. And they publish an edited collection. And honestly, if I want to get into a PhD program and eventually get a job, this is a make-it-or-break-it opportunity."

What he didn't add was what he'd been thinking to himself more or less since he'd gotten the acceptance email: *to get someone to take me seriously as a scholar.*

"Why in the seven fucking hells would you do a PhD program in the humanities? Look at Theo. Look how well that turned out for him." Emery seemed to consider it for a moment. "Why don't you get a PhD in biology?"

"Oh, sure, get a PhD in biology."

"I didn't say it was easy. But at least it would be worthwhile."

"I don't know, I'm kind of busy right now. Maybe I'll get one next year."

Emery gave him a flat look.

Ahead, the campus of Chouteau College was taking shape. The old limestone buildings stood apart from more recent construction—in contrast to the towers of glass and steel, the campus, with its neogothic turrets and spires and leaded-glass windows, looked like a place outside of time. Part of that, Nico had to admit to himself, was the tangle of excitement and nerves in his gut. But part of it was the chilly sunlight, and part of it was the confetti of brightly colored leaves papering the old brick walkways, and part of it was how, when the wind moved the branches of the old trees, the shadows rippled, and it made him feel, only for a moment, like they were underwater.

"Do you have your wallet?"

"I don't carry a wallet. And you know that."

"I was hoping you'd come to your senses. Do you have your license?"

Nico waved his phone to display the cardholder attached to the back.

"Credit cards?"

"Ready to go and loaded with debt."

"They'd better not be after I spent three Saturdays in a row helping you consolidate—"

"It was a joke!"

Emery glowered at him. "Cash?"

"Nobody carries cash anymore."

"You should always have a couple hundred dollars in case of emergency."

"I've got Apple Pay, Em. I'll be fine."

"Textbook?"

"Believe it or not, nobody writes textbooks for seminars on Christian existentialism."

Emery thought about that. "They should. That seems like an untapped market."

The next stoplight flicked to red. The campus was cattycorner to them now, and on the sidewalk, a young woman in what Nico thought of as a pioneer-type dress (to the ankles, to the wrists, gingham, even a bonnet) had set up a makeshift plywood stall with a sign that said GOATMILK FOR SALE – NO FREE SAMPLES. Next to her, chomping on what appeared to be the college's expensive landscaping, was a goat.

"She'd better have a permit," Emery muttered. "And a pasteurizer." His gaze flicked to Nico, cool amber chips raking him up and down. "Did you pack warm clothes?"

Nico touched the corduroy shirt jacket, worn over a favorite Kumbia Queers t-shirt. "This is super warm."

"Real clothes, Nico."

"These are real clothes."

"Those jeans are riddled with holes."

"That's how kids wear them these days."

Emery snorted.

The light changed, and they drove on.

"Condoms?"

Nico choked on his spit.

"Do not make me ask again," Emery said.

"This is why I should have driven myself."

"You can't drive yourself because your car is in the shop because you refused to let me take it in for an oil change, and then you refused to let me put a reminder in your phone to have the oil changed, and then you refused to tell me how many miles you'd driven—"

"All right, all right. I know. It was my fault. I was irresponsible and immature, and I screwed up, and you're being so generous, and I totally appreciate it."

"You didn't answer my question."

"Oh my God."

"I'm going to take that as a yes."

"No, Em. I didn't pack condoms. Believe it or not, I don't go to prestigious seminars to hook up."

Emery looked at him.

Heat rose in Nico's face. "That was one time. And I shouldn't have told you."

"Then allow me to remind you," Emery said drily, "that on the off chance opportunity strikes—"

"It won't. This is important to me, Em. This is a big deal. And I'm not going to screw it up."

"Perhaps your goal should be not to screw anything. Not until I've completed the full vetting process."

Nico sank down in his seat. He reached over as unobtrusively as he could and tried the door handle. Still locked.

"We're still in the maintenance phase on Prowler," Emery said, reaching back to grab The Binder off the seat behind him. Nico could only think of it in capital letters now: The Binder, Emery's contribution (if that was the right word—single-minded mission might have been a better description) to get Nico happily paired up. It was approximately four inches thick, stuffed with printouts—articles and research and a surprisingly large number of photos of porn stars, which Emery had once, disastrously, used to try to figure out "Nico's type." They'd been sorted by body type and then by dick. There had been organizer tabs. "But," Emery continued, "it wouldn't hurt you to start thinking about how you want to tweak your Hinge profile. You liked that marathoner. His average mile time—"

"Okay," Nico said, yanking on the door handle again. "We're here."

Emery held out The Binder.

"Uh, you know, I'm going to be super busy."

Emery pushed The Binder at him. Well, pushed sounded like something a normal person would do. Emery pressed The Binder against Nico's body until Nico gave up and took up. "I want you to send me a list of the changes and a draft of the new profile. Maybe you should mention running; that can be your hobby."

Fortunately, the next turn took them onto the campus proper, and the next brought them to a stop directly in front of Harlow Hall. Like the rest of campus, it was an imposing limestone building with pointed windows and architectural elements that Nico guessed were supposed to suggest flying buttresses. A couple of boys—undergrads, clearly, with their flannel and beanies and, unmistakably, clove cigarettes—stood outside, but otherwise campus was empty. Fall break meant the perfect opportunity to hold the seminar on a beautiful campus without the inconvenience and distraction of, well, students.

Emery parked, and together, they got Nico's luggage from the back of the van. The flannel boys were laughing and talking to each other in low voices, and from the snatches Nico caught, they thought it was fucking hilarious that Emery was dropping Nico off.

With a glance at the suitcases, Emery said, "I could help you get everything upstairs." A smile teased the corner of his mouth. "I promise I won't embarrass you."

"I'll be fine, Em. Thank you again for the ride."

"Of course."

They shared an uneven beat of silence, and then they spoke at the same time.

"Be careful—" Emery said.

"Have a safe drive—" Nico began.

Nico laughed. Emery didn't, but Nico recognized the amusement in the cold autumn fire of his eyes.

He had barely made it halfway to Harlow when Emery called after him. "Did you remember clean underwear?"

The boys in flannel cracked up over that one.

Nico turned back, and at that distance, he honestly couldn't tell if Emery was giving him shit or, worse, this was a legitimate question. The boys in flannel were practically crying. One of them dropped his clove cigarette.

"I'm all set, Daddy," Nico called back, and it was worth it when one of the flannel boys actually fell over. Doubly worth it because of the unmistakable tightening of Emery's jaw. "Love you!"

2

Jadon

At shift change, the station was a madhouse—even in the relative isolation of the detectives' bureau. Phones rang. Officers shouted greetings or goodbyes as they passed each other in the hall, and as often, yelled updates in passing. "We had a pisser," one of them called out, with what sounded like glee. Schroeder, Jadon thought. That sounded like Schroeder. Another man groaned, and Schroeder added, "Have fun." A woman handcuffed to the desk in the corner was singing "Ave Maria," but, as she had explained to Vaughn, "the way a dinosaur would sing it." And she wasn't wrong, Jadon thought; it did kind of sound like how a dinosaur would sing it.

All sorts of well-meaning people in Jadon's life, he knew, would have pointed to this particular observation as further proof that he worked too much.

It was worse, of course, near Halloween. The crazies (to use a term that was strictly not department approved) came out en masse this week, and bad behavior tended to escalate in general. Even though the holiday itself wasn't until Saturday, the weekend before, Jadon had seen two slutty Taylor Swifts being dragged toward the holding cells, and a Tiger King had gotten into a fight with a Joker in the lobby. That kind of thing made it hard to get into the spirit of the season, although somebody had strung paper jack-o'-

lanterns around the doorframe, and spider webs made from black construction paper had been taped to the front of the detectives' desks.

Jadon scrubbed backwards on the video he was watching. When he reached the beginning, he let it play again. The footage was from an emergency call box on the campus of Chouteau College. As a result, it wasn't exactly the best quality—colors washed out by the low light, the resolution grainy. On screen, a young man in nothing but a silver jock and fairy wings followed one of the campus's many brick footpaths. Another night, this would have been occasion for nothing more than a chat about public indecency and the fact that you couldn't let your ass hang in the wind, even if you were going to a Halloween party.

The young man—Dalary Lang, a freshman who hadn't declared a major but had been thinking about theater studies, who had sobbed uncontrollably when Jadon had taken his statement in a hospital cubicle, and who had texted Jadon the day before to tell him that he was withdrawing from college and going back to Perryville (population 8,500, if you added in the cows) to be with his parents—passed the call box without even looking at it. He'd almost reached the edge of the screen when another figure appeared. This one was a man, but the only reason Jadon knew that was because of the victim's statement. On camera, he was dressed all in black, a hood up to conceal his face. The clothes were baggy, making it difficult to determine his build, but Jadon pegged him at around the same height as Lang, the victim. Then he corrected himself: the most recent victim. Because, if Jadon was right, this suspect was responsible for a string of assaults on campus.

On screen, Jadon watched as the man followed the path, staying a few dozen yards behind Lang. He looked for anything that might give the man away—a hint of jewelry, a glimpse of a tattoo. But, as with the previous ten times Jadon had watched the video, he saw nothing. The closest he came to something identifying was the man's gait. Shoulders back, posture straight, even stride. The suspect wasn't afraid; far from it. It told Jadon a couple of things. This wasn't the suspect's first time; there was none of the nervousness or uncertainty that might have suggested inexperience. It was also likely that the suspect was, in the real world, someone who was confident, successful, perhaps in a position of power. Likely was the key word, though—some men turned to assault to live out the power fantasies that went unfulfilled in their daily lives.

A hand appeared above Jadon's screen and moved down, as though about to close the laptop.

With an annoyed noise, Jadon waved the hand away and, to be safe, pulled the laptop out of reach.

"Give it a rest."

Cerise Cao was thin, with old acne scars and a too-tight ponytail. She was also a grade-A chef, kept a box of Trivial Pursuit questions from the '80s in her desk drawer, and had a disgustingly wholesome relationship with her boyfriend, Dhanvin. Which meant Jadon was, as her partner, regularly supplied with "leftovers" that, he was told, he'd be doing her a favor if he'd eat them, and he was bombarded with questions like *How many feet are there in a fathom?* and *How long is "Camptown Racetrack"?* and *What's the only house in England that the Queen may not enter?* The House of Commons, it turned out. It meant Jadon faced an unending series of kind, generous, sincere invitations (many of them proffered by Dhan), and he knew he was a dick for turning them down.

She had been his first real partner since *then*. He didn't have a good word for *then*. It was *then*. Before. A flash of bad memories: Barr laughing, tobacco flakes caught in his teeth while winter sunlight lay on his neck like a hand; the hospital room, and the smell of his unwashed body and a powerful antiseptic; the night of cuts and burns and questions, the hours strung out like those paper jack-o'-lanterns, full of glowing eyes until finally the gunshot, darkness. But all of that was too much to put into words. He could say, *My partner betrayed me.* He could say, *I was a fucking idiot.* At night, in the last few minutes before exhaustion blanked everything out, he could admit, *It was my fault.* But he had learned to keep all of that in the box and call it *then*.

"I'm serious," Cerise said. "How many times have you watched that thing?"

"A couple."

"A couple dozen, maybe."

Leaning back in his seat, Jadon shrugged. "It's all we've got."

And that was true. The assault had happened a hundred feet past the call box, in an alcove formed by two of the old limestone buildings. Minimal struggle because Lang was barely more than a kid, because he'd been surprised, but mostly because he'd been hurt and disoriented by a blow to the head. No DNA had been collected. No one had heard Lang's screams, if he had screamed. That was one of the things that had made Lang sob—he didn't remember if he had screamed, and if he had, he hadn't been loud enough. Jadon had tried to tell him about the faculty party. About the music so loud it had resulted in a noise complaint. But Dalary Lang, like many victims, had blamed himself.

After, Lang dragged himself to the call box—the same one where they'd gotten the security camera footage, the same one he had passed not fifteen minutes before. But the suspect hadn't appeared on camera again—not on any of the cameras, not anywhere on campus, not anywhere in the Central West End, which was tony enough that just about everywhere had cameras. And that told Jadon something about the suspect too, just not enough to find him.

"And there's nothing there," Cerise said. Jadon opened his mouth, but she spoke over him. "You need to call it a night. You've watched it. I've watched it. Vaughn and Duke and Rios have watched it. If there were something there, one of us would have seen it."

Jadon nodded. "I know. You're right."

"Great. So, turn off your computer, and grab your jacket, and let's go." She looped a scarf around her neck—more seasonal affectation than necessity; it wasn't that cold outside—and directed a flat look at him. She didn't say *now*, but he heard it anyway.

"I'm going to finish up some paperwork."

"Jadon."

"Twenty minutes. Half an hour, tops."

Struggle showed in her face. She must have lost whatever battle she was fighting, though, because the words came spilling out. "And then?"

"What?"

"What are you going to do when you finish?" Her tone turned scornful when she added, "In twenty or thirty minutes."

Jadon rocked back in the chair. Inside the detectives' bureau, the temperature simmered from too many bodies and an old boiler. They'd cracked a window (that was, per regulation, supposed to be sealed shut), and drafts of cold air limped into the building, an occasional whisper on the back of Jadon's neck. We should get a fan, he thought. A fan would help.

"Are you going to hit the gym," Cerise asked, "for the second time today? Or do you have a Brazilian jiujitsu class? Let me guess: you're going to go home and stare at a blank wall for six hours and shower and get here before anybody else."

He had a headache, he realized, and he wondered how long that had been going on. A while, he thought. It was one of those things, like the full-body aches, that became background noise eventually. His eyes felt gummy, and he rubbed one now. He couldn't quite bring himself to look Cerise in the face.

"I'm sorry," she said.

"No."

"That was super shitty."

"No, I get it."

Cerise sighed. She looked him over, and then she said, "Jay, people are starting to talk." And then she must have heard it and she said, like she was editing, "People are worried."

"I'm fine."

"Are you? Because it's okay if you're not."

He cracked a smile. "I'm fine, Cao. Scout's honor."

"When was the last time you went out with friends? Or slowed down long enough for a real meal? Or—"

He made a warning noise.

As usual, Cerise ignored it. "—went on a date?"

"I appreciate this. I do. But I'm good. And you can tell all these other people who are worried about me that I'm good. Okay?"

The sound of traffic filtered in through the open window.

"Come to Halloween."

"Oh God."

"Dhan is begging you. Well, technically, he's begging me."

"That's nice—"

"And you're not the one who has to come up with excuses all the time. He's starting to think you don't like him."

Jadon gave her a level look. "That's a low blow."

But, as usual, Cerise was unfazed. "You're hurting his feelings."

"Cheap. That's real cheap."

"So, I'll see you there?"

Helpless, Jadon stared at her.

"Don't come as a cop," she told him. "It's tacky."

"I don't have time to come up with a costume."

"You're spending three days at a glorified sensitivity training. You're going to be bored out of your mind. Be a real person for once and sit there and pretend to listen while you shop online."

He opened his mouth to object to the *real person* comment, and then the rest of the words hit him. He glanced at the calendar. He forgot what he'd been about to say.

Three days.

Three goddamn days at a symposium he'd been ordered to attend. For LGBTQ+ law enforcement officers. Even though he'd objected. And explained how much work he had to do. And, in the end, pleaded.

"You forgot?" Cerise said.

"I can't spend three days at a training. Shit, Cerise, I've got—" He gestured at the stacks of folders. "How the hell am I supposed to take three days off from this?"

"Believe it or not, Jay, people find a way."

"We're ten days behind on the Lang kid, and we still don't have anything. The trail is going to be ice after three more days; what am I going to turn up then?"

"What are you going to turn up if you don't? We worked that case the way we were supposed to. We didn't get any hits. It's not magic, you know. Pounding our heads against a wall isn't going to change anything." She softened her voice. "I'm sorry for that boy. You know I am. But Jay, you've got to think about yourself for change."

"He withdrew from school. He went back to fucking Perryville!"

The woman dinosaur-singing "Ave Maria" broke off to stare at them.

Jadon mumbled, "Sorry—"

But Cerise bent over her desk and spoke in a low voice. "Jadon, listen to me. You need to get your head on straight. And you need to do it fast. Two days ago, the captain hauled me into her office and asked me if you were having personal problems. I said no, and the captain started pressing. Was everything okay with Detective Reck? Had I noticed anything unusual? The whole thing like we were one big happy family, like she was so worried about you. When I kept saying you were fine, the questions got more specific. Were you sleeping at the station? Were you sleeping in your car? How was your mental health?"

For a moment, the words didn't make any sense. "What are you—" The headache throbbed, and it was like a noise, swallowing up everything else. "Why didn't you tell me?"

"I'm telling you now. Ever since Barr, you've been a black mark for the department. I'm sorry. That's bullshit, and it's not fair to you, and it's not how it should be. But it's the truth. I'm telling you, the questions the captain was asking—and the fact that she was the one asking them, and not trying too hard to hide what she was doing—that's a bad sign. They're done waiting for you to self-destruct, Jay. They want you out, and if that means making a case that you're not fit for duty, that's what they're going to do." She swallowed and stood straight again. "And that's why you're going to go to this stupid symposium, and you're going to use the next few days to pull your life together, and you're going to make sure these assholes don't have a single thing they can use against you. Understand?"

Jadon nodded, but it felt like someone else was doing it. The draft was cold on his neck.

"Please, Jay," Cerise said. And then, with an effort at good cheer, she added, "See you on Halloween."

3

Nico

Nico was willing to admit the glasses might have been a bit much. He checked himself in the mirror, though. Decided to keep them. Fixed a stray lock of hair. Carefully mussed another. The slim button-up. The unadorned cardigan. Plain navy trousers that even Emery would have been proud of (or, at least, satisfied with). He looked like a responsible, respectable grad student.

You look like a nerd, said a voice remarkably like Marco's. Show them tiddies!

True, he did look a little...basic. A little...boring, maybe. The glasses swallowed up his whole face. For a moment, his hand hovered over his placket, as he considered the fourth outfit change of the day. And then Nico stopped. He would not show them tiddies, not when he was busy building a career for himself. He double-checked the buttons to be sure. He took an extra moment to pick yesterday's clothes up from the floor (he'd been working on that, among other things), and promised himself, next time, he wouldn't leave them on the floor at all.

By the time he got out of Harlow Hall, it was after eight, which meant he ran across campus. The morning was bright, the sky clear, ivy flaming across the old limestone walls. His breath clouded in the frosty morning air and caught the light and blazed white. Emery might have been on to something; the cardigan definitely wasn't heavy enough for this morning.

With fall break in full swing, the campus was quieter than it ought to have been. Nico passed an old white guy bundled up in a parka, his bald head gleaming and then snuffing out as he walked a little terrier from sunlight to shadow to sunlight again. A wiry Indian grad student jogged past Nico in the opposite direction and gave him double thumbs up. A pair of thirtysomething women in business casual emerged from the student union building, one of them laughing so hard she had to hang on to the door to stay upright while the other simultaneously laughed with her and tried to shush her. Professional, Nico thought, and he adjusted his glasses as he slipped through the still-open door and into the union.

Waverley Center was warm, thank God, and like the rest of campus, it had a kind of dark-timbered, iron-fixtured gravity that made it hard to imagine undergrads filling the space. The warmth fogged his glasses for the first few seconds—that was new—and Nico wiped them on his cardigan as he did a quick scan.

"Can I help you, sir?"

The voice belonged to a Hispanic guy who, in spite of the lingering baby fat in his face, was a certified hunk of meat in a security guard's uniform. His hair was buzzed, his mouth hard in a way that made you think things, and his tawny eyes were frank and assessing. Right then, they were assessing Nico, and Nico had been on that end of the camera long enough to have an idea what this guy—whose name tag said Heeley—was thinking.

And that was most definitely, most certainly, not why Nico had come to this seminar.

"I'm good," Nico said. He held up the glasses, as though that explained anything.

Heeley's hard mouth cracked at one corner—not a smile, but something even more interesting. Tawny eyes flicked up and down. "Can I help you find something?"

Well, Nico thought, if that wasn't an opening, he didn't know one.

"I'm good," Nico said again. He strode off into the union, pretending he hadn't seen the way the corner of Heeley's mouth twitched, pretending he couldn't feel Heeley's eyes following him.

It didn't take him long to find what he was looking for — the stream of people, more than he would have expected during the campus's fall break, led him straight to the coffee shop. A long room, complete with vaulted ceiling and oil paintings, more in line with a *Harry Potter*-style banquet hall than anything else, served as a coffee shop, and it was surprisingly busy. Nico got in line behind a muscularly built man, put his glasses back on, and scanned the menu.

His basic bitch mode activated almost immediately: pumpkin medley latte.

They couldn't call it a pumpkin spice latte. Or maybe they didn't want to. It was one way to be different from all the bougie white ladies with their seasonal Starbucks cups. But they could call it whatever they wanted; it didn't make any difference to Nico.

More men queued behind Nico. Big guys. Muscular. And then a single Latina who Nico would have bet his left nut was a lesbian. Something ticked in the back of his head. He gave the room another long look. A lot of beefy guys in polos and khakis—business white dude's equivalent of an invisibility cloak. Not much talking. Even the ones sitting in pairs were looking at their phones. But Nico had spent enough time around cops — around one cop in particular — to recognize the breed.

When he turned back, the man in front of him was holding a boxed cinnamon roll, studying it. Then he looked at Nico. He was shorter than Nico, his skin a deep brown, and he had strong features set in a wide face — a wide nose, a wide mouth, a wide jaw. He had to be a cop too, and the way he held himself, the thick hands, the strong fingers, gave him an unexpected air of roughness, somewhere on the scale between boyish and thuggish.

Then he smiled, revealing the deep tear troughs under his eyes, and Nico inched him toward boyish. Trouble, but definitely boyish.

"This is way too big for one person," he said, displaying the cinnamon roll.

Nico made a noncommittal noise.

The man's smile got bigger. "Okay, that was weak."

Nico raised his eyebrows.

"How's your morning going?" the man asked.

"How's my morning going?"

It only made his smile get bigger. "Come on, that was polite."

"The line is moving."

The man shuffled backward, still keeping an eye on Nico. "You're not going to make this easy on me, are you?"

"You're definitely not making it easy on yourself."

"Vic," he said and held out his hand.

"Hello, Vic," Nico said. "It's your turn to order."

Vic gave him a final, appraising look. Then his grin flashed to a hundred. "Could I buy you a coffee?"

"No, thank you."

"Sir?" the barista asked.

Vic shrugged. "Can't blame me for trying. Have a nice day."

He ordered, and then he moved down to the pickup area with a parting wave for Nico. Nico placed his order next (ignoring the face the barista made when he asked for the latte at kid temp). He snuck a look at Vic, who was playing on his phone now. He was a nice-looking guy. More attractive than handsome, but confident and polite. He'd taken the losses with good humor. Hell, he'd wanted to split a cinnamon roll, and most of the guys interested in Nico thought he should be living on air and water to keep himself thin. Would it be so bad to have coffee with a guy who was interested in him? Maybe—just maybe—to share a few bites of the cinnamon roll?

Yes, Nico decided. It would. Because the minute Nico let his guard down, Dr. Chapman would appear, or Dr. Young, or Dr. Meza, and they'd see him flirting and hanging out and wasting seminar time, and that would be the end of it.

He waited until Vic had collected his coffee before moving down to the pickup area.

By the time he got his pumpkin medley latte, it was almost eight-thirty. Nico hurried toward the exit. The security guard, Heeley, caught his eye. That was all, a look, but it was the kind you felt in your belly, and Nico had a hard time dragging his gaze away.

Which was why he didn't see the man barreling through the doors until it was too late.

They crashed into each other. The paper coffee cup collapsed in Nico's grip. Pumpkin medley latte (kid temp) fountained out. And then Nico's head cracked against the other man's, and they both went down.

He was still sorting himself when a familiar voice said, "Oh my God, I'm so sorry—Nico?"

Nico stared at the vaulted ceiling above him. Because maybe some sexual ley line had gotten crossed. Maybe a horny ghost was determined to mess up his life. Because this was, apparently, the theology seminar of potential hook-ups.

Including Detective Jadon Reck.

Jadon squatted next to Nico, peering down at him. As usual, he looked...well, perfect. Even in autumn, his coloring made Nico think of the beach: darkly sandy hair, darker eyebrows, even darker eyes. His white dress shirt, dripping with coffee, clung to his sculpted chest. It was, admittedly, a look. It didn't seem fair that a detective should be handsome to the point of having perfect nipples.

"Are you okay?" Jadon reached down, hesitated, and then touched Nico's head. Nico flinched. "You've got a goose egg," Jadon told him with a small smile. He rubbed above his hairline. "I think I've got one to match."

With Jadon's help, Nico got to his feet. He did a quick check and was amazed to find that, aside from a few drops of coffee spattered on his button-up, he was unscathed—it would be easy enough to button the cardigan and hide the stains. Jadon, on the other hand, had taken the brunt of the coffee. Following Nico's gaze, he plucked at the shirt and said, "It's totally fine."

"Jadon, oh my God."

"It's fine, I promise."

"I ruined your shirt."

"I didn't even like this shirt. I hated the tag. You did me a favor."

"You can cut out a tag, Jay. You'll never get the coffee out of this."

"Sir." Heeley stepped into Nico's peripheral vision. He didn't look happy. "Are you all right? Should I call an ambulance?"

Jadon gave him a quick look and said, "We're good here."

Heeley didn't like that; Nico could see it in his face. "Maybe you should sit down, sir."

"I'm okay." Nico even managed a smile. "Thanks."

"I think—"

"Why don't you radio for a cleanup?" Jadon said, nodding at the coffee. "You don't want somebody to slip."

Heeley's jaw tightened at that, but after another long look at Nico, he stepped back and reached for his radio. Jadon guided Nico away from the spill. The feel of his hand on Nico's arm—warm, solid, strong—shook Nico out of his daze.

This was Jadon.

Jadon was here.

And then it all came rushing back: that first, chance meeting at North and Shaw's house; the first, awkward conversation; the way Jadon had looked in shorts and a tee—the lines of his arms, the muscled thighs, the way he spread his legs, his large, powerful body sprawled and at ease. And then months of texting, the short, flirty messages building into something more, the things Nico never said to anyone, the things, he thought, Jadon might not say to anyone else.

And then it had stopped.

No explanation. No answer. Nico's final text left hanging there.

And Nico refused to make a fool out of himself.

He pulled his arm away from Jadon.

Jadon let his hand drop as though it had been his idea; he might not have even noticed because all his attention seemed to be on Nico as he asked, "What are you doing here?" And then, his voice dropping, "Are you in disguise?"

"Am I in disguise?"

Nico had to admit, as he heard himself, that his tone might have slipped a bit.

Some microcalculation took place on Jadon's face, and he said, "Sorry, I—" Then he grinned, and it was like someone had flipped a switch, because he looked relaxed and — well, if Nico weren't a total idiot, happy to see him. "What are you doing here?" And then, "I didn't know you wore glasses."

"I don't, usually," Nico said. Which was, technically, the truth. But he took the glasses off, folded them, and tucked them into a pocket of the cardigan. "And I'm here for a seminar."

"You are?"

Nico stood a little straighter. "Believe it or not, Jadon, yes. I actually do go to seminars. They even let me present papers once in a while."

"Uh, okay. I mean, I thought it was more of a police thing, but that's great that they're letting private investigators attend too."

Nico stared at him.

"What?" Jadon finally asked.

"What are you talking about?"

"What are you talking about?"

"I'm talking about the theology seminar I'm attending this week. Here. At Chouteau College."

Jadon's smile grew. "Ah. I thought—there's a symposium for LGBTQ law enforcement professionals. Well, you don't have to be gay, but a lot of the attendees are."

"That explains the sexual ley line," Nico said under his breath.

"What?"

"Nothing."

A group of men passed, suspending their conversation as they stared at Nico and Jadon—particularly at Jadon, in his coffee-soaked clothes.

"It's not a fucking strip show," Nico snapped. "Put your eyes back in your fucking heads."

The men—more of the burly, police types—exchanged startled looks and walked a bit faster toward the exit.

When Nico turned back to Jadon, he was smiling.

"You're here all week?" Jadon asked. "Why didn't you tell me?"

"Figured you were busy, like always."

Jadon's smile dropped.

"Don't worry," Nico added, "I won't hold you to your promise."

"Hold on—"

At that moment, Maya passed them. Nico called her name, and when she turned around, he jogged to catch up.

4

Nico

"No," Nico said. "No, no, no, no, no."

"But why not?"

It was a typical Maya question: smart, logical, ruthlessly practical. As they approached Eldridge Hall, where the seminar was being held, she checked her sectioned Afro in the door's glass. Then she looked at Nico.

"Because he's a cop."

Maya didn't snort, but the cool non-response sounded like one anyway.

"And I don't date cops. Not anymore."

"Not after big, bad, and brooding, you mean."

"Not after Emery. Exactly."

"That's not a reason. Why not?"

Nico scowled and yanked the door open for her. They'd been friends since their first year in grad school together, and while Maya had, since then, finished her master's degree and started a Ph.D. program at Notre Dame, they'd stayed close. It helped that their overlapping research interests brought them together—there weren't that many people working on Christian existentialism.

The downside was that she'd known Nico long enough to have seen some of his less desirable phases. And, of course, that she could call him on his bullshit.

"Because," Nico said, lowering his voice as he followed her inside, "I'm busy. Did you think about that?"

"Oh my God."

They followed the hall, checking room numbers as they went. Like the rest of the campus, the old neogothic building was chilly even with the heat (theoretically) on, and their steps rang out on the ancient flagstone floor. It even smelled cold, if that was a thing—which Nico was pretty sure it was.

"I'm serious. I've got to finish this degree; I can't keep dicking around forever."

"He said."

"Excuse me?"

"Nothing." She offered a saccharine smile. "Go on."

"I've got to finish my paper for the seminar."

That stopped her.

"I mean—" Nico tried.

"You haven't finished your paper?"

"I wrote—"

"For this seminar? The one that we're at? Right now?"

"See—"

"Where you're going to have a chance to submit said paper to be included in a collection edited by some of the top scholars in our field?"

"Yes, but—"

"But only, Nicolás, after you present said paper in seminar and have it ruthlessly ripped to shreds. In a loving and constructive way. That paper?"

Nico's shoulders sagged. "Yeah, that paper."

"You're self-sabotaging. That's always been the problem." And she whirled away.

"I'm not self-sabotaging," Nico said as he trailed after her. "I'm almost done. It's, like, ninety percent done. Ninety-five. And it's good. I mean, I know it's still going to get ripped apart, but it's good, Maya."

"He's an adult," Maya said when Nico caught up to her.

Nico groaned.

"He wears real clothes, and he's got a real job."

"We're not doing this."

"He's not a barista. He's not a server. He's not a bartender."

"Those are real jobs. It's classist of you to say those aren't real jobs." Maya shot him a look, and Nico raised his hands in surrender. "I'm saying the guys I've gone out with—"

"Exclusively, Nico. You exclusively go out with guys like that. Because at the beginning, they're easy, and they're uncomplicated, and they want to fool around, and their lives aren't going anywhere. I know those are real jobs, Nico. But it's not a real job when Chase's life plan is to 'open his own gay bar' when his dad still does his taxes and he spends all his tips on clothes, and it's not a real job when Marcus wants to get high and go out and has nothing lined up on the horizon. This guy is gorgeous—"

"He's not that handsome."

"I saw him, Nicolás, with my own two eyes. In the coffee equivalent of a wet T-shirt contest. And he's totally into you."

"He's not—"

"Did you see how he was looking at you? Because I did. It was like a puppy that got hit in the head."

"Actually, we did hit our heads—"

She stopped at the door they'd been looking for. "What are the red flags? What am I missing?"

"He ghosted me. Stopped texting me, totally. Out of the blue, Maya. I mean, things were going, or I thought they were, and then...nothing."

Maya's face softened for a moment. Then it hardened again. "Did you ask him why?"

Nico felt his jaw go weak. "Why should I—"

"You are unbelievable," she said and pushed into the room.

The classroom that had been given over for the seminar was large, with desks rising in tiers toward leaded glass windows at the back. Cloud-colored light traced the patterns of the cames on the worn carpet squares. A Bunn coffee urn sat on a cart near the door, and Nico caught an acrid whiff as he passed it.

Three other grad students were already there, and because Nico had seen their emails and stalked them, he recognized each of them. Ridson was Black, with an oval face and his hair in short twists. Kaylee was white, her chestnut hair in a long side part, her eyes and mouth quick and expressive. Giovanni (Gio, who posted almost exclusively videos of himself doing yoga in nothing but a pair of tiny bike shorts) looked like Daniel Radcliffe meets Frankenstein. (A voice that sounded a little too much like Emery's corrected, *Frankenstein's monster*). Skinny, with glasses, his complexion the color of ceiling paint, he'd sent everyone an email inviting them to read "my latest piece in the *New Yorker*" before the seminar. Nico, channeling earth-shattering levels of pettiness, had checked—*latest piece*, it turned out, was only technically correct because it was also Gio's only piece.

After murmured hellos, Maya continued in a whisper, "You are going to talk to him, Nico."

"Will you knock it off? He's cute, fine. He's obviously not into me—"

Maya gave him laser eyes.

Nico stammered through the rest of it. "—and I've got to focus. I need to make a good impression, okay? I need to get into a doctoral program. I need publications, and letters of rec, and, you know, a reputation. I don't need a random hookup."

"Oh," a familiar voice said. "Hookups. Nico, do tell."

"What," he managed in a strangled whisper, "the fuck is going on? Is this the fucking ghosts of hookups past?"

Maya smiled, even though she was clearly trying to look sympathetic. Then she said, "Hi, Clark."

Nico forced himself to turn around. Clark Beaumont was white-bread money: movie-star hair, A-lister scruff, and he wore cardigans the way God had intended. He wasn't handsome, not really, but he had an appeal. Nico remembered, his face heating, that the little cleft in Clark's chin was eminently kissable.

"Why are you here?"

A tiny smile darted across Clark's face as he sat at the desk with Nico and Maya. "Hello, Nicolás. Good to see you too. I thought maybe you'd be doing a shoot."

Nico glanced around to see if anyone had heard, but no one seemed to be paying attention. He stared daggers at Clark.

"Oops," he said.

"You weren't on the email chain. I would have seen your name."

"I found out about the seminar late." The smile was more of a smirk now. "Thank God Dr. Perry and Dr. Meza are friends. I would have hated to miss out on this opportunity."

Branches scraped the leaded glass window. The silence in the room—particularly from the other three students—had dialed in on Clark.

"You mean you didn't even apply?" Maya asked.

"I found out too late," Clark said. Nico remembered that too-smooth tone. "I would have applied, of course, if I'd known."

Across the room, Kaylee blurted, "That's so unfair."

Ridson shook his head.

"It's the way the world works," Gio said. "I didn't know anyone at the *New Yorker* when I submitted my latest piece—"

"Was that Karl Jaspers thing yours?" Clark said. "That was cute."

Say one thing for Clark Beaumont, Nico thought. He's good at putting people in their place.

While Gio apparently died a slow death by humiliation, Clark turned back to Nico and Maya. He set his hand on the back of Nico's chair—just casual enough that it could be taken for friendliness, but the way his thumb traced Nico's shoulder blade, anything but. "Don't tell me you're fucking him, please. I've seen his videos; you can do better."

"Not that it's any of your business—" Nico began.

There was the smirk again. The spark of suggestion in Clark's blue eyes. His thumb moved again, millimeters, and Nico remembered what it had felt like when Clark had bit down on his collarbone.

"—but no. I was telling Maya that I don't think it's smart or appropriate or professional to do that kind of thing at conferences." And he added a long, warning look for Clark.

"I don't think that's necessarily true," Clark said. "Obviously you should be circumspect. But what you do on your own time, well, it's your business. Personally, I think conferences are great opportunities to meet people. I mean, we're all so specialized, and we're in this intellectual hothouse, and how often do we get to spend time around people who share our interests—" His thumb scritched at Nico's shoulder blade again. The corner of his mouth quirked. "—and passions?"

"And how much do you want to be labeled," Maya asked drily, "in not so many words, as a poser fuckboy who's wasting everyone's time?"

"I'm not saying—"

"I know what you're saying. And did you ever think about the fact that there are a lot of double standards in place? It's fine for a straight white man. It's probably even fine for a gay white man. But if you're a person of color? Or if you're a woman? All you're doing is throwing fuel on the fire that a lot of these bigots already have burning. You're speaking from a position of privilege, and you don't even know it."

A hint of color came into Clark's cheeks. He shifted in his seat, his body squared up with Maya's now. "Nothing's going to change if we all keep pretending things are okay and do whatever they expect us to do. There's nothing wrong with meeting someone at a professional event and, at an appropriate time, pursuing that relationship. We should be pushing back on anyone who says otherwise."

"Great point, Clark," Nico said. "That'll be my subversive agenda: get plowed at every possible work event."

"Excuse me?"

The voice belonged to an old man with dandelion-fluff hair. Nico recognized, from his publicity photos, Dr. Chapman. Behind him was Dr. Young, dressed in a butterfly-patterned muumuu, and Dr. Meza, fiftyish and practically throbbing with silver fox energy. Meza gave Nico a tiny, crooked smile before he rolled his eyes.

"I'm sorry—" Nico stammered. "We were—I was—"

"I don't believe," Dr. Chapman piped as he moved into the room, "I should have to explain to a roomful of rising scholars the kind of behavior— and discourse—that's appropriate for serious professionals."

5

Jadon

"Unh-uh," Jadon said. "Nope. No way."

"Because you're intimidated by him," Allison said.

Vic shook his head. "Because he's scared."

"Fuck you," Jadon said. "And fuck you. Respectfully."

Allison laughed. Vic shook his head again, grinning.

The buzz of conversation filled the multipurpose room in the student union as they waited for the symposium to begin. Unlike the rest of the campus, with its turrets and buttresses and age-dark limestone, this space looked like it had been lifted out of an office supply catalogue: rows of laminate-top tables and plastic chairs that could be stored when they weren't in use; a drop ceiling with fluorescent panels; blandly patterned carpet squares. Hints of the old design still showed in the windows and the mahogany trim. Jadon could hear the slightly accelerated rumble of his own heartbeat. He felt like everything had slowed down, or he'd sped up. Hyperaware—of Vic's knee bumping his, the sound of a chair being dragged across the carpet, the smell of a woman's perfume, summery, melon-y, out of season. The morning's light was the color of eggshells, and he wondered why he'd never seen light that beautiful before.

Vic leaned in and whispered, "Reck, that kid is some grade-A pussy. I saw that tight little ass."

"Vic!" Allison said.

Shrugging, Vic added in a slightly louder voice, "I'm serious: that thing would choke the life out of your dick."

"Don't talk about him like that," Jadon said.

Vic smirked and spread his hands.

"Actually," Jadon said, "don't talk about anyone like that."

"It's a compliment—"

"It's not a compliment. It's objectifying, and it's sexist, and it's inappropriate. Especially for a law enforcement officer. And especially in a professional setting. And especially when you're here because you run your mouth when you shouldn't, and you're talking to two people on the LGBTQ task force."

A flush rose, only barely visible under Vic's brown skin. The tear troughs under his eyes deepened. He sat back, hands up again, and said, "What crawled up your ass?"

"Just say you're sorry, Vic," Allison said.

"I'm sorry, Jesus Christ."

Jadon held Vic's gaze for a moment longer and then turned his gaze forward again. It was bad enough to be here, forced to sit and listen while self-proclaimed experts (experts on what, Jadon wasn't exactly sure—being a gay cop, maybe?) yammered and yakked and went on and on for days, while the Lang case, and a dozen other cases, slipped out from under him. It was worse, though, that he had to do it with Vic Serrano sitting next to him. Vic wasn't exactly a bad type, but he was an unrepentant asshole (as his most recent comment proved) whose career had stalled at detective and whose frustration was always finding new outlets. He'd been sent to the symposium, apparently for sensitivity training, after informing half of patrol that Captain Weaver had only made rank because he was a cocksucker and, on top of that, a citizen complaint that had suggested, without using the word, harassment. Jadon figured Vic's biggest complaint about being sent for sensitivity training was that it was fucking up all his free time during his suspension.

Out of the corner of his eye, he caught Allison's questioning look and gave back a tiny shake of his head in answer.

Vic shifted around in his seat a few times and finally said, "Well?"

"Well what?"

"Why aren't you going to hit that?"

"Do you want to try that again?"

"Climb off the stick, Reck. I said I was sorry. He's here. He couldn't peel his eyes off you." Vic smirked and gave Jadon's new ensemble — Chouteau College sweats, fresh from the campus bookstore — a once over. "And you two have a vibe."

"We've got a vibe?"

Allison nodded. "There's definitely chemistry."

"Who are you trying to help here?"

"Vic might be a dumpster-mouthed asshole of a savage —"

"Thank you," Vic said.

" — but he's not wrong. And you still haven't answered his question: why not?"

"How about he's out of my league?"

Allison rolled her eyes.

Vic's voice softened. "Aww, Reck, buddy, you're hot stuff." He cupped himself. "I'd let you swing on my knob anytime."

"How about you fuck off for five minutes, Vic?" Allison gestured toward the doors. "Why don't you find a traffic cone to hump or something?"

"I'm going to get a coffee," Vic said, giving himself a final jiggle. As he left, he added, "It's to drink, Reck, not to wear, so don't get excited."

Jadon watched him go and shook his head. "That's a walking case of sexual harassment."

"Are you going to report him?"

"Are you kidding? He'd probably molest the HR person."

With a quiet laugh, Allison shook her short bob of wavy blond hair. She was one of those women who were cursed to be both good at their jobs and unwilling to put up with bullshit, which meant that instead of being a lieutenant or even a sergeant, she was still a detective. She'd told him over too many margaritas, once, about the time she'd punched a drone from the Public Information Division who'd told her she was too pretty to waste on patrol.

For a few moments, the hum of background conversations filled the air between them. Then Jadon said, "I need to stay focused right now."

Allison nodded.

"I've got a lot on my plate. The captain is gunning for me, I found out, and I've got these campus assaults going on that nobody seems to care about except me—"

"Which is why you're here," Allison said, "which is why you're—how did Cerise put it? Getting your shit together. Right? Because you're not going to give that fuck-off any more ammunition."

"—and it's not a good time for me. I can't afford to get distracted."

He didn't say *again*. But Allison knew; everybody knew. He'd met Shaw Aldrich, and he'd been head over heels. He'd been in love, actually. And that meant he'd had his head in the clouds. That was why Barr was able to get away with what he did—the kidnappings, the torture, the killings. And that was why Jadon hadn't had any idea what his partner was up to, not until it was too late.

Allison made a soft noise. "Jay, I get it, but—"

She cut herself off, and Jadon made a gimme gesture. "But?"

"I don't know. Did you ever think that maybe—just maybe—you need to blow off some steam?"

"I'm sorry, are you telling me I need to get laid?"

"Well, you do." Allison's laugh had a trace of defensiveness, but it was still a laugh. "You've been running yourself into the ground; everybody can see it. You're not taking care of yourself. You're—" She stopped again.

"Falling apart?"

"Not happy. And you deserve to be happy."

They'd put a bag over his head; he remembered that. Even when they'd used knives, even when they'd used jumper cables, the real fear had been the crinkling plastic. Every time he tried to take a breath, the plastic had sealed itself around his mouth and nose. He still dreamed about it.

"Yeah," he said. "Well." And then, still trying to shake off the memory, too late he heard himself say, "Nico's such a great guy. He's not a hookup. And that's why I stopped texting him—"

Horror frosted Allison's voice. "You ghosted him?"

"I didn't ghost him. I just stopped texting him. Without any warning. Oh my God, I ghosted him. Okay, in my defense, he ghosted me too. I mean, it's not like he tried to keep texting me."

"Because you ghosted him! You can't mutually ghost each other, Jadon."

"I didn't mean to ghost him. I...got busy."

Allison reared back, studying him like she'd discovered a new kind of bug. "You're an asshat," she informed him.

"It's not like I—"

"No, you are an asshat. And you're taking him to dinner."

"He doesn't want to go to dinner with me."

"Oh please. Vic was right, you know. He about licked your shirt off you. And he does have a cute butt."

"Would you keep it down, please?" Jadon glanced around, an automatic check to see if anyone was listening. Then he hesitated. Near the door to the multipurpose room, a man in a security guard's uniform slouched against the wall. Jadon pegged him at early twenties, maybe even younger, but he had a man's body, hard and developed and packed into that navy uniform, with an uncompromising line of a mouth. For a moment, their gazes met. The guard pushed off from the wall, his movements casual as he let himself out of the room. But a little too fast. And a little too soon after he'd noticed Jadon watching him.

"What?" Allison asked, craning her head. "Something wrong?"

"No. I don't think so."

"Is this one of those tricks to make me forget what we were talking about? Because it's not going to work. At a bare minimum, you owe him an apology. Especially if you want a second chance."

Jadon pulled his gaze back to Allison. "I don't want a second chance. Haven't you been listening?"

"Yeah, I've been listening. You're being a pussy."

"We're literally at a sensitivity training. You realize this is why they sent you and Vic here, right?"

"Here are the facts: you need to pull your life together, fast. You need to get laid, fast. And you've got this total babe practically melting every time you look at him. Plus, you need to apologize for being an asshat."

"This is why they sent you to sensitivity training. You get that, right? You're a bully. This is emotional abuse."

"It's dinner, Jay," Allison said as a woman stepped up to the microphone. She turned forward with a tiny smirk. "You have to eat sometime. It might as well be with a guy whose ass can strangle your dick."

6

Nico

By the time the seminar ended on the first day, Nico felt like someone had put him in the dryer to tumble for a couple of hours. All he'd done was sit, take notes, and occasionally try to answer mind-bending questions (scrambling, of course, to make a good impression while the other grad students in the room tried to do the exact same thing). But his body ached, and his head throbbed, and he had a mountain of reading to do overnight.

All of which meant that, when Kaylee said, "We should all go out for drinks," Nico began thinking of excuses.

"Wipe that look off your face," Maya murmured.

Nico whispered, "We've got two hundred pages of reading. For tomorrow, Maya."

"This is a networking event, isn't that what you said?"

"I could use a glass of wine," Gio announced.

"There you go," Nico whispered to Maya. "That's the answer. Hard pass."

"Nico and I are probably going to hit the library," Clark said, his hand coming to rest on Nico's shoulder again.

Nico shrugged him off. "Maybe I will get that drink."

At least Maya had the decency not to laugh.

They emerged from Eldridge Hall into the evening gloom. It was a little past five, but in another hour, it would be full dark. Old-fashioned lampposts made islands in the evening, and every so often, the familiar blue light of an emergency call box broke the gathering shadows. A guy in Chouteau sweats sat on a bench, watching something on his phone. The smell of the leaves whisked past them on a breeze. Ridson and Gio were arguing about something that had come up in the seminar, and Kaylee was tapping on her phone (looking for a wine bar to impress Gio, Nico guessed), and the sounds seemed louder because the campus was so still.

"Are you sure you don't want to have a study sesh in the library?" Clark asked in a low voice as he strode along next to Nico. "It could be like old times."

"I'm sure."

Clark laughed quietly.

"Nico?" It was the guy on the bench. And then, Nico realized with a start that the guy was Jadon. He jogged toward them, a smile forming on his face. Nico had forgotten how big he was—tall and muscled and solid. Right then, it felt disorienting.

Nudging Nico, Clark whispered, "Who's he?"

"Hey, sorry." Jadon thumbed at the bench. "I didn't want to interrupt."

The murmurs between Ridson and Gio faded. Maya was watching Nico with bright eyes. Kaylee's gaze whipped up from her phone and then back down again. The humor faded from Clark's face, and he examined Jadon.

Then he stepped forward and held out a hand, "Clark Beaumont."

"Hey, man. Jadon Reck."

And because he was Jadon, he shook hands and smiled.

"We were going to get a drink," Clark said. Now Clark was smiling, and it had a strange cast to it that Nico hadn't seen before. "You're a friend of Nico's, right? Why don't you join us?"

"Uh." Jadon swung his gaze to Nico. "Well, I was hoping I could talk to you for a minute. If that's all right."

"Anywhere around here you recommend?" Clark asked a little too loudly.

Maya shoved Nico, and he stumbled and barely caught himself. With a glare back at his alleged friend, Nico straightened up and managed to say, "Just for a minute."

"There's this place called Allure." Jadon gestured. "Just a few blocks that way."

Clark stared at him. Then he said, "Nico, don't take too long. It's chilly out here."

Nico moved down the sidewalk. He chafed his arms, wishing he'd brought a heavier sweater and, as an added bonus, mentally cursing Emery for being right. Again. Jadon kept pace with him until they stopped under the next lamppost. The yellow light dusted Jadon's hair, the bridge of his nose. It glistened on a full lower lip. He smelled a little like a warm male body and a little like new clothes that hadn't been washed yet.

"If it's about your clothes, I can Venmo you—"

"Would you like to have dinner?"

"What?"

Jadon's shoulders relaxed, and his smile stretched wider. "Dinner. It's this thing where two people eat food together."

"I already told you, I don't expect—"

"But I promised, right? I told you next time you came to St. Louis, I'd take you to dinner. And I meant it. And we're both here, and we both have to eat, and you don't know St. Louis." His grin flashed out again. "And I've got a car, so we don't have to stay on campus."

"You realize that's basically a pickup line for undergrads."

Jadon's grin slanted into a smirk. "Plus I know this great bar where they don't ID."

In spite of himself, Nico laughed. Then the cold settled over him again, and he shifted his weight. "I've got a lot of work to do."

"Nico," Clark called. "We're waiting."

A furrow creased Jadon's brow. "Are you—" He stopped. "None of my business."

"No," Nico said in answer to the half-asked question. "God, no."

The smirk slipped across Jadon's mouth again. "I promise we'll be fast."

"He'd love to go," Maya shouted.

"You don't even know what he's asking," Nico snapped back. "He might be asking if he can harvest my organs."

"Please," Maya called. "Get him out of here."

"It's my duty as a police officer to help citizens in distress," Jadon said.

Nico chose to ignore that. He eyed Jadon and said, "Aren't you cold?"

"A little." Then, with a quiet laugh, "I'm freezing."

"How long have you been waiting out here?"

Jadon groaned. "Please don't make me tell you."

Nico almost laughed at that; it was a close thing, and he was still fighting to smooth out his mouth when he asked, "How'd you find me?"

"I'm a little offended. I am a detective, you know."

"Or a stalker."

Darkly sandy eyebrows arched in amusement. "I can have hobbies."

"Have a great time," Maya called. "See you tomorrow!"

"Nico." Clark's voice was crisp. "We're leaving."

"I—" Nico's gaze swung from Jadon to his friends. "I think I'll see you tomorrow."

Clark's—what was it? disapproval? anger?—hardened the lines of his body, visible even in the dusk. He turned and strode away, followed in a ragged line by the rest of the grad students. Maya was last, and she gave a little finger wave in parting. Nico thought she might have been laughing.

"Ready?" Jadon asked.

Nico managed not to sigh. He nodded. "Starving."

7

Jadon

They lucked into street parking on Delmar before Jadon realized he might have miscalculated.

"Dang it. I didn't even ask about dietary restrictions."

Nico gave him a sidelong look, but all he said was "That's all right, because I don't have any."

"Are you sure? I mean, I know a couple of good vegan places, and there's this great spot that does clean food."

Dusk was settling into dark, and all along the street, lights hung in hazy spheres. The Delmar Loop, as it was called (which was not, as far as Jadon could tell, a loop in any discernible fashion), was a strip that featured restaurants, vintage clothing boutiques, a (mostly shuttered) old theater, boba, and more. It catered to the college students at Wash U and Chouteau, but people from all over the metro area drove here for a night out. Fortunately, on a Wednesday, it wasn't too busy. Already, traffic was starting to thin, the sidewalks beginning to empty.

"I'm fine with whatever you picked," Nico said. The words sounded a bit stiff. "Let's eat."

"Is there something you like to eat when you're traveling or—"

Nico made a noise in his throat, unbuckled himself, and got out of the car.

Jadon got out more slowly. He joined Nico on the sidewalk, waited a beat for both of them to catch their balance, so to speak, and then said, in as even a tone as he could manage, "It's right up here."

He led the way, and Nico walked with him, chafing his arms through the thin cardigan. He looked, well, stunning. Still. Even at the end of a long day. The wavy black hair. The dark coals of his eyes. Coppery skin and the long, slender lines of a dancer. The cardigan and button-up accentuated his build, and Jadon caught himself thinking about Nico's waist, about how his hands would look there, wrapped around his hips, his thumbs pressing lightly into the pale brass sheen of Nico's belly.

Jadon pulled his thoughts away from that and promised himself, for the millionth time, he would unfollow Nico on Instagram and delete his account. Permanently.

"What are these stars?" Nico asked. And then, "Tina Turner is from St. Louis?"

"I think that one might be a stretch," Jadon said. "She went to high school here."

"That's pretty cool." Nico's stride turned into an amble, and although he continued to chafe his arms, his hands slowed. They moved from star to star in silence, Nico reading each entry in St. Louis's Walk of Fame. And then Jadon had an idea. A change of plans. A pivot.

Ahead of them, Blueberry Hill's enormous sign flashed WELCOME TO THE LOOP. Above the words, the images of a man and woman, both dressed in old-fashioned clothes, were frozen in a dance. When Jadon touched Nico's arm, he looked up, and then he said, "Here?"

"I bet we can get a salad —"

Nico pulled away from him and headed for the door.

Inside, music played loudly from speakers overhead — classic rock, something by the Grateful Dead, even though Jadon couldn't remember the name of the song. It was a large space, the lighting low, filled with bodies and voices and air that felt hot and close after the ripped-open cool of the

October evening. Jadon's stomach grumbled at the smell of seared onions and ground beef, but he pushed that thought down. A salad. No dressing. Extra protein.

The wait for a table was almost an hour. When the hostess offered them a seat at the bar instead, Nico said yes before Jadon could answer, and the hostess swam off into the crowd. They found themselves sitting side by side, shouting to be heard by the young Black woman tending bar. After some back and forth, Nico ordered a 4 Hands, one of their IPAs. Jadon got the Urban Chestnut STILPA.

Nico sat, looking straight ahead. He took a long drink of the beer, his throat moving with each swallow, his Adam's apple prominent against his slender profile. I've got to get out of here, Jadon thought. The music got louder and louder until it seemed like the only thing he could hear. He couldn't tell Nico this was a mistake, but he could say—what? He had an emergency?

But he heard himself ask over the din, "How was your seminar?"

For a moment, he thought Nico hadn't heard; he stayed as he was, unmoving, the glass hovering at his lips. Then he turned, the movement abrupt, almost hostile. "We talked for two hours about whether Augustine could be called a Sartrian existentialist or if that was anachronistic."

Jadon took a drink. Augustine. Sartrian existentialist. Maybe ask a question, his brain suggested. Maybe say, Tell me more.

But before he could, a mocking little smile raked across Nico's face, and he said, "How was your seminar?"

"Good."

Nico cocked his head.

"Good," Jadon said again more loudly.

Annoyance streaked across Nico's face and was gone again as he nodded.

"It's important," Jadon said.

"What?"

"It's important!"

Again, that slight tightening around Nico's eyes and mouth. "I'm sure it is."

Before Jadon could ask what that meant, though, the bartender was back, asking for their order. Nico turned his attention to the menu again, so when the woman looked at Jadon, he said, "I'll do this house salad, no dressing, add chicken."

Nico's head came up. He must have heard him over the music because he turned slowly toward Jadon and said, "You don't have to get a salad."

"Huh?"

"I'm not getting a salad."

"Okay?" It shouldn't have sounded so much like a question, but it did.

"I can eat whatever I want."

"I know—"

"I want the Western burger. Can you add an extra onion ring? And what are toasted ravioli?"

The bartender began, "You've never had toasted ravioli? They're a St. Louis thing. It's like a regular ravioli, but—"

"They're deep fried," Jadon said. "Delicious, but super unhealthy, so—"

"Perfect." Nico shut his menu with a snap. "We'll have those."

Jadon took a drink of his beer. A long one.

After that, neither of them had much to say. Jadon tried a few more times to start a conversation—he had no idea who Augustine was or what Sartrian existentialism might be, but he asked how school was going, and he asked about work (one of the things he'd picked up on, during those late-night texts, was that Nico loved his job and loved his boss and still managed to complain about both of them). Nico parried the questions, or answered with scything sarcasm, or—more and more as the meal went on—simply ignored them. By the time the check came, they were both facing forward, and Jadon had ordered a second beer.

"My treat," Nico said, handing a card to the bartender.

"No, I invited you."

"I insist."

They went outside. The street was all closed doors and bleached light, and the cold cut at Jadon's cheeks. When they got to the car, he went to open the door, but Nico got there first. He yanked on the handle. It didn't open.

Down the street, leaves skittered along the gutter.

Jadon unlocked the door with the fob. As soon as the car beeped, Nico opened the door and got into his seat. He slammed the door.

In the car, it wasn't cold enough to see his breath, but Jadon felt it, the cloud of invisible heat brushing his face, like someone was stoking a furnace in his belly.

"Are you okay?"

"I'm great. I had a great meal. It was a great night."

Jadon sat there for a moment, keys in his hand. Then he started the car and drove back to Chouteau.

When he found a parking spot at the edge of campus, he looked at Nico. The cool light from the dash gave him luminous cheekbones, taut, gleaming skin, and the dark coal-fire of his eyes.

"I feel like I did something wrong."

Nico was already opening the door, and his words ghosted back. "You were a perfect gentleman."

The door shut hard, and Nico strode off into the night.

Jadon reached for the shifter, watching him go, already chafing his arms. Nico disappeared into a pool of shadow. Then the blue of an emergency light glimmered in his hair. Then he was gone again. Jadon thought of Dalary Lang, going home alone one night. And calling himself every kind of stupid, he killed the engine and got out of the car.

Just making sure, he told himself. until he gets to his dorm.

He kept his distance. Nico already didn't like him; no point in confirming his fears that Jadon was some sort of stalker. For the first thirty yards, the cold cut through the Chouteau sweats. Then it settled into him, and the pressure in Jadon's chest eased, and the ache in his head quieted. It was better things had turned out this way, honestly. It had been a clusterfuck of a disaster, in technical terms, but this was actually better because—

Something moved in the darkness.

At first, Jadon thought it was his eyes playing tricks on him. But then a figure took shape in the darkness. The man—Jadon decided it was a man— stepped onto the path and followed Nico. A black hoodie. Dark jeans. It was a college campus, and dark, hooded clothing wasn't exactly uncommon. But one thing you learned, if you were a detective and you took your job seriously, was that people had all sorts of tricks for disguising themselves, but they often forgot one thing: the way you walked could be as identifying as anything else. And right then, Jadon recognized the gait of the man ahead of him. Confident, almost relaxed. Sure. And moving straight after Nico.

Questions spiraled: why Nico? That one, at least, had a possible answer: now that Jadon thought about it, he could see the physical similarities between Nico and Dalary Lang. But why now?

As quickly as the questions had come, Jadon filed them away. The upper levels of his brain turned off, and what remained was dark, oiled gearwork. He picked up his pace, careful as he set his feet down so that his soles wouldn't scuff the brick pathway, not quite breaking into a jog, but certainly passing the mark of a power walk.

Ahead, the suspect kept a comfortable distance from Nico. They passed in and out of pools of light. Nico had to be freezing in that ridiculously thin clothing; even at a distance, Jadon could see him huddling into the breeze. But if he noticed the man following him, he gave no sign of it.

Harlow Hall came into view—in the dark, feathered by security lights, shadows seemed to ripple over the buttresses. The suspect started to move faster. Then, between one heartbeat and the next, he was running.

Jadon sprinted after him. His shoes slapped the pavement, but he was past caring. He shouted, "Stop! Police!"

The suspect gave a startled glance back, his pace faltering for a moment. And then he buttonhooked right, darting down a narrow alley between two buildings. Jadon had a glimpse of Nico backlit by one of the security lights, staring. Then his vision tunneled to the alley, and the deeper darkness within it.

A knife coming out of nowhere. The heat of steel opening a path across his belly, up his chest. Hands holding him down. Ropes that wouldn't give.

They were only memories, but they went off in his head like fireworks. He couldn't breathe. His heart hurt like someone was squeezing it.

And then, somehow, it was over.

He stood in the alley, in the dark, alone. And the wind was like the flat of a blade.

8

Nico

Nico slept poorly, and when he woke, a distant, rational part of him realized he was what Emery would have called *on one*. It took him an extra fifteen minutes to get his hair right, and by the time he got dressed, he hated the rust-colored sweater. After ripping it off, he had to fix his hair again. The blazer, which had seemed playfully boxy when he'd bought it, now looked like a pool cover.

The whole time, he kept thinking about the night before. Not only the train wreck of dinner, although that had been strange enough. But the end of the evening too: Jadon sprinting out of the dark, chasing off a man in a hoodie, and then mumbling an apology before he left, white-faced and sweating in spite of the cold.

In some ways, that part actually made the most sense. Nico had learned a lot about Jadon over those midnight texts. Maybe it would have been different if their texting had taken place during the day. But Jadon's schedule meant that his messages had always come late, when Nico was caught between the luxury of a grad student's late nights and the harsh reality of Emery Hazard as a boss in the morning. And because the messages had come late, they had come when both men—or so Nico believed—had their guards down, their inhibitions lowered. With the world shuttered in darkness, the texting had felt confessional, a place Nico—and Jadon—could say things he never said to anyone. It had felt safe, too, if Nico were being honest, because Jadon lived a hundred miles away, and because the distance was a barrier that kept it from becoming real. And the safeness of it, the ability to say what he wanted to say and, to his surprise, discover that Jadon was both supportive and understanding, had only made it worse when one day, without explanation, Jadon had stopped answering. Because the message had been clear: something that Nico had revealed about himself, some confession or truth or secret, had been too much, and whatever Jadon had learned about him, it had made him want to end things.

So, Nico understood—or thought he understood—why Jadon's face had been the color of chalk, and why he'd been breathing those awful, ragged breaths like he wanted to throw up. He even understood, with a kind of compassion he hadn't expected, why Jadon had left so abruptly, without explaining anything. But all of that only took up part of his attention. Because he couldn't stop thinking about Jadon waiting in the cold for a chance to talk to him. And Jadon making that stupid joke about a place that didn't ID. And the way Jadon had waited while Nico read each star on the Walk of Fame. And then Jadon had ruined it all. And Nico couldn't stop being angry with Jadon, and he couldn't stop being angry with himself, and he couldn't stop being angry because he felt guilty.

Finally, he ended up in a navy quarter-zip, gave up on his hair, and rushed out the door. He was, without a doubt, going to be late.

For the second time in two days, he almost crashed into Jadon. And, for the second time, coffee was involved. The detective was leaning against the wall opposite Nico's door, and he looked—well, not quite as great as the day before. His eyes were shadowed, his hair lank, and he was wearing the Chouteau College sweats again. In one hand, he held a cup of coffee; a second waited at his feet. He was scrolling on his phone when Nico almost ran into him, and he used the hand with the phone to steady Nico as Nico hit the brakes.

"Easy there," he murmured.

"Jadon."

Those darkly sandy eyebrows went up.

"This is my dorm," Nico said.

"I told you I'm a detective. See how good I'm doing?"

"What are you doing here? The doors are supposed to be locked, and it's—oh God, I am going to be so late." Nico scooted around Jadon and headed for the stairs. "Do you realize how weird this is?"

"In my defense, I brought you coffee. And I'm not wearing it this time, so I think that shows both thoughtfulness and an ability to learn from my mistakes." Jadon caught up with him and held out the second cup. As they took the stairs—Nico bounding two at a time and annoyed that Jadon kept up so easily—Jadon continued, "Also, I want to reiterate that I'm not a stalker, although I can see how this might appear to undermine my case."

Nico shouldered open the door at the bottom of the stairs, took the coffee, and was surprised by a blast of kid-temp pumpkin latte. He forgot what he'd been about to say.

"I know it's weird showing up here like this," Jadon said, and he lowered his voice as a pair of men emerged from a door down the hall. "But I need to talk to you."

"Look, I appreciate, uh, whatever this is, but we don't have to have a talk. Nothing happened. Thank you for dinner. You seem sweet, but I'm not at a place in my life—"

"Oh my God, Nico."

Nico stopped talking.

A radiator pinged. Jadon rubbed under his eyes. He didn't look tired; he looked like he'd been dragged behind a car and then forced to do calisthenics in vintage college gear.

Finally, Nico shifted his bag and said in the most controlled voice he could manage, "I'm late."

"We can talk as we walk."

That didn't seem to be a question, so Nico pushed out into the hard slap of the autumn morning, Jadon glued to his side.

For the first few steps, the only sound was a warbling birdsong, and a little brown-and-yellow bird flitted from bare branch to bare branch ahead of them. Nico glanced over. Then he said, "Did you sleep last night?"

"I caught a few hours in my car."

"Outside my dorm."

Jadon's droll little smile was another surprise. "Yes, Nico. I hear it. I understand the pattern." The smile faded, though, and again, Jadon seemed to disappear inside his thoughts.

"Okay," Nico said. As usual, he was going to have to be the communicator in the—well, relationship didn't seem like the right word. Stalker-stalkee thing they had going? That was closer. "Why didn't you get any sleep last night?" In a rush, he added, "And I'm sorry if I upset you—"

Jadon actually groaned at that. "I didn't sleep because I spent two hours fighting with the ancient security system this campus has, trying to get a decent shot of the suspect from last night."

"What suspect? What happened? Did someone get hurt?"

"The guy? Last night?" Jadon waited, but when Nico didn't say anything, he added, "The one who was following you?"

"Huh?" Then memory clicked. "Jadon, he wasn't following me. I didn't even know he was there until you started shouting."

"That's not exactly a point in your favor."

"He was some guy walking across campus."

"He wasn't walking. He was following. And then he was running."

"It's a tiny campus, Jay. It probably looks like we're following those guys." He indicated the men ahead of him. "And maybe he was out for a run and taking a breather, then he decided to start running again."

"At night?"

"I run at night."

"You shouldn't."

Nico rucked his bag up. "Goodbye, Jadon."

"There's been a string of assaults on campus," Jadon said. And then, as they walked, he told Nico about it, laying out the basics, sketching out his investigation. "I'm fairly certain the man I saw last night is the same suspect from the other assaults."

"Okay, but—" Nico tried to pick from a dozen different responses. He settled on "Then we need more police on campus, right? Until he's caught."

"That'd be nice, sure. It's not going to happen." Jadon's dark eyes moved restlessly, as though he were reading some invisible text of the world. "For one reason, the Metropolitan PD is, as usual, stretched thin. For another, nobody happens to believe that the same perpetrator is behind these assaults."

"But they're all happening on campus!"

"And, as you pointed out, there are a lot of ways of explaining this away. The most obvious one is that most sexual assaults on campus happen in fall semester—early in the semester, actually. Do you know why?"

Nico shook his head.

"Because there's a new group of eighteen-year-olds who go to parties and drink too much and end up in bad situations. So, if you're a lieutenant and you're looking at Chouteau College and you have a choice between believing this is a normal pattern of assaults, with the usual suspects—the normal pieces of shit, in other words—or believing this is a series of carefully planned assaults by a single, calculating individual, which one do you think you're going to choose to believe?"

"That's awful."

"That's reality, unfortunately. Lieutenants are experts in reality; that's pretty much their whole purpose."

Their steps clipped the bricks for a few yards. Ahead of them rose Eldridge Hall, but instead of walking faster, Nico slowed his pace. "I don't understand. It's not like this guy could be targeting me specifically. I mean, you dropped me off. Nobody could have known I was going to be where I was."

"Nico, that's not how it works. He doesn't have to know where you are. He has to know where you're going. Harlow Hall. Eldridge Hall. Waverley Center. Sterling Library. And you're right: it might not be you, not specifically."

The cold made Nico's ears feel, strangely, hot. "But?"

"But I'm not willing to take that chance."

"What?"

A hint of color dusted Jadon's cheekbones, and he gave a tiny shrug, but he didn't look away.

"So, what?" Nico looked around. "You're going to sleep in your car and watch my dorm and walk me to class?"

"If you promise me you won't leave your dorm at night, I won't have to sleep in my car."

"Do you think this is funny?"

Nico wasn't sure he'd seen Jadon angry before, but he saw it now: the way his whole body tightened, and the easy happiness in his face crystallized into something harder, sharper. Nico liked it. He was also fairly sure he was going to hell.

"No, I don't think this is funny. Do you think this is funny?"

"I think—" Nico shouldered his bag higher. "—I don't need a bodyguard. I can take care of myself."

"Great. I've got no problem being redundant."

"I don't need some walking alpha-male stereotype trying to tell me what I should do and how I should live my life."

"I think you can handle it for a few days."

"If this is some weird, psycho way of trying to get me to, I don't know, be with you, it's not going to work."

"Believe it or not, Nico, I don't want to 'be with you.'" The way Jadon drew the air quotes, the way he cut a tiny, icy smile at him, made Nico flush. "That's why I stopped texting you, remember?"

That tiny bird warbled again. Then the morning seemed still.

"You're a fucking asshole."

"From what I hear, you've got plenty of experience with that." Jadon folded his arms, planting himself, and chinned toward Eldridge Hall. "I'll see you at five. Have a great day at school, honey."

9

Jadon

The day passed in a blur. After what had felt like a surge of wakefulness and clarity that morning—an illusion, he knew, that was common following a sleepless night, and which had been compounded by the argument with Nico—he found himself in a kind of fugue state, moving from workshop to workshop, head nodding as he tried to keep himself upright and at least appear to be paying attention. The rooms, warmed by the radiators and crowded bodies, made it hard to stay awake, though, and more than once Jadon's own sleepy breathing roused him from the edge.

Vic told him he looked like shit.

Allison asked twice if he needed to go home.

At the end of the day, he mumbled excuses and managed to escape while Vic was bragging about his conquest from the night before and Allison was pretending to vomit. He made his way to Eldridge and sat on the bench where he had waited the day before. The shadows were long, and the stone was ice, freezing his ass to the bench. Over the turrets and spires of the college, beyond the oaks and maples of Forest Park, the sky was the red of spaghetti Westerns. His head dipped again, and instead of uncomfortable, the cold felt like a hand catching him. If I fall asleep out here, he thought in that jumbled way of half-waking, Nico will leave me to die of exposure.

The sound of doors opening and animated voices roused him, though, and he wiped drool from his chin and straightened up on the bench. Nico and his friends emerged from Eldridge Hall. Nico looked good; maybe not how Jadon remembered him, not how Jadon had thought about him when they'd been texting. But there were reasons for that. They'd met during the summer, when Nico had been wearing a T-shirt and shorts that left a lot of smooth, coppery skin exposed. And when they'd been texting, it had always been at night, and the occasional selfie had always been sleep shorts (so tiny, Jadon had to admit, they barely qualified as underwear) and old tanks washed to the point of translucency. The image he had carried in his mind of Nico for months didn't quite line up with the starched professional in front of him—a microdot button-down, a navy quarter-zip. He was wearing the glasses again, the ones Jadon didn't remember. The images overlapped: the Nico who had worn a tank top that said, MY OTHER DADDY HAS A MOTORCYCLE; and this Nico, the one who looked like he'd been shopping in the straight bro aisle at J. Crew. (Maybe, Jadon considered, that was all the aisles?)

The grad students came down the steps from Eldridge, several of them talking animatedly—a Harry Potter type with a Bart Simpson haircut, the girl Nico had called Maya, and Clark, the boy Jadon had thought—still thought—might have something going with Nico. Nico didn't even look at Jadon. He moved along with the others, his head locked forward, even though several of the students glanced at Jadon and turned questioning looks at Nico. When they'd gone a few yards, Jadon got to his feet and went after them.

He was close enough to hear when Maya said, "Nico, your friend is here."

Nico stopped abruptly. He turned to look at Jadon. For a moment, he said nothing, obviously struggling between the desire to make a scene (something Nico had confessed, in those midnight texts, to doing because it gave him a feeling of control when he felt powerless) and his desire to maintain a professional demeanor. Finally, body stiff, he stalked toward Jadon.

"What?"

"Nothing. You go do your thing; I'm not going to bother you. You won't even know I'm here."

It looked like it took Nico an effort to rein himself in, and by the time he opened his mouth to speak, Clark was walking toward them as he said, "Is there a problem?"

"No," Nico snapped. "I'm fine, Clark."

That's right, Clark, Jadon thought. We're fine.

"What's going on?" Clark said when he reached them.

"Nothing," Nico said.

With an appraising look at Jadon, Clark said, "Can I help you?"

"No, thanks. I'm checking in with Nico."

"And you are?"

"A friend."

Nico shifted his weight to angle his body slightly away from Clark. "I'm handling this."

"I don't think you are," Clark said. To Jadon, he added, "I think you're bothering Nico. I think this is starting to constitute harassment."

"I appreciate that you're trying to protect your friend," Jadon said, "but you don't know what's going on here."

"I know exactly what's going on." Clark took Nico's arm. "Come on, Nico."

But Nico wrenched free. "I told you I'm fine, so stop it."

From the crowd of grad students, Maya called, "Nico?"

"I'll see you guys later," Nico shouted back. He said in a softer voice to Clark, "You'd better go."

"I don't like this," Clark said. "This is weird, and you're being weird. If you're scared of him, I'll call the police right now."

That seemed to undo some of the tension in Nico's body. He gave a small laugh and shook his head. "I'm fine, Clark. I promise. Go catch up with the rest of them; I'll see you in the morning."

"Text me when you get back to the dorm," Clark said. "I want to know you're safe."

Nico rolled his eyes, but finally he nodded. Clark slunk off after the rest of the grad students, darting poisonous looks back at Jadon.

"Ex?" Jadon asked.

"He wishes," Nico muttered. Jadon cracked a smile, but Nico's expression stayed flat. "I don't need a bodyguard."

"I heard you say it the first time. I understand how you feel about the situation, and I'm sorry you're frustrated."

For a moment, Nico stared at him. "Was that a fuck-you apology?"

"No." Jadon thought about it. "Well, a polite one."

Nico walked off, and Jadon gave him a few yards before following.

Instead of hurrying after his friends, though, Nico headed north. He passed Waverley, where a few students waited for shuttles as the October dark closed around them. They passed more buildings—dorms, Jadon guessed, based on the orange-and-purple lights strung in the windows, and the cardboard sign that said JESUS LOVES YOU, and, on the fire escape, a jack-o'-lantern with an electric candle illuminating the words FUCK TRUMP. The dark closed like a slipknot. Somewhere nearby, an oboist was practicing scales.

Unlike most of campus, Sterling Library was a grim, hulking building shorn of its neogothic trappings. It looked like a glass-and-concrete cube that could have been plucked from take your pick of post-Soviet states. Nico still had a lead on him, so he was already inside by the time Jadon caught one of the glass doors. His reflection flickered, and he decided Vic had been right— he did look like shit—and then he was stepping into warm air and a mixture of odors: wool that had been warmed by body heat, and aging book bindings, and something that made him think of mothballs.

Nico had a card that let him past the security gates, while Jadon had to stop and explain why he was on campus (the symposium) and what he wanted in the library (a totally made-up journal article he needed for the next day). The guard, a short, stocky twentysomething in need of a powerful exfoliant, finally buzzed open a gate, and as Jadon went in pursuit of Nico, he wondered if Nico would go so far as escaping out a fire door. Probably, he thought.

Like the exterior, on the inside, the library was severe, everything lines and angles and brown: brown linoleum in the lobby, brown carpet in the halls, brown bookcases, brown plastic furniture, all of it showcased by banks of fluorescent lights and, of course, more concrete. He wandered each floor and then climbed to the next until, on the fourth floor, he spotted Nico. He was so deep in a study carrell it looked like he might be trying to crawl inside it. The floor was unoccupied, as far as Jadon could tell, except for an Indian girl who was staring at a laptop and chewing her nails, and a white guy in a shapeless smock and hemp pants—he was (because why wouldn't he be?) barefoot. Jadon took a seat at a table with a good view of Nico, and then he took out his phone.

He'd been reading for about five minutes when Nico stood and came to the table. He had a hint of a flush under that coppery skin, and his shoulders were locked and loaded. He stared down at Jadon until Jadon put his phone on the table and looked up.

"As you can see, I'm fine. I made it all the way across campus without being attacked. So, now you can go home, and you can take a shower, and you can sleep in a bed, and tomorrow, you can go to your symposium and look like a human being."

"I appreciate the concern."

Nico took a deep breath, but it didn't sound like it helped much. The glasses started to slide, and he resettled them. "I'm going straight back to my dorm after this."

"Good."

His volume rose a notch, and the words took on a staggering, insulting choppiness. "I want you to go away. Do you understand?"

"I do."

Nico made a —admittedly soft—screaming noise.

"Have you eaten today?" Jadon asked. "I could pick up something from the vending machines. I bet they've got some healthy options, maybe some nuts—"

"What I eat isn't any of your fucking business!" The shout echoed through the large, open space. It bounced back from the raw concrete. "And I don't need you following me around while I'm trying to look like a professional!"

It was exhaustion. And frustration. And the jangle of nerves like far-off alarm bells, the ones that never went quiet. Jadon stood up so fast that he thumped onto the carpet behind him, and he shouted back, "I don't care! And you know what? It's hard to take you seriously when you're wearing those stupid fucking glasses!"

Behind the frames, Nico's eyes got huge.

"Hey!" the Indian girl shouted. "This is a library!"

Jadon couldn't explain the wave of giggles that rolled over him. He barely fought them back. Nico made a strange noise, and in a moment of disbelief, Jadon realized Nico was fighting the giggles too. Somehow, they both made it to the stairwell, and when the doors swung shut behind them, they dissolved into laughter. Jadon sank down onto the steps, and Nico leaned against him, laughing so hard that he was practically draped over Jadon. And even through the laughter, Jadon was painfully aware of the warmth of lean muscle, the almost-forgotten casual pleasure of skin on skin as Nico's hand brushed his nape.

Eventually, they quieted. Nico took the glasses off and held them in one hand, a wry smile creasing one cheek.

"You look cute in them," Jadon said. "If it's any consolation."

"They're so stupid. This was so stupid." He was still leaning against Jadon, sitting so close that heat stitched a line up Jadon's side. "God, I feel like I'm going crazy. I'm sorry. I shouldn't have yelled at you."

"I'm sorry for—uh, offering you a snack, I guess?"

Nico tapped his head with the glasses.

"Ow," Jadon said, but he laughed. "What?"

"You know what drives me out of my fucking head? Guys who think they know everything about me because I did some modeling. Did, Jadon. Past tense. I don't need you picking a restaurant because you know I can get a salad there that'll be under five hundred calories. I don't need you worrying about when I ate. I don't need you controlling how much I eat, or worrying about portions, or any of that bullshit. I'm an adult, and I spent way too much of my life letting what other people thought about my body control me, and I do not fucking need that again."

His volume rose again at the end, and Jadon waited until the echoes in the stairwell died before saying, "Is that why you were grumpy last night?"

"Grumpy? I was being a world-class bitch. And if you say I wasn't, I'm going to be offended."

The grin broke out before Jadon could stop it. He was fairly sure, even though he couldn't see, that Nico was grinning too. "Okay, here we go, for the record: first, I was going to take you to Salt + Smoke, which is my favorite barbeque place in the city. I didn't switch to Blueberry Hill because I thought you needed a salad. I switched to Blueberry Hill because you seemed so interested in the Walk of Fame, and Chuck Berry used to play there every month in the Duck Room. Which, you know, was kind of hard to explain when we were sitting at the bar."

"And when I was icing you out so hard your balls froze off."

"My balls are fine, thanks. And second, I'm not trying to control what you eat. I'm trying to control what I eat. I keep myself on a pretty strict diet, and it's hard to eat out. And also, even if you don't want people controlling what you eat, I think I deserve a little credit for trying to be considerate. I mean, I was being polite, Nico. The same way I'd worry about taking a friend who ate vegan to a place where they could get something they'd enjoy."

It seemed like a long time before Nico said, "You have friends who are vegan?"

"I dated Shaw, remember?"

"Yeah, how in the hell did that happen?"

Jadon laughed. "We met on a case. And believe it or not, not everybody finds me to be an unmitigated asshole. At least, not on first sight."

A door on a landing below them opened and closed. Footsteps pummeled the stairs.

Nico straightened, pulling away from Jadon, and the side of Jadon's body felt cool now. "I'm sorry. Again. Officially, totally, completely sorry. I didn't—yeah, I'm the unmitigated asshole, and I shouldn't have, um, projected my bullshit onto you."

"Well, we've got a problem."

Nico glanced sidelong.

"It's super hard to get me to accept an apology," Jadon said. "Like, almost impossible."

"I'll buy you pizza."

"Imo's."

"What is Imo's?"

"You, my friend, are in for a treat."

It turned out that libraries had strict policies about large, greasy, cheese- and sauce-covered pizzas being carried through their stacks, so when the delivery came, they had to take it to Waverley. They ate on a battered sofa outside the closed coffee shop.

"It's not pizza," Nico said. "It's a cracker."

"Aren't you supposed to be groveling?"

Nico flicked sausage at him. It struck Jadon's cheek, and he rocked backward, like the impact had bowled him over, as he cleaned up the spatter with a napkin.

"It's not terrible," Nico said after three more squares. "It's weird."

"Uh huh."

"What?"

"It's hard to hear you with all that pizza crammed in your mouth."

Nico's grin was surprisingly boyish. "You noticed I can fit a lot in my mouth."

Jadon choked on a slice of pepperoni.

They were quiet on the walk back to Harlow Hall, and as they climbed the steps to Nico's floor, Jadon felt a moment of unreality. It was hard to remember, but maybe this was what it was like to have a normal life: pizza with a cute guy, watching the way his hair moved in the wind, discovering the little mole behind his right ear, realizing that he had an impossibly sexy neck. Like, who knew vertebrae could be hot? Then a quiet walk back to his place. Suddenly Jadon felt hot, sweat like pins and needles under his arms, sweeping across his chest. And his mind started to play out the rest of the scene: the lingering moment at the door, the silence that was a question you were both asking the other, the way sometimes you knew (or, if you were Jadon Reck and you were nineteen, you didn't know, and you tried to kiss Brit Booth, and he pulled back and you chipped your tooth on the doorjamb).

Nico pushed through the door at the top of the stairs and turned down the hall.

They stopped at his door. Nico took out his key. He looked at it. He looked up. He looked over Jadon's shoulder, like there was some safe spot he could focus on. He stood hipshot, those dancer lines perfect even in a quarter-zip and chinos, and he still hadn't said anything. His lips were parted. Jadon thought he could hear those soft, small breaths. He thought he knew what they would feel like if he were close enough. The heat, the hint of the taste of him brushing his lips, before breath joined to breath. A promise.

"I won't leave the dorm," Nico said, and although the tone was light, his body was still asking the unasked question. "Swear to God."

Jadon managed a loose, marionette nod. He was too hot in these sweats. He wasn't sure he could feel anything below the knee.

"So, you're going to go home," Nico prompted. "Shower. Bed. A full night's sleep."

The dreams, Jadon thought. The plastic bag over his head like a second skin across his mouth and nose. He nodded.

Neither of them said anything. The clockwork of Jadon's body told him a million years had gone by, a million years standing here, Nico's eyes still coal-fires, but softer now, a place to be warm. Nico's lips still parted. The question still hanging between them.

"Well," Nico said, "goodnight."

Jadon gave another of those wobbly nods and backed toward the stairs. His heart was running so fast he thought he might be sick, and distantly, he thought it had been a test, the whole thing had been some sort of test, and he had no idea if he'd passed or failed, if it had been Nico testing him, or if Jadon had been testing himself.

Nico paused, hand on his door as he pushed it open, and looked down the hall to where Jadon was trying to reach the stairwell. "See you in the morning?"

Jadon didn't trust his voice, but the words that came out were surprisingly smooth. "Of course."

Nico crooked a rueful smile at him. And then he was gone.

10

Nico

"You have got to be kidding me," Nico said as he stepped out of his room.

He'd slept better—slept great, in fact, and woken before his alarm, the gray predawn buoying his room up like a fog bank. His bad mood from the day before had evaporated. He'd felt light, energized, alive as he'd pulled on his running gear. And now this.

Jadon leaned against the opposite wall, a cup of coffee in hand, another cup on the floor beside him. He looked rested, or at least, more rested than he had the day before, and he was dressed in a suit that, although not expensive, was clearly good quality—and, on top of that, had been tailored. Nothing major, but in a few places, it had been taken in or adjusted for a better fit. The result was that it showed off Jadon to perfection: his height, his build, that slab of a chest. Navy wool. A white broadcloth shirt. A garnet-colored tie. He'd confessed, in one of those midnight missives, to being a bit of a clothes horse, but seeing him now, Nico decided he understood why. Clothes looked good on Jadon—some people were born that way. Although Jadon probably looked fine naked as well.

Nico didn't like where that thought had come from, so he squashed it.

"It's six o'clock," Nico said.

"Good morning," Jadon said. "Going somewhere?"

"For a run. By myself. Before you get here and engage babysitter mode."

Jadon raised those sandy eyebrows, but all he said was, "I've got my gym bag in my car."

"What time did you get here?"

But Jadon was already handing him both cups of coffee, and as he walked to the stairs, he shot back, "Please don't make me chase you down."

Nico scowled until the door swung shut behind him. It was a few minutes before he caught himself smiling, and he decided to put a stop to that immediately.

Like a gentleman, he waited in the hall while Jadon changed, although he had to admit to some thoughts about that expanse of defined chest, the way his arms would look, biceps popping when he pulled off his shirt, the powerful thighs flexing. Maybe, Nico decided, he needed to take Clark up on his offer. Maybe he needed something quick and easy, no strings attached. Maybe he just needed to clear his head.

Last night, he certainly hadn't been thinking clearly. He blamed it on the cracker-like pizza, and on the bad sleep, and on the annoying revelation that, now that they had passed that weird threshold of spending time together in person, Jadon was turning out to be as funny and sensitive and...Jadon as he had been over text. That was the only way he could explain the near disaster when Jadon had walked him to his room. He had almost said, *Do you want to come in?* And the part of him that was a good read of this kind of thing thought Jadon would have said yes. And that would have been—

Well, a part of Nico thought treacherously, would that have been so bad?

Yes, he told himself. It would have been—

Jadon's hand at the small of his back, raising his hips, his fingertips brushing electricity into Nico's spine.

—a disaster.

The door opened, and Jadon stepped out. The shorts hit him above the knee. The shirt looked like it was glued to his chest, even under the hoodie. All of it was the kind of high-tech athletic fabric that went perfectly with the expensive-but-broken-in running shoes. Good Lord, the man even had calf muscles. And Nico was immediately aware of his own skinny calves, the ratty shorts, the Nirvana tee that had been a Target find.

"It's chilly," Jadon said. "You might want a jacket."

"I'll be fine."

A little smudge of a furrow appeared between Jadon's eyebrows, but Nico didn't give him time to object. He headed out of the dorm, and they emerged into the October morning. It was cold beyond crisp, full of the sweetness of damp earth, the sky like a ring of lead, and it made him think of biting into an apple that had been kept at the back of the refrigerator. It also made him think Jadon had probably been right about the jacket.

But he took off at a jog, and Jadon paced easily alongside him. They followed Kingshighway for a block, and the street was empty at this hour except for a lone Escalade, white, buzzing every time the beat dropped. They crossed at a light, ignoring the WAIT sign, and started into Forest Park.

"You're now officially a criminal," Nico told Jadon. "You're a felony jaywalker. You're going to be stripped of your badge."

"I'm going to be stripped, huh?" Jadon said. And he didn't do anything—his face didn't change at all—but it was like he was smiling. Or maybe that was because Nico was smiling, and when he realized it, he forgot he was supposed to be annoyed at Jadon showing up so early today.

Before Nico could reply, Jadon moved into the lead. He was only a couple of inches taller than Nico, so Nico didn't have an easy excuse like Jadon had longer legs or anything like that. The fact was that Jadon was strong and athletic and conditioned, and it showed as they ran. Nico kept up, but only barely—and, he was aware, only because Jadon allowed it. *Don't make me chase you down.* Nico shivered, and it was only partly from the cold. Part, he could admit in the silence of the morning, was the thought of Jadon catching him.

They ran past lakes, where rushes bristled with frost and cattails exploded in fluffy white seed heads that, at first, Nico mistook for snow. They ran down footpaths, the gravel puffing dust under every step, and on either side, prairie grass grew to Nico's shoulders and stirred like something sleeping. The park wasn't empty — they passed another runner, a Black man with a tiny Bluetooth clipped to his belt, a Miley Cyrus song carrying him in the opposite direction. A bird wheeled over head — something large and strong and beautiful, but in a way that suggested the capacity for violence. It made Nico think of the way Jadon opened and closed his hands sometimes. The way, when Jadon stood suddenly, he remembered how big he was. A white-tailed doe broke trembling from a stand of oaks and stared at them, breath steaming from her nose, before running toward the next tree line. The sky was melting into blue.

A massive stone colonnade led into a building with the words MUNICIPAL THEATER written above the entrance. Then they cut away from the paved road again, following the bank of a creek. The illusion that they'd left the city only lasted a few moments: the beat of their footsteps echoing back from trees and sedge and water. Then a horn honked, and they reached pavement again, and Jadon led them along the sidewalk. An enormous basin opened on their left, the water hard and gray, cigarette butts bobbing against the walkway. Then a hill that left Nico's legs burning. The Art Museum, with its stern Roman lines. The Zoo, with its humped wire baskets — the aviaries, Nico guessed.

At the rise of another hill, Jadon slowed. He wasn't breathing hard, of course, but Nico was drawing in deep lungfuls of the cold morning. His body was pleasantly loose and warm, and as it usually did, the rush of the endorphins had left his brain quiet. For a moment, they walked together. And then Nico saw it.

His first thought was that it was something out of a fairy tale—or a Disney movie. An ice castle, maybe. But then his brain caught up with him, and he realized it was some kind of greenhouse. The entrance was the same limestone he'd seen elsewhere in the park. But after that, the building was all glass—panels joined by verdigris copper strips, rising in tiers like a wedding cake. The sun was starting to come up, and it painted the topmost tier with fire, except in a few places, where it caught the edges of the glass and broke into a rainbow.

"Holy shit."

Jadon laughed quietly.

"It's beautiful," Nico said. Then he shoved Jadon. "Why didn't you tell me?"

"Tell you what?"

"That we were going somewhere cool instead of, I don't know, trying to give me a heart attack."

Jadon answered with a small smile.

They kept walking, moving around the building. The inside of the glass was beaded with moisture, and lush, tropical greenery filled the space that Nico could see.

"I love coming here in the morning," Jadon said. "It's a little too far for a weekday run, but I used to come here on the weekends. Kind of a treat."

Nico hopped up onto the edge of one of the planters. It was cold, but the sun fell on his face, and he closed his eyes. The breeze picked up, flash-freezing the sweat on the back of his neck. He shivered.

The sound of a zipper made Nico open his eyes. Jadon was turning himself out of his hoodie.

"Oh no," Nico said, hugging himself. "You told me to bring a jacket, and I acted like a brat, which means I'm going to suffer the consequences."

"That seems pretty silly," Jadon said as he draped the hoodie around Nico. He gave him a one-sided smile and tugged the hood up over Nico's hair, and for some reason that made Nico laugh. "And I don't think you were being a brat."

Nico gave him cock-eyed as he fixed the hood.

"Okay," Jadon said with a laugh of his own. "Maybe a little."

He sat on the planter next to Nico. Their legs brushed once. The hoodie was warm and smelled a little like Jadon's sweat—and it wasn't exactly unpleasant. Jadon looked at the building, and his voice was softer when he said, "It's called the Jewel Box."

There were so many things Nico wanted to ask. *Why didn't you tell me about this?* That was one of them, and although it seemed like such a small thing, he wondered—they had told each other a lot during those late-night texts. Why not this? And why had everything changed when Jadon had given Nico his hoodie? Nico couldn't put his finger on the exact difference, but he felt it, the way he had felt the smile that hadn't made its way to Jadon's face earlier. *I'm going to get stripped, huh?* The silence, maybe, was deeper. Or something else. Something about the way he craned his head. The way he was framed against the sun, the lines of his neck on display. The way their breathing seemed to line up. Heat, Nico thought he had learned in school, was a hundred thousand million particles moving around like crazy. He felt like he was sweating again.

Which was why he said, "That's not a treat, by the way."

Jadon made a sound that suggested he'd already forgotten his own words.

"Coming here to run on the weekends. That doesn't count as a treat. A treat is, like, a brownie sundae. Or a ginger-cranberry whiskey sour and a ribeye as big as your head. Oh, and mashed potatoes. Oh! Or a treat is ordering an entire birthday cake from the Piggly-Wiggly, and you make them do the birthday writing on it, only you tell them some other name and have a whole story about how you're doing the Big Brother program, and won't he be happy, and then it takes you three days to eat that cake by yourself."

Jadon gave him a look.

"Don't judge me! It was an emergency!"

"An emergency that could be fixed by cake?"

"The emergency was that I wanted cake, so, yes, smartass."

Jadon laughed. Sweat and the breeze had mussed his hair, usually spiked to GQ perfection. One little spike had somehow fallen across his forehead, and it lay there now, dark with sweat. The way his cheek shifted when he smiled. Everyone's cheeks moved when they smiled, Nico knew; that was basically the definition of a smile. But the way Jadon's did...

Nico resettled himself on the planter. And, in the process, his shoulder came to rest against Jadon's.

He liked the idea that they might have sat that way forever if someone hadn't interrupted them. A man strode past, phone pressed to his ear, shouting, "I don't care whose funeral it is. I need those numbers by tomorrow! Then get yourself a new fucking job!"

As the man's tirade faded into the distance, Jadon made a face. "Glad everybody's enjoying the morning."

"Kierkegaard says truth is subjectivity," Nico said without meaning to. "And subjectivity is truth."

Jadon raised an eyebrow.

"That was super nerdy," Nico said. "I am so sorry. It's this seminar; I've been quoting Kierkegaard reflexively, and apparently I can't turn it off. It won't happen again."

Jadon's eyebrow lowered. That little smudge of a furrow was back. In the distance, a woodpecker was going to town on a tree.

"What does it mean?" Jadon asked.

With a laugh, Nico shook his head. "That's nice, but I promise, I don't need to talk about my research. It's, like, soul-crushingly boring to anyone who has a life. I appreciate that you asked, though."

"I didn't ask to be nice. I want to know."

"I promise, you don't."

"And I'm telling you I do. So, either you're calling me a liar, or you don't believe me, and I don't like either of those options."

The change in tone caught Nico off guard. "No, I didn't think—I mean, I thought you were being polite."

"I'm not."

"Obviously."

That made Jadon huff an amused breath, and some of the tension went out of the air, but the expectancy on his face was still a kind of demand.

"So—do you know much about Kierkegaard?"

"Nothing."

"Okay, well—do you know what existentialism is?"

"I mean, I've heard of it."

"Okay." Nico thought for a moment. "Kierkegaard was a philosopher, I guess. But mostly he was a theologian. And one of the things he struggled with was why people believe in God, or I guess, how people have faith might be a better way to put it. And he believed that faith is, well, absurd. That's not what the word he uses, but, like, it's irrational. And so one of his big ideas is that faith requires believers to make a leap of faith—that's his term, by the way. They have to make an irrational jump beyond reason. Faith means acknowledging that there's something beyond reason, something greater."

Jadon was quiet for a long time. The woodpecker, in contrast, was having its way with that tree.

"I thought you were an atheist," Jadon finally said.

"I am. I think." Nico laughed, and Jadon laughed too after a moment. "I mean, I'm not into any organized stuff. I don't even know if I believe in God. But I find the idea of something more than reason compelling. And Kierkegaard, what he says about angst, about this existential dread connected to freedom and infinite possibilities and how our own life is limited and finite—I don't know. I found him when I was going through some hard stuff, and it changed a lot of how I see the world." Nico shook his head and gave another quiet laugh. "Kind of like this weird conversion that wasn't, you know, religious."

The silence felt longer this time.

"Sorry," Nico said. "I told you this was boring. And, I am now realizing with exquisite horror, super weird."

"It's not weird. Or boring. What about that quote you said? What does that mean?"

"Oh. Well, a big deal for Kierkegaard is that truth might not be subjective, but we reach it through subjectivity. So, objective fact—kind of like reason—aren't the most important thing in determining the truth. Individual experience affects how facts are integrated into someone's life. And our individual experiences carry their own form of truth. So, I can sit here, and I can have this beautiful morning, and I feel connected to—" Nico barely stopped himself from saying, *You*. "—everything around me, and I know, in this fundamentally indescribable way, what it feels like to be alive. And an asshole on a phone walks by, and he doesn't get any of that."

Jadon nodded slowly.

"I know," Nico said. "Weird."

"What's weird is that you lied about the birthday cake, Nico. It's not like someone was going to check your story and verify that the cake was for a terminally ill child."

"I never said—" Nico stopped, mouth open in outrage. "You asshole!"

With a smirk, Jadon slid off the planter. He held out a hand. Nico let him help him down, aware of the strength in Jadon's grip, aware—in a way that sent all those molecules into a frenzy of spinning again—of how gentle he was. Then Nico shoved him.

Jadon staggered back, the big faker.

"You are an asshole," Nico said and shoved him again.

"I give up! I surrender!"

Scoffing, Nico turned and started toward the sidewalk.

Jadon, the dumbass, was chuckling when he caught up.

"Your turn," Nico said as they started down the hill.

"For what?"

"To expose some embarrassing secret vulnerability. Let's go back to the potty-training years."

"Good Lord," Jadon said under his breath. In a stronger voice, he said, "Just so you know, I like learning stuff, believe it or not. And I like—" The hesitation was so slight that, if Nico hadn't been a hundred percent attuned to Jadon and hyperprocessing every cue—he might have missed it. "—learning stuff about you."

"Quit stalling. How about embarrassing boners, the middle school edition?"

"Oh my God, one time when we were running the track."

"Big deal. It happens to everyone in gym class."

"The entire time you're running the mile? The gym teacher said I broke a school record."

Nico laughed. The breeze picked up in the trees ahead of them. Branches moved. Light flashed on mottled bark. Pompom clusters of seeds drifted out across the sky. Put your arm around me, dumbass, Nico thought. Hold my hand.

But instead, Jadon said, "Do you remember I asked you for a favor?"

"You told me going to dinner with you would be a favor. Which—keep this in your back pocket—is actually a terrible pickup line. Next time, try telling me how you're so desperate for me that if I don't go to dinner with you, you won't eat or sleep, you'll waste away because all you'll be able to do is think about me."

"Yeah," Jadon said. "That doesn't sound psycho at all."

"A little psycho is cute."

"You might be a niche audience."

"Tell me about the favor."

"So—" Jadon hesitated, and it was hard to tell because of the run, because the whole world seemed pink in the sunrise, but it looked like he might be blushing. "So, I've kind of been going through it. Okay, not kind of. I'm a mess." And then, like a man plunging off a cliff, "And that's part of the reason I stopped texting, which I realize was a shitty thing to do, and I'm sorry."

Their footsteps rang out against the pavement for a few yards before Nico said, "Okay."

"You're not going to scream at me?"

"I don't think so."

"Make a scene?"

"Maybe later."

"I was under the impression there would be...consequences."

Jadon's words carried a note of humor, like he was trying to keep things light, but he wasn't joking, not entirely. That had been one of those sleepless confessions, Nico explaining—why, oh God, why had he decided to explain—all the stupid things he did when he felt scared and threatened and vulnerable. But he'd been working on them. He'd been working on himself. And, more to the point, he didn't feel vulnerable right then. If anything, the opposite—because he could tell, from the way Jadon's shoulders hunched, the way he hugged himself, the way he turned his head slightly so his breath steamed off to the side, that Jadon was feeling vulnerable and exposed and maybe even a little frightened. And Nico wanted to make that better for him.

"Okay, so, you're a wreck."

Jadon groaned.

"Get it? Wreck. Reck. Jadon Reck."

"I've never heard that one before."

Nico shoved him. In a supportive way. "Keep talking, dummy. Don't make me pry it out of you."

"Okay, well, I haven't been handling...life, I guess. Not well, anyway." He drew in a slow breath, and Nico thought of how Jadon had looked the day before, bags under his eyes, his color bad, the hundred little tells of a man hanging on by his fingertips. "And apparently, there are going to be consequences if I don't pull it together. Like, I'm going to be found unfit for service." A white cloud of laughter exploded out of him. "Jesus Christ, I can't even believe it, hearing it out loud."

"God, Jay. I'm so sorry."

With a grimace, Jadon shrugged. "I'll figure it out. Cerise is probably right; I guess I've been letting things…slide."

Nico thought about how *letting things slide* didn't quite explain how Jadon looked hollowed out, run down, worn to the bone.

"You know, John-Henry, Emery's husband, he's got all these gay romance novels."

"Huh?"

"Like *My Gay Christmas Prince*. And *My Gay Christmas Billionaire*. And *My Billionaire Bear*. Oh, and *Alphas under the Mistletoe*. That one was raunchy."

Jadon's eyes narrowed.

"So," Nico said in what he considered his most helpful tone, "if you're going to try a fake boyfriend stunt, you should probably borrow some of his books. Because the fake boyfriend thing shows up all the time."

Another laugh escaped Jadon, and even after it faded, little crinkles remained around his eyes as he studied Nico. "So, I need a fake boyfriend, huh?"

"You obviously need help. And I'm your friend, so I'm helping." Then Nico smirked. "Besides, I notice a significant lack of real boyfriends."

"You're not wrong there."

They crossed one of the old, graceful bridges, and Nico let his hand trail over the pebbled concrete of the parapet. The roughness of it, the cold, they seemed to wake him up. The sun slanted through the trees in long, pale shafts, and everything was still touched by that rose-colored light. It was like he hadn't been awake in a long time.

"It's hard, you know," Jadon said, but it sounded like he was talking to himself. "Being police. Seeing the stuff I see. Bringing it home to someone else, making them share it."

"Someone who loves you, someone who cares about you, you're not making them share it. The right guy is going to want to share it, because it means sharing more of your life, and it means another way he can support you."

Jadon made a noise that could have meant anything. "It's the hours. That's what it always comes down to."

"I thought it was bringing bad stuff home."

"The work never stops. Even when I take time off, I get calls, or I have to follow up on a witness, or a report is due. It's not the right time in my life; I'm too busy."

Nico didn't say it, but it sounded like bullshit.

"Well, I don't know why I'm single," Nico said, "because I'm a gem."

A huge grin spread across Jadon's face.

"Something to say?" Nico asked.

Jadon shook his head. He even raised his hands in surrender.

Nico snorted. He stopped to lean against the parapet. Cold soaked into him, and even inside Jadon's hoodie, he shivered. Jadon hadn't complained about the cold, but he folded his arms, and his nipples looked dark and stiff under the athletic fabric of his tee.

"Do I have to?" Nico asked.

"What?"

"No, it's okay. I have to." He blew out a breath. "I don't know. I mean, I got so sick of it. Dating, I mean. And then even hooking up started to feel awful. I mean, there's only so many times you can see a guy's eyes light up because you tell him you used to model underwear and then, over and over again, see how disappointed he is when the fantasy doesn't live up to the reality. Not to mention the whole I-give-high-maintenance-a-new-definition thing."

He tried to smile, but he was surprised that his face felt stiff. The cold, maybe.

For what felt like a long time, Jadon looked at him. Then he said, "I don't know. You don't seem high maintenance to me."

Nico's eyes felt hot. The cold again.

"Really," Jadon said to the silent question, and then he chuckled. "For example, you've never asked me to do a dopamine detox with you. And you never asked me to help you put together your hope chest. And you never once asked me to use my official police resources to investigate the Silicone Butt Plug Killer."

Blinking his eyes clear, Nico loosed a wet laugh. "You're making that up."

"Hello, I dated Shaw. He got super high and watched something about Brazilian butt lifts. Don't ask me how it turned into butt plugs."

"I think I have an idea."

That made Jadon grin. Then something else appeared in his expression; for lack of anything else, Nico would have called it surprise, as though something had startled Jadon—snuck up on him and caught him unaware. His face smoothed into troubled stillness.

"You can, uh, talk to me, you know," Nico said. "About stuff. Work stuff."

Jadon stared at him.

"If you want to talk to someone, dummy! Like, if you need to talk when you get home at night. I mean, I'm still awake, you know. And you still have my phone number."

Down below, a flock of Canada geese shuffled along the edge of the stream, making geese sounds to each other, the whole lot of them sounding like malcontents. After approximately an eternity, Jadon nodded. "Thanks."

"So, text me. Or call me. Or something. You know, so you don't turn into a shambling disaster of a human being."

"This might not sound as supportive as you think it does."

"Of course it does," Nico said loftily. "Being supportive is what I do."

Rather than give Jadon an opportunity to debate that—and before Jadon's nipples froze off—Nico started walking again.

They didn't make it far. On the other side of the bridge, a Canada goose waddled up from the stream and glared at Nico. Then it honked.

"Jesus Christ," Nico said, skipping down from the sidewalk and moving halfway into the road. The goose kept glaring at him.

Jadon, the big asshole, started laughing.

"What the fuck is wrong with you?" Nico asked. Loudly. "That thing tried to kill me, and you stood there laughing!"

Jadon laughed harder.

"Here I am, being the single most supportive man in your life, and you're going to stand there and shit yourself laughing while a goose disembowels me!"

Somehow, Jadon managed to quell his laughter. Giving the goose a wide berth, he moved down into the road. His movements became watchful and guarded, and he took Nico by the back of the neck and forced him into the crouch. He scanned the area around them. He pretended to speak into a mic. "The eagle is under attack. Repeat, the eagle is under attack."

"Get off me!"

"Swarm, swarm, swarm!"

Nico was still trying to wrench himself free from Jadon when Jadon pulled him into a stumbling run. They looped around the goose, sprinting down the asphalt until, laughing again, Jadon towed Nico up onto the sidewalk. Nico was laughing too, but he swatted Jadon until he released him.

"Asshole!"

"All clear," Jadon said. "Repeat, the eagle is all clear."

"You are such a jerk! And you think it's funny, and that's so much worse!"

The laughter had faded into a glimmer of a smile. Nico was suddenly aware of Jadon's quiet breathing, the tiny plumes of white, the way his chest rose and fell evenly. That single lock of hair was still stuck to his forehead. It was unfair and unjust and a sign of how messed up the universe was that when everybody else (i.e., Nico) was a sweaty mess after a run, Jadon looked like his shirt had been painted on, the definition of pecs and abs visible through the thin tee.

"I've been thinking about last night," he said. "About that guy following you. I want to show you something."

"What?"

Jadon took him by the shoulders and turned him. Then his arms slid around Nico's waist, and the length of his body pressed against Nico's, and Nico had enough blood left in his brain to think, That is definitely his dick, before Jadon started to speak, the words low and buzzing against Nico's ear.

"If someone grabs you from behind, there are a few simple ways to escape."

"Oh."

Nico's brain told him, a moment later, he had said it out loud, which was a good sign his next calendar appointment would be to crawl into a sewer and die of sheer and total humiliation.

Fortunately, Jadon either didn't hear or didn't care because he kept talking. "You can go limp and drop to the ground. He won't be expecting that, and most likely, you'll slip free and be able to run. Go ahead."

"I don't need you to—"

"The more you argue, the longer this is going to take."

"Excuse me?"

A tiny rumble of laughter, and—that was definitely Jadon's dick. Like, one hundred percent.

"Nico?"

"Hm?"

"Drop to the ground, please."

"Uh—oh."

Out loud. Again.

Nico let himself fall. Jadon didn't drop him, but he did, with a kind of exaggerated showiness, lower Nico and then release him. Nico got to his feet, and Jadon motioned for him to turn around again. His arms wrapped Nico a moment later. And Nico realized, with the inevitability of somebody watching a rocket launch, that he was chubbing up.

"Another option," Jadon said in that same low, firm voice, "is to fall forward. Go ahead and try that one too."

Nico did. And he stayed on the cold concrete, hoping for frostbite and shrinkage and anything, basically, that would save him from the embarrassment of that particular moment.

"Nico?"

"Right. Getting up now."

Once again, Jadon's arms encircled him, the hard lines of Jadon's body tight against him. Do not, Nico told himself. Do not. Don't you dare—

"You can also stomp on their foot." When Jadon nudged the back of Nico's knee, Nico pretended to bring his foot down on top of Jadon's. "Good. Or you can go for their ears, their eyes, their nose, or their throat."

He made Nico try each one, although fortunately, Nico wasn't required to actually stick a finger up Jadon's nose.

"If they grab you like this—" Jadon said, and he wrapped one hand— one big, strong hand with unmistakably masculine fingers—around Nico's throat.

And that was when Nico lost yet another battle.

"—you can try any of the techniques we talked about, but you can also grab their fingers. You want to try to bend them back as far as you can, as hard as you can. Try to break them if that's possible. Go on."

It shouldn't have had this effect on him. It shouldn't have made him tent his shorts, made him aware of the blood pounding in his ears, embarrassed by his body's reaction and unable to do anything about it. It shouldn't have been so fucking hot. But when he grabbed one of Jadon's fingers and pulled lightly, arousal washed through him again, even as Nico tried, desperately, to remember why it had seemed so important, not so long ago, to prevent anything like this from happening.

Jadon let Nico peel his hand away, and then he stepped back. The cold pressed against Nico's back like a flat, hard hand. His cheeks were hot. He shoved his fists into the hoodie's pockets and prayed to the saint of unruly boners that the old middle-school trick would provide cover once again.

"How do you feel?" Jadon asked when Nico finally turned around.

Nico's voice sounded thick when he said, "Fine."

"Any questions?"

Nico shook his head.

That little smudge of worry was back. "I'm sorry if that wasn't appropriate. I—I thought of it, and I didn't actually stop to think if it was a good idea."

"No." That was better—a little more normal, a little less like a teenage boy whose voice was about to break. "No, that was—thank you."

Behind them, a goose honked furiously. Jadon's mouth slanted into a smirk. Nico shoved him off the sidewalk.

Then, with a backwards grin for Jadon, Nico took off running back to the dorm.

11

Nico

By the time the seminar ended that afternoon, Nico's head was pounding. He followed the other students out into the blustery gray, the sky full of scudding clouds, leaves whipped up into tiny whirlwinds that spun away and died. One more day, he told himself as the breeze raked his hair. One more day. He could do one more day.

It wasn't simply the amount of new information he was learning from the professors—and, he reluctantly admitted, from the other grad students. It was the questions. The on-demand critical thinking. The passages of text presented and then, after barely a moment to read (or, if Nico were lucky, re-read) them, the dissection, anatomization, analysis. The fact, at the bottom line, that the whole thing was such a fucking performance.

Gio always had something brilliant to say, of course—a grudging admission, but one that Nico couldn't avoid. As did Clark. Between the two of them, they probably answered sixty percent of the questions. But Kaylee, when pressed, came up with excellent answers (for which she would then, every single time, apologize profusely). And Ridson had a trick of staying silent until delivering a bombshell response. Maya, of course, was crushing it—sliding in after Gio and Clark had blathered on to say something incisive and succinct. Nico tried to say something when he could, but that was becoming less and less frequent.

And, of course, it didn't help that he was supposed to present his paper tomorrow, on the final day of the seminar. It was probably a good thing. Probably a great thing, actually. Because it would be Saturday, and the seminar would end, and he could go get tanked and forget about how he had epically failed at this big opportunity.

Because the reality was, Nico wasn't going to finish his paper. He had drafts, sure. He had ideas. And now, after three days of pounding his head against indecipherable glosses of Augustine and Plotinus and Hegel and Nietzsche, he realized he had nothing. Scrap. Shit.

Maya elbowed him, and Nico brought his head up. He opened his mouth to ask what she wanted. And then he saw Jadon.

They hadn't seen each other since the fumbling awkwardness of the dorm showers, where they had cleaned up after the run. To Nico's simultaneous relief and disappointment, the showers featured private stalls, and he'd gotten no closer to seeing Jadon naked—not that he wanted to— than his silhouette through the thin curtain. Now, seeing him again in the navy suit and the garnet-colored tie, with his hair back to its sandy-dark perfection even after a day spent in trainings and round tables and whatever else police officers did at a symposium (maybe talk about their favorite time they handcuffed someone?), Nico forgot what he'd been about to say.

Laughing, Maya gave him a push toward Jadon.

"What—" Clark said behind Nico. And then, "You've got to be kidding me."

"Hey," Nico said.

"Hey yourself," Jadon said as he stood. "How was the seminar today?"

"Oh my God, I don't want to talk about the seminar. Also, it was great. And horrible."

"That is a confusing series of words."

For some reason, that was enough to make Nico smile. "How was the symposium?"

"Oh, that's easy: super boring."

Nico laughed.

The cluster of grad students was already moving off again, talking in low voices, and Clark called, "Nico, we're not waiting for you today."

Nico gave a wave without glancing over.

"You can go with your friends," Jadon said. "I told you, I'm not trying to mess up your life."

"Jesus, no. I've spent all day with them. If I hear Gio say one more time, 'Yes, but have you considered —' I'm going to blow my brains out."

"Well, we don't want that."

"Besides, I have to work on this paper. Which I will not finish. Which means tomorrow, I will give a live performance of complete academic self-destruction. And then I will blow my brains out."

"I liked the first part, but you lost me at the end."

He was still laughing as Jadon chivvied him toward the library. When the door to Eldridge Hall opened, Nico glanced over out of reflex. Dr. Meza stepped out, and his sharp, inquisitive eyes landed on Nico. It was different from how the professor had looked at Nico in the seminar, and Nico recognized that look. He'd seen it across a lot of bars, in a lot of clubs. He'd seen it on runways, at photoshoots, in agencies. His mouth did what he'd trained it to do a long time ago: a perfect smile that wasn't a promise but that...suggested.

Interest quickened in Dr. Meza's face.

And then Nico realized what he'd done. His cheeks heated, and he turned away and walked faster.

"Everything okay?" Jadon asked.

"Yeah."

"Did you know that guy?"

"He's a professor."

Jadon didn't say anything, and his silence grew as they crossed the quad. The sounds of traffic filtered in from Kingshighway —horns and engines and tires and, of course, ambulances. A group of men and women emerged from Waverley, two of the men shouting over each other about where to get the best wings while the rest of their group was engaged in the kind of collegial conversation that meant none of them knew each other. A girl pushed a cat in a stroller, occasionally stopping to bend and say something to the cat. The sky had deepened to the color of old ash, and for an uncanny moment, it was the same color as the campus's stained limestone, and Nico couldn't tell where stone ended and sky began.

He told himself not to look back, but of course, he did. No Dr. Meza. Relief loosened Nico's body, and then he told himself he was being silly. Nothing inappropriate had happened. Dr. Meza had looked at him, and Nico had smiled back. That was all. It wasn't like they'd been flirting in class. It wasn't like Dr. Meza had shown any kind of interest at all.

Not unless you counted the way he looked at Nico. Not unless you didn't know what that kind of look meant.

And what was he going to do, anyway? Follow Nico into the library and—what? Flirt with him some more? Make a pass? Demand sex in exchange for professional favors? Nico shook his head at himself. The whole thing was ridiculous.

But when he checked behind them again, he saw Heeley. The security guard was skulking in a narrow passageway between two buildings, but Nico was sure it was him. Although—Nico frowned through the gloom, trying to make out what he was wearing. Dark clothes. But they didn't look like the uniform he'd been wearing the other day. But that could have any number of explanations. It might be the gloom, playing tricks on Nico's eyes. It might be that Heeley had ended a shift, or was about to start one, and he was in his civvies. Did security guards call them civvies?

"Everything okay?" Jadon asked.

Nico whipped his head forward and managed some sort of noncommittal response. He could have told Jadon about Heeley. He could have mentioned, in passing, that it was strange. But what if it wasn't strange? What if Heeley had a perfectly innocent explanation for following them?

Nico dragged his gaze forward again, his mind racing as he tried to keep his body language normal, his stride smooth. They reached the edge of the quad, and when he looked a third time, Heeley was still back there. Moseying along, yes. But there. And this time, Nico was sure he made eye contact.

He opened his mouth to tell Jadon, and before he could say anything, he thought of how, only a moment before, he'd been worried about Meza. And how there were a million reasons Heeley might be crossing campus right then. He might be going to the gym. He might be going to meet a friend—he was young, the right age to have friends on campus. Hell, he could be a student here, and he was going back to his apartment or dorm. Nico wrestled with a nervous giggle. He could be going to the library. Maybe he and Nico could be study buddies.

At the glass doors to the library, Jadon paused, studying Nico's face in the panel of light that fell from inside. Then he said, "Are you sure everything's okay? If you want to go with your friends—"

"They're not my friends. Well, Maya is. And no." Nico softened his voice. "Thank you, but I've got to get this paper done. Or, at least, I've got to print it off so, after they massacre me tomorrow, they can shred it and bury me in the strips of paper."

Jadon nodded. "Like a giant litter box."

For a moment, Nico forgot about Heeley. "What is wrong with you?"

Jadon opened the door, grinned, and made a courtly, after-you gesture as Nico stomped past.

This time, Nico waited while Jadon got a pass, and they went up to the fourth floor together. Instead of the large, open study space, Nico made his way through another fire door and into the stacks. This was the heart of the library, where the collection was housed. The floor was sealed concrete. The walls were concrete too. The shelving units were a dull, serviceable gray that probably would have brought fond memories to the heart of a rear admiral. Fluorescents buzzed steadily overhead, their light sterile and strangely depthless, and even with the HVAC system circulating air, it smelled of moldering cloth bindings and old paper and something else, a smell Nico associated with freshmen dorms and finals week and unbrushed teeth.

Carrels were spaced throughout the stacks, and Nico found one close to the section of books he needed. He slung his backpack from his shoulder, pulled out the chair, and made quick, efficient work of laying out pencils, notes, his laptop. When he looked up, Jadon was grinning.

"Message received," Jadon said.

"What message?"

The grin got bigger. "I'll let you work. Let me know if you need to go anywhere."

"Yes, Dad."

"You know, I like it when guys call me daddy," Jadon said. And he did some sort of stretch, arms over his head, that pulled his shirt tight against his chest and made Nico think wet, thirsty thoughts. And then, still grinning, he sauntered off.

"Asshole," Nico said by the time he recovered the power of speech.

But Jadon was gone, and it was too little, too late.

Nico set to work. None of the farting around that—if he were being honest—typically took up ninety percent of work sessions. He didn't check his mail. He didn't look at campus news. No scrolling the *New York Times*. No checking JSTOR "just one more time" to see if someone had miraculously published a new article since yesterday. No phone.

It was hard. And tedious. And it was probably why so many people, grad students among them, had such a hard time finishing what they set out to do. But deadlines had always been a motivating factor for Nico—lose five pounds by Friday or don't come back; complete your thesis by December or be asked to leave the program; finish this paper or be a laughingstock on the final day of the seminar, kiss this golden opportunity goodbye. And then what? Get a real job? Spend the rest of his life mastering the ever-evolving intricacies of the Emery Hazard filing system (patent pending)?

He was still working when, unmistakably, he smelled smoky, savory meat. He lifted his head and glanced around. The stacks were silent. Then ductwork boomed as the HVAC came on again, and Nico startled. People brought food into the stacks, of course. They weren't supposed to, but until the university started employing a dedicated task force of police librarians (which, Nico thought with the typical mixture of fondness and low-grade annoyance that accompanied every thought of the man, was probably the job Emery Hazard had been born for), students were going to do what they wanted. So, someone had brought their meal into the stacks so they could keep working. Nico's stomach grumbled. It wasn't a bad idea.

Then someone whispered, "Boo."

Nico jumped in his seat. He twisted in the chair: the shelving units, the long empty aisle, fluorescents streaking the concrete—

"Dumbass!"

Jadon had shifted the books on the shelving unit and made an opening to stick his head through. He looked both amused and incredibly self-satisfied as he put a finger to his lips and—a tad dramatically for such the butch cop type—whispered, "We're in a library."

"I know we're in a library!" It wasn't exactly a yell—more like a whisper if somebody had it by the balls. "Do you know how I know? Because I'm working. Here. Silently. Studiously. In the library. Not—not screwing around scaring people half to death! You almost gave me a heart attack!"

Jadon's smile was big. And silly. And bizarrely confident. And in the light of all those late-night texts, Nico suddenly understood what he was seeing: Jadon Reck, the man, the one who wasn't dragging around whatever had made him decide the only fit punishment was working himself to death. It surprised Nico, how young Jadon looked, and it surprised him again that Jadon was young—that he was, in fact, almost a year younger than Nico.

Before Nico could process the thoughts, plastic rustled, and Jadon pulled his head back enough to display a bag through the opening.

"You're not allowed to have food in here," Nico said, but his stomach rumbled so loudly that he was pretty sure Jadon heard. "And you have to put those books back."

Jadon did something with his eyebrows, but he put the books back. Plastic rustled a few more times. The smell of meat and wood smoke grew stronger, now mixed with something else—something, Nico's body told him, undoubtedly fried. Nico's stomach decided to try to turn itself inside out in anticipation. And still Jadon didn't appear.

"Jay?"

No answer.

Nico heaved himself out of the chair, his joints crackling from the time in the chair—God, had it really been three hours? He pushed aside the irrelevant, impossible, ludicrous thought that maybe he was getting old.

He came around the corner of the shelving unit into the next aisle, and then he stopped. Jadon had spread a tablecloth on the floor, and he sat there, takeout containers dotting the pristine white fabric. Paper plates. Eco-friendly disposable utensils.

"Jesus, Mary, and Joseph," Nico said. "If that's a beer, I will love you forever."

Laughing, Jadon popped the top on a can of—well, Nico hadn't heard of Schlafly Summer Lager before, but it did taste a little like summer, bright and citrusy and refreshing. Like it wasn't October, with the dark and the cold clenched tight around everything.

"We can't do this," Nico said. His stomach gurgled a protest.

A tiny smile hooked the corner of Jadon's mouth. "I can pack it up."

"No! I meant, we can't do this again. Just this once. That's it."

Jadon nodded.

"Because this is wrong."

"So wrong."

"There are rules."

"That's what makes it so exciting."

"Stop!" Nico laughed. "You're making it sound porny, and this is a library. It's a sacred space."

"You've never read Shaw's stories about Emery," Jadon asked drily, "have you?"

"God, why did you bring that up? It took me months to use a self-checkout again." Nico lowered himself to sit cross-legged on the tablecloth. He touched the fabric, and then he looked up at Jadon. The detective had lost his jacket, and the white broadcloth of his shirt had ridden up from his waistband to expose a hint of skin as he leaned back on his hands. The top button of the shirt was undone too, and Nico realized that, in a weird way, the hollow of a throat could be muscular—defined, anyway. And it was patently unfair that Jadon could even be buff in his neck. Where his collar lay open, it exposed a patch of paler skin, where most days it must have been hidden. That seemed unfair too. Nico took another drink of the beer. You need to eat something, a voice in his brain told him. You're drinking that too fast.

"All right," Nico said, gesturing with the can. "How?"

"A magician never reveals his secrets—ow!" With a laugh, Jadon pulled back the leg that Nico had kicked. He rubbed his shin and gave Nico puppy eyes. Then it was gone again, and the young, bright, smiling Jadon was back. "You wouldn't believe what you can get away with if you're a cop." Then he held up three fingers like a Boy Scout. "But I promise to only use my powers for good."

"Requisitioning the college's table linens," Nico said with raised eyebrows. "And don't give me that line about being a cop; I saw the security guard when you tried to get a pass tonight. He wanted to strip search you."

"But he was much friendlier after I gave him fifty bucks."

"Jadon!"

"Are you going to yell at me every time I tell you something?"

"Very possibly."

"So," Jadon said, "this is the place I was telling you about, before I changed my mind when I saw you looking at the Walk of Fame."

"Before I was a colossal brat, you mean."

"Before Saladgate. It's my favorite barbeque in the city. And these—" He held up what Nico now knew was a toasted ravioli. "—are toasted ravioli stuffed with brisket, so basically, they're the food of the gods."

Nico reached to take it from him, and at the same time, Jadon held it out, and somehow, instead of taking the ravioli, Nico found himself opening his mouth and accepting a bite. Jadon's knuckles dusted his chin, and the dark, dark sandiness of his eyes was so unbelievably...calm. Nico chewed mechanically, with absolutely no idea what the ravioli tasted like. It could have been delicious. It could have been school paste.

"Well?" Jadon asked.

"It's good, but I think I like the regular ones more."

"Try it with this sauce."

Nico did. And now that he wasn't—what? staring into Jadon's eyes, his whole body responding to that casual brush of skin on skin like it had been an electric current?—he could taste the brisket, the smoke, the vinegar and garlic. He nodded. "It's growing on me."

"And I got all the best stuff. They've got popovers, and pulled pork, and oh God, I'm going to have to run a marathon to burn off this mac and cheese, but it's like crack."

"What's a popover?" Nico asked, grabbing a plate.

The conversation moved easily after that—although Nico still didn't have any idea what a popover was besides buttery, airy, carby goodness. Nico asked about Jadon's day. Jadon asked about Nico's. Nico surprised himself by talking about his frustrations with the seminar, and it was oddly gratifying to make Jadon laugh. And when Jadon talked about how frustrated he felt, unable to make progress on his investigations while he was stuck at the symposium, Nico nodded and made understanding noises and, before he realized what he was doing, put a hand on Jadon's leg, the muscle warm and firm under his touch. And Jadon didn't even blink; he put a hand over Nico's, like it was supposed to be there, and kept talking.

This is the place I was telling you about. Jadon's words echoed in the back of Nico's head. And then, a voice like Nico's saying, This is a do-over.

This is a date.

Instead of the rush of dismay or panic or, frankly, annoyance, Nico found that it didn't seem to change anything. He was here. He was sharing a meal with someone who was funny and generous and kind. And, with a kind of wonder, Nico realized he was happy. It was like something loosening inside his chest. It wasn't the kind of manic restlessness and hilarity he remembered from his undergrad days, when everything had been going a hundred miles an hour, and happiness had seemed to mean something like screaming with laughter and drinking and parties and yes (he sounded a little defiant as he addressed the inescapable Emery-voice that had taken up permanent resident inside his head), even a little coke. This felt more like what he had with Emery, when things had been good. This felt — it came with a wave of heat that rose in his body — better.

Nico's phone buzzed, and Jadon stopped in his description of a woman he'd had to arrest for taking a dump in the middle of a Dollar Tree.

It was a text from Clark: *Whare are you?*

Nico shook his head, and Jadon started to speak again.

The phone buzzed again.

"Sorry," Nico said.

Jadon opened his mouth, and the phone buzzed again. With a sheepish smile, he said, "Are you sure you don't need to handle that?"

Nico shook his head, but he did check the phone:

Where are you/

Where are you??

He stared at the screen, his heart hammering in his ears. And then he silenced it and turned it facedown on the tablecloth.

"Everything okay?" Jadon asked.

Nico gave a frustrated toss of his head. "Clark."

"Ah."

"We're not together. Or hooking up. Or anything."

"You told me."

"We did hook up. Once. It was over a year ago. And it was stupid, and I've regretted it ever since. I mean, God, I don't even like him. And now this bullshit."

"Nico, you don't have to explain yourself to me."

"No, I'm sorry. I—we were having such a nice time, and now it's ruined."

"I'm still having a nice time." Jadon leaned back on his hands again. The darkly sandy eyes made Nico think of water, the sound of the surf, the way the sun caught grains of mica and spent them like matches. "Tell me about this big paper you're working on."

"Working on might be a loose description," Nico said. "I don't know. At this point, I might be banging my head against a wall."

"It's a big deal?"

"It could be. I mean, if I want to get into a good doctoral program, this could do it. I'd love to have a solid publication when I apply. And maybe a letter of rec from one of these professors."

"What's the paper about?"

"Kierkegaard," Nico said with a lopsided smile. "It's so boring; you don't want to know."

"Didn't we go over this?" Jadon said, and his tone was still gentle, but there was steel there too—a reminder that Jadon was, along with whatever else he was becoming for Nico, still a detective. "I asked you a question. That means I want to know."

"Okay. Um, so, let's see." Nico worked to sort out the threads of the argument in his head; he'd been living inside the paper for so long that it had become a jumble. "So, my research is about Kierkegaard's role in developing an aesthetics of Christian existentialism."

"Aesthetics like, what? Why things are beautiful?"

"Mmm, kind of. Why is part of it. But it's broader than that. What it means for something to be beautiful. What beauty means in the larger framework of Christian existentialism."

"Truth is subjectivity."

Nico gave him a startled look.

"Okay, that's a little insulting," Jadon said, eyebrows curved to take the heat out of the words.

Laughing, Nico shook his head. "No, I—oh my God, I'm sorry."

"Well, it was only this morning, Nico. I'm not a genius, but I can remember that far back. Keep going."

"Right. Well, the question of aesthetics and subjectivity is a huge one, way beyond Kierkegaard, and that's partly what I'm interested in. But for this paper, I'm interested in a different side of his work. Kierkegaard is…um, complicated? I mean, that's a way of saying his writings are convoluted, and sometimes they seem contradictory, and in general—"

"It feels like pounding your head against a brick wall?"

"Pretty much. But one of the questions that comes up is the way Kierkegaard uses the language of the aesthetic to talk about love, which again, isn't exactly unique—I mean, most of the Western tradition has some conflation of love and beauty—but the way Kierkegaard does it is fascinating."

Jadon's smile was like something Nico had drawn as a child, his best, most determined efforts to capture the essence of a smile, and somehow getting it right even though all he'd managed were the lines of it.

"Sorry. You're—"

"If you tell me I'm bored," Jadon said, "we're going to have a fight. What does Kierkegaard say about love?"

"The problem with the aesthetic—with beauty, for Kierkegaard—is that it's sensual, it's unstable, it's often selfish, and it's right now, a pleasure that distracts us from what matters, which is the eternal. And if we're caught up in the aesthetic, and aesthetic love, which a lot of people take to mean sexual love, or love with a sexual component, then we're not going to make that leap of faith that takes us from reason to beyond reason."

"Because we already have something we want, something here."

"Exactly!" Nico sat up a little straighter. "So, Kierkegaard says there's ethical love. Because loving our neighbor is a commandment in the scripture, so he can't say love in general is a problem. Ethical love is a duty. It's an obligation to care for people, and it transforms love from something based on feelings, which are sensual and changing, to a commitment. It's also something we choose, which means that even though it's an obligation, it also emphasizes our moral freedom. True love is freely given and freely chosen."

"But no sex?" Jadon said dubiously.

"I heard that."

"It's a philosophical question."

"Sorry, Kierkegaard didn't cover being called daddy."

"Hey!"

Nico shrugged and spread his hands.

"Hey," Jadon said again, and this time he laughed. "So, that's it? Ethical love? A moral commitment to care for the person you choose to love? That seems kind of...I don't know. Cold."

"Kierkegaard isn't a straightforward writer. He talks about romance and the reality of human relationships that begin in the aesthetic mode. But he believed that ethical love was higher, and he tried to live that way. Struggled with it. He was engaged, and he broke off that engagement, which was a big deal for him." Nico was silent for a moment. "Anyway, I'm writing about the absurd and the leap of faith, kind of this mixture of ideas, playing around with how Kierkegaard's ideas on non-rationality might actually resolve some of the contradictions in his ideas of aesthetic love."

"That sounds so interesting."

"No, it doesn't."

"Yes, it does. And it's intimidating. Here you are, you speak five languages, and you read like twenty more, and you're writing this paper about stuff I can barely wrap my brain around, and it's—it's incredible."

Nico tried not to. Then he smiled. He shrugged.

"This is going to sound so stupid," Jadon said, "but how did you get interested in this stuff? I mean, how did you even learn about it in the first place."

"Like, when I was a braindead model, how did I ever manage to stop doing coke and blowing agents to start a rigorous investigation of Kierkegaard's theory of the aesthetic?"

Jadon's face closed.

"I'm sorry," Nico said. "I didn't mean that. I—it's automatic."

"It's all right."

"Jay, I'm super sorry. I hate doing that, the knee-jerk response. It's so immature. It's a good question."

"I know you weren't braindead." Jadon's expression softened. "For God's sake, you were at Columbia."

"Yeah, well, that doesn't always mean as much as you think it does," Nico said with a grin. "But thank you. I guess I was...I guess I was in a bad place, actually, although at the time, I didn't realize it. I was in my second year. At Columbia, that's when you have to declare your major. I had no idea what I was going to do. I was picking up modeling jobs as fast as I could, convinced that was...I don't know, the right thing to do. My parents." He stopped. He felt hot, and he found the tab of the zipper on his sweater and clutched it. Stop, he told himself. This isn't cute, not on anybody. So, stop right now. But the words kept tumbling out. "I'd moved off campus and into an apartment that the modeling agency provided. Three of us to a room. In bunk beds, my God. And it was a shithole. And I never knew when I was going to get paid, never knew when I was going to have money, and the other guys were such bitches, and I got so weird about food, which, yeah, it was definitely the start of an eating disorder, even though the other guys made it all seem so normal." He stopped. Tried to. It was like trying to brick up a dam as the water came pouring through. "One time, I heard one of the guys say we were just hangers for the clothes, and that's right. You'd show up for a shoot, and they'd take one look at you and send you home. Or you'd wait hours to be considered — because for that job, they couldn't go by the agency photos — and they'd say, 'Too brown.' Or 'Too tall.' Or, I swear to God, 'Too skinny.' And I started having these epic meltdowns. It was this vicious circle, because then I'd be nervous the next shoot, or I'd make myself sick, or God. And then one day —" Stop, he thought. This is when you have to stop. " —one of the assistants for the photo shoot took out a measuring tape and started checking my wrists and ankles and calves. I shit you not. And they had this whole discussion while I was standing there about the ratios, calf to ankle, wrist to ankle, if they could find a way to make it work because I wasn't what they wanted. And I stood there, listening to them, already starting to meltdown. They sent me home, and I stayed in bed for two days. And there was this voice in my head, telling me how shit I was, how worthless, how ugly."

"Nico—" Jadon began.

But Nico spoke over him. "But this other part of me, this part of me that was trying to stay alive, was reminding me that at one point, I'd been proud of the fact that I was smart, that I did well in classes, that I had goals and ambitions that had nothing to do with whether my fucking calves were too big for my fucking ankles." He shook his head. "Thank God I hadn't dropped out of school. I'd been going to classes, although I was doing terribly in most of them, and I decided I was going to start getting good grades again. It was a lifeline; I can see that now. I took fewer jobs. I stayed in the library as long as I could because I didn't want to go to that apartment.

I was in a philosophy elective, and we were reading Kierkegaard, and it was like he was talking to me. Despair and angst, being confronted with your failure to live up to your potential." Nico waited until his throat relaxed enough for him to continue. "At semester, I moved into the dorms, which felt great as a sophomore. I declared a philosophy major. I kept taking modeling jobs, but it was a job now. And holy shit, I cannot believe I said all of that out loud. If you need to run for an exit, I think there's a fire escape that way."

Jadon didn't smile, though; he watched Nico with an unsettling intensity, the silence growing until it prickled. When he spoke, his voice was rough, "I am so sorry."

"It's okay. It's fine, actually. I'm fine. I'm here now, and I'm happy— well, I'm not unhappy—and I learned some heavy shit about myself, which is apparently the whole fucked-up purpose of life."

"But I'm sorry you had to go through that. I'm sorry you were alone. And I think it's amazing that you took all that pain and suffering and found a way to use it to make yourself stronger." His voice softened. "I think you're amazing."

"You should think I'm crazy," Nico said. "Or nuts. Or psycho; a lot of people like to tell me I'm psycho."

The only answer was more of that intensely earnest study.

"Now you're supposed to tell me the tragic secret of your childhood," Nico prompted.

Jadon laughed quietly. "No tragic secrets, unfortunately."

"Bullshit."

"Scout's honor."

"God, of course you were a Boy Scout."

"Actually, I wasn't. My moms wouldn't let me." His voice took on an amused note as he added, "Trust me, I asked."

Jadon wasn't sure what had been most surprising, in those under-the-cover-of-darkness conversations via text: learning that Jadon had grown up on an organic farm outside of Iowa City with two moms, or that Jadon seemed so surprised by Nico's surprise when he'd learned it. In hindsight, Nico recognized the hippie-ish thread to Jadon's character—the quirky T-shirts about tea and beets and Santa Fe; the sneaking suspicion that Jadon aspired to drive a Subaru; the improbability of how well Jadon and Shaw had fit as a couple (which, yes, Nico had done all sorts of snooping about, to the point that Emery had started to get suspicious about all the questions).

"Why?"

"Why did I want to be a Boy Scout? Or why wouldn't my moms let me?"

"Both, I guess."

"My moms have strong opinions. I guess I should say strong beliefs. They're the ultimate hippies—anti-war, anti-corporation, anti-government. As an adult, I can look back and see that they were two young women trying to figure out how to run a farm with zero experience, zero money, and a brand-new baby boy. I mean, it's ridiculous; one of my moms was an honest-to-God debutante. What did she know about farming? And, of course, they were terrified about raising a boy."

"Because they're lesbians?" Nico asked doubtfully.

Jadon gave him a look.

"I don't know," Nico said with a laugh. "I'm trying to be an active listener."

"Not because they're lesbians. Because they didn't know anything about boys, and because they were already overwhelmed, and because, if I'm being honest, they've got—"

"Beliefs?"

Jadon smiled. "Yes. They've got beliefs about men. So, when I was growing up, there was a lot of talk about toxic masculinity, although they weren't calling it that back then. A lot of conversations about how to be a human being—not 'a man'. And I love them for that; I'm glad they worked so hard to try to teach me to be compassionate, not to buy into stereotypes about gender."

"Not to be another tool for the patriarchy."

"Yep, not to be another tool for the fucking patriarchy." A wry grin crossed Jadon's features. "But at the time, it pissed me the hell off."

Nico burst out laughing. "What?"

"Oh God, by the time I was a teenager, I hated it. Hated them, or that's what it felt like. Because it was hard enough going to school and being the kid from the hippie-lesbian-organic farm commune, when everybody else had a mom and dad. And then, on top of that, I wasn't allowed to do Scouts, wasn't allowed to go camping, wasn't allowed to shoot guns or bows or go hunting. They were hardliners about not letting any 'masculine energy,' as they called it, into my life."

"Let me guess: good little Jadon Reck did exactly what they said."

"Hard to remember since I was stoned from 2007 to 2013."

Nico laughed so hard he had to lie down. Somehow, his head ended up next to Jadon's leg. Jadon laughed too, although softly. When he drew his fingers through Nico's hair, it was like someone tightened a wire that ran from Nico's chest down, down, down.

"They actually didn't care so much about the grass, as they called it, but God, when they found out I'd shot a turkey. One time in my life, my mom hit me. Once. She had this leather strap, God knows why. I didn't sit down for a week. I heard them crying about it later, and now, it's heartbreaking. At the time, though, it made me mad."

"Please tell me more about rebellious Jadon. Please tell me you did something wicked like pee standing up or mansplain or use gendered language. Did you call a flight attendant a stewardess?"

Jadon tugged on his hair and, the next moment, ran a soothing hand over it as he said, "Smartass."

"Did you hear a name like Dr. Murray and automatically assume it was a man?"

"Forget it. Never mind. I decided you are a brat."

"No, please! You have to tell me how you went from stoner turkey-killer to the pillar of law and order."

"Oh my God."

"Please!"

It was, admittedly, too loud and too long for the stacks, and Nico could only giggle when Jadon put a hand over his mouth.

"No more beer for you," Jadon said. "And no more toasted ravioli. They're making you wicked." He gave Nico's head a little shake for emphasis. "Two things happened. One was Robbie. And the other was college."

"Oh my God, Robbie."

"Yes, Robbie. He was a college student interested in organic farming, and he spent a summer doing an internship — which mostly meant smoking a lot of 'grass' with my moms, providing free labor, and —" Jadon cut off.

"You had sex with him?"

"A little more quietly," Jadon half-whispered and gave Nico another of those tiny shakes. "He was gorgeous. And bi. And yes. And if you laugh when I tell you our first time was in a hayloft, I'm going to leave."

"I'm dying. I'm dead. I'm literally so happy that my body has perished."

"Okay."

"Tell me everything. Was he wearing plaid? Did he have a big —" The pause lasted long enough. "—belt buckle? What kind of boots was he wearing?"

Jadon pulled his hair again.

Laughing—and crying out in pain—Nico batted at his hand. When Jadon finally released him, Nico said, "Fine, fine. Tell me about Robbie."

"I'm certainly not going to tell you about Robbie." But his hand came back, stroking the side of Nico's head again, and after a moment, he drew a deep breath. "I was in love with him, of course. I mean, he was gorgeous.

And the sex was—I mean, I'd never had anything like that, although I'm guessing it was a pretty underwhelming fifteen seconds for him."

Nico giggled into Jadon's thigh.

"I was eighteen, and when he left, my heart broke. I honestly thought I was going to die. I didn't, obviously. But when I could think clearly again, I remember—I remember thinking that I was going to have to leave. I hadn't put it to myself that way before, but I knew. I wasn't going to find someone to love if I stayed on that farm. So, I applied all over the place, and believe it or not, I got a full ride to UMSL. I started the next fall."

"And you stayed in St. Louis?"

"I did. I figured out a lot of stuff in college. How to dress. How to act. I found guys I wanted to be friends with."

"And guys you wanted to fuck."

"Them too."

"So much masculine energy."

"God, yes. And what's the butchest job? I mean, the most macho, the most sexist, the most—"

"Guns?"

Jadon laughed. Nico could feel it reverberate through his body, into Nico's body, and he thought, That's a part of him that's a part of me now. And he thought, We're touching. And it sounded silly because of course they were touching, with Nico's cheek against Jadon's thigh. Of course they were touching. But that was the thought, as the laughter vibrated into Nico: We're touching.

"Are you seriously telling me that you are the first person in the history of the world to become a police officer to piss off your parents?"

"Believe it or not, I'm not the first."

"Jadon!"

Another easy chuckle passed through his body, into Nico's. He stroked Nico's hair. "I mean, the criminal justice major was to piss off my moms. By the time I was a couple years into it, though, I'd matured."

Nico made a skeptical noise.

"But by that point, I'd also realized I didn't agree with some of what my moms believed. They raised me with a lot of good values, things I'm happy they taught me. But I'm not a pacifist. And I'm not anti-government."

"And you're definitely not a vegetarian."

The laugh, this time, was richer, deeper, and that wire running down from Nico's chest drew tighter and tighter. "Definitely not."

The silence that came after had a quality that Nico wasn't used to — easy, comfortable, and yet also charged with a potential that he couldn't quite name. Jadon was still stroking his hair, the movements slow and relaxed.

Nico was speaking before he realized he meant to say anything. Whispering, really. His eyes on the ceiling, because it felt like too much to look at Jadon right then. "I'm happy you are who you are, Jay. I think you're a good person."

"I'm happy you are who you are, Nico. And you are a good person."

"I'm not," Nico said. "But I want you to think I am." Nico sat up, blinking his eyes clear, trying to draw a deep breath. He fought for a normal voice as he said, "And I've got to finish my paper, or we'll be here all night."

"Go on. I'll clean this up, and when you're ready, I'll walk you home."

"It's late, Jay. You need to sleep."

"Well then," Jadon said from behind him, and Nico could hear the smile, "you'd better get to work on that paper."

"You could come hear it." As soon as the words were out of his mouth, Nico decided the best and only option was to find a section of movable stacks, stick his head between two units, and become the first official library decapitation. "Never mind; I forgot you've got your symposium, and you're too busy anyway, and it's definitely not like anyone dreams of spending a Saturday talking about Kierkegaard."

Jadon didn't say anything.

Eventually, because no decapitating bookshelves appeared to be within reach, Nico craned his head.

Jadon wore a tiny smile. "That sentence kept getting better and better."

Because he was full of toasted ravioli, Nico permitted himself an outraged noise.

"I'd love to listen to your paper," Jadon said. "I didn't know people could attend."

"Ridson's wife sat in when he read his the other day. Not that you're my wife. Oh my God."

Not quite laughing now, the sandy gold of Jadon's eyes was definitely amused. "Thank you for inviting me."

"It was an accident. I didn't mean to."

"Too bad."

"You're uninvited. I uninvite you."

With a nudge to the shoulder, Jadon said, "Finish your paper so we can get out of here."

To Nico's own surprise—and, for that matter, the universe's as well—he had a draft that was barely, marginally acceptable completed within an hour. The background noises of Jadon cleaning up their picnic in the stacks faded to nothing, and before long, he was sending the paper to the printer out in the study space. He packed up his laptop, collected his pages from the printer, and found Jadon lounging in one of the seating areas near the stairs.

"In case you tried to sneak out," Jadon said without absolutely zero shame.

"Charming."

For a moment, the flash of a grin lifted the mask of weariness and—what? despair?—from Jadon's face, and Nico tried not to think about what it meant when he caught himself smiling on the stairs a few moments later.

They walked back to Harlow Hall under the hazy glow of the security lights and the scrim of thin, gauzy clouds. Their steps sounded louder in the stillness, the crunch of a brittle leaf, the snap of a dry twig that had fallen across the path. Neither of them spoke, and Nico found himself listening to the movements of Jadon's body. Strange, wasn't it, that already he could recognize the cadence of Jadon's gait, the whisper of his breath, the way he took up space in Nico's world. The universe's default state, he had learned as an undergrad, was a vacuum.

Harlow rose ahead of them, the limestone cloaked with shadows, the neogothic adornments lost in the darkness. A few solitary windows glowed; everything else had given in to the night and disappeared. It took Nico a moment to realize what was different: the security light at the front door had burned out.

"Wait here," Jadon said.

"You're not serious."

He put a hand on Nico's arm, the touch firm, a silent command. Nico rolled his eyes, but he let Jadon stop him. After a moment, when Jadon must have felt sure Nico wouldn't bolt, he drew back his hand and started forward again.

"You're being silly," Nico called after him.

A breeze picked up, sending more leaves skittering. Branches creaked overhead. Jadon didn't respond, didn't even turn to answer back, and Nico shivered and chafed his arms.

It was sweet, of course. But it was silly, too. Even if Jadon were right, even if, by some bizarre chance, someone had followed Nico across campus the other night, it couldn't have been more than bad luck. Nico didn't go to school at Chouteau. He didn't know anyone here. And, therefore, he couldn't be a target. For that matter, Nico would be gone in a couple of days, which meant—

Well, what did it mean?

The future was like a movie screen, images flickering across it: Jadon laughing, Jadon with his long legs kicked out in a vee, Jadon's mouth twitching with amusement when he was trying to be professional and Nico got that obstinate itch to break the façade. Jadon naked. The strong calves and thighs. The sculpted definition of chest that every shirt seemed determined to show off. Big arms—powerful and toned. He'd take up too much of the bed, Nico tried to tell himself, through the heat-shimmer of the fantasy. He'd elbow you in your sleep.

And then, clearer, a vision of the next few minutes: they'd walk upstairs, and they'd stop at Nico's door, and Jadon would look at him, and Nico knew—because he could always tell—that something would happen. He didn't know if he would move first, or if Jadon would, or if it would be both of them. He liked it best when it was both of them, when they both seemed to know. Last night, it had felt like that, but at the last minute, something had changed. Tonight, though—his lips, the taste of his mouth, and beer, and the leftover smokiness of the barbeque.

Oh my God, Nico thought with something like despair. I'm going to kiss him.

Jadon's steps rang out against the brick pathway as he returned. "Sorry, but it seemed a little too convenient that the light burned out tonight."

"Lights burn out, Jay."

"Uh huh."

"Does the eagle have permission to land?"

His hand settled comfortably on Nico's nape, and he steered him toward the building.

At the door, Nico turned and planted a hand on Jadon's chest. Dense. Warm—to his chilly fingers, in fact, almost hot. He gave a tiny push and said, "Thank you for dinner."

One of Jadon's eyebrows went up, but he said, "You're welcome."

"And thank you for being worried about me."

"Of course."

Nico shivered, and he wasn't sure if it was the cold or the words, the way he had said them like he meant them. *Of course.*

"I'm going to go inside now," Nico said, fumbling the door open with his free hand. "And I'm going to say goodnight to you right here."

"I'd like to walk you to your room."

"I'm giving my paper after lunch, around one. If you want to come."

"Don't be silly; I'll go upstairs with you and make sure you get into your room." A hint of a smirk. "I'm not going to try anything."

"I've heard that before," Nico said as he slipped through the door.

That brought a laugh. "Excuse me?"

"Goodnight," Nico sang softly.

Jadon did a big production: arms across his chest, a pointedly unhappy look straight at Nico. Nico gave him a little finger wave. Jadon just doubled down, arms tightening, scowl deepening. Fighting a laugh, Nico blew him a kiss and headed for the stairs.

He caught himself thinking, as he took the steps two at a time, of how it had felt, his head resting against Jadon's thigh. He shook that off, but on the next step, he caught himself thinking about strong fingers moving over his hair. The way it had felt when Jadon laughed, and the sound rippled from one body to another. It's been a long time, Nico told himself. You're going through a dry spell. Touch, anybody's touch, is going to feel amazing because it's been so long. He caught himself thinking of how Jadon had felt under his hand, of the rise and fall of his chest. Absolutely not, he told himself. And, with a kind of bumbling adolescent indecision, he thought maybe he should jack off.

When he reached his floor, the lights were off except for the lone EXIT sign at the end of the hall. Nico hadn't known the lights turned off; he'd been vaguely aware, the last couple nights, of a strip of light under the door, like in a hotel. Someone bumped a switch, he guessed. Or the custodial crew had someone new on it, someone who didn't know the dorm was in use during fall break. Nico reached for his phone to turn on his flashlight.

The EXIT sign shed a faint red glow, and something passed beneath it—only an impression of black against black, texture, like velvet rubbed the wrong way.

"Hello?" Nico said.

Nothing. The red glow of the sign was undisturbed now. Your imagination, Nico told himself. You're tired. Your eyes are tired.

The whisper of a sole against carpet.

That had not been his imagination.

For one paralyzing moment, he was back in the sub-basement at Wroxall, the smell of damp, raw stone, the aching heaviness of his body as he fought the drugs, the disorientation as he woke to darkness. A serial killer who called himself the Keeper of Bees had kidnapped Nico. It had been easy for him; Nico had made it easy for him, because Nico had liked him, trusted him, had maybe even thought the relationship was going somewhere. He remembered the crushing silence, the way it had caved in on him until he wanted to scream just to hear something.

And then the moment broke, and Nico turned, trying to find the door to the stairs in the dark. He found the thin paneling. The whisper of steps came again, faster. Running. Nico's hands slid over the door, trying to find the handle. The running steps were louder now, closer, closing in on him. A white fog of panic filled Nico's head. Where the fuck was the handle?

Then the door swung open, and in the stairwell lights, Jadon stood there. He seemed to take in Nico, and he said, "What's—"

And then his face changed, and he yanked Nico toward him. Nico stumbled down several steps, catching himself against the railing, as Jadon shot past him into the hall. Jadon's shout rang out—"Stop right there!"—and racing footsteps hammered away. A door slammed, and it sounded like a gunshot. Adrenaline spiked, waves of pins and needles rolling over Nico, and too late he tried to remember all the self-defense he'd learned. He worked the keys through his fingers into an improvised weapon. He was shaking so badly that he leaned against the rail to keep himself upright.

It was hard to say how much time passed. Nico stayed where he was, under the dim glow of the stairwell's emergency lights, until the door at the top of the stairs swung open again. Panic dug its claws into his guts for an instant. And then it was Jadon, his face contorted with fury.

"He got away."

12

Jadon

He'd gotten away.

Again.

Jadon tried to tamp down his fury as he escorted Nico—pale and trembling—to his room, but it felt like a losing battle. The suspect had been here. Inside the dorm. Waiting. He'd planned the whole thing. He'd been waiting. He'd watched them approach the dorm. If Nico had returned alone, Jadon guessed the assault would have happened near the entrance. But Jadon had ruined that plan, and so the suspect had retreated and gone with his backup plan: the lights on Nico's floor. And in spite of Jadon's best efforts, the man had escaped again—in Jadon's memory, the chase was a blur of impressions: the sky a gray smear of light pollution, the branches of old trees swaying overhead, the narrow passageways between the old campus buildings, and then emerging, his body hot from the run, his breath steaming, into the emptiness of the quad.

When they stopped at Nico's doors, Jadon waited for Nico to unlock it, but Nico only stood there. After a moment, Jadon took Nico's hand and slowly worked the keys loose from between his fingers. Nico's breathing stuttered, and tears rushed into his eyes. He blinked them away, and as he released the keys, shook out his hand like it was aching.

"That was smart," Jadon said as he opened the door. "The keys were a good idea. You kept your head, and you remembered how to protect yourself."

Nico's little noise was half laugh, half sob. After Jadon gave the room a quick look, Nico didn't resist when Jadon put a hand at the small of his back and walked him inside.

He'd been in Nico's room earlier that day, but it seemed like it had been so much longer. The morning, and that run through Forest Park, and the moment that had flowered between them, with the Jewel Box like a giant prism, and Nico talking about subjectivity and truth, and the way Nico had seemed brighter, more alive as he talked — all of it felt like it had happened ages ago. Sparkling, Jadon thought, remembering how Nico had looked with the sunrise lighting his face. Like Nico was a prism too, and people only saw the sharp edges, the glass, until light hit him at the right angle, and then there was so much more.

"Why don't we pack your clothes," Jadon said as he helped Nico sit on the bed, "and we'll get out of here? You can stay at my place —" Nico opened his mouth, and Jadon rushed to add, " — in the guest room. Or if that makes you uncomfortable, I'll get you a hotel."

"What?" Nico stared at him blankly.

"You can't stay here, Nico. I'll pack your stuff. Tell me if I miss anything."

"I can't leave."

"What do you —"

"Do you know how that would look?"

"How it would look? What —" Jadon stopped himself from saying, *What does it matter how it looks?* Instead, he managed "Right now, the most important thing is that you're safe."

"The most important thing that matters is giving my paper tomorrow, convincing one of the professors to write me a letter, and making sure they include me in the edited collection." Nico's voice got stronger as he spoke, and some of the color was coming into his face. He pushed his shaggy hair back with both hands and said, "It's fine. I'm fine. I'll lock my door or something and—"

"Nobody is going to care if you sleep somewhere else tonight. They're certainly not going to be upset that you took steps to keep yourself safe when you're clearly in danger."

Nico shook his head. "You don't understand."

"You're right about that. I don't understand."

"Dr. Chapman, he—God, it's a long story, but he heard me saying something stupid about hooking up, and you don't know how he is. He's this terror of a dinosaur, and he, I mean, he's going to say it's my fault or something. That I shouldn't have drawn that kind of attention, or—or I don't know."

Jadon breathed slowly. He studied Nico's wide eyes, his shallow breathing, the restless hands that plucked at hair and clothing. "I understand that right now, you're upset, and you've been through a lot. But you're not thinking clearly. What matters—"

"I already told you what matters!" Nico recoiled from his own shout, making himself smaller, arms wrapping around his stomach. In a quieter voice, he said, "I'm not leaving."

After a long ten-count, Jadon said, "I've got to call this in."

Nico nodded without looking up at him.

Jadon called campus security first. Then he called Cerise. In actuality, everyone responded promptly, but the process was long and onerous, with Jadon briefing the campus security guards who arrived, and then telling his story to Cerise, and then Nico, withdrawn and still hugging himself, delivering his statement in a monotone, without looking anyone in the eye.

When it was finally over, one of the campus security guards offered to patrol the area for the rest of the night. Cerise lingered with Jadon near the stairs at the end of the hall. Her eyes cut to Nico's door, still open, and she lowered her voice. "Anything else you want to tell me?"

"No."

"He should go to a hotel."

"I told him."

"I can tell him if you want."

Jadon shook his head.

A radiator rattled to life nearby, pinging and creaking and groaning. Cerise's face was a maze of questions, but finally she said, "Don't fuck yourself over, please."

"I won't."

"I'm begging you."

Jadon surprised himself with a quick smile. "I appreciate the concern."

"I don't want to break in a new partner," Cerise said as she pushed open the door to the stairwell. "Dhan's excited to see you tomorrow. At our Halloween party. On time."

Jadon tried to swallow a groan.

"I believe the invitation includes a plus one."

"Goodnight," Jadon said, and he chose not to acknowledge the smirk as Cerise cut her eyes toward Nico's room again.

Jadon made his way down the hall and stopped in the doorway. Nico stood in the middle of the room. He was still in the trousers and quarter-zip, staring at his suitcase on the floor. After what felt like a long time, he looked up, his face was unreadable.

"If you're staying here," Jadon said. "I'm staying here."

Nico opened his mouth.

But Jadon spoke first, pointing to the second bed. "It's not a discussion, Nico. Right there."

Nico pushed fingers through his hair. Then he nodded.

"I'll let you change—"

"I'm sorry I shouted at you." Nico shifted his weight. Some of that shaggy hair fell over his eyes. "Will you please come in and not stand there?"

So, Jadon stepped into the room. It seemed smaller with the door shut. The two of them taking up almost all the space. But fitting, somehow. Like their bodies were lock and key. Like everything lined up the way it should.

"I know you think I'm overreacting," Nico said. "I know I'm overreacting. I—I—" For a moment, he looked like he was about to cry.

Jadon moved before he could tell himself not to. He slid his arms around Nico, and Nico melted into him. He wasn't shaking anymore, but his breath came in little bird-wing flutters, and Jadon made soothing noises as he rubbed Nico's back.

"I told you," Nico finally whispered. "About what happened. With that guy."

Those three little bursts of words contained a lot: being betrayed, being drugged, being kidnapped, being forced to endure darkness and isolation and mind games, thinking you were about to die. Nico had told Jadon some of it in those strangely confessional texts. Other parts, Jadon had learned on his own, piecing together the story. Because it had mattered. Because it had happened to Nico.

Still rubbing Nico's back, Jadon said, "This isn't the same, okay? I want you to understand that. You're not alone. You're not on your own. You're going to be safe."

Nico's breathing slowed. The air that moved across Jadon's neck was hot and dry, and the skin there was sensitive to each tiny puff, to the faint hint of stubble on Nico's cheek when he burrowed more deeply into Jadon, to the contact of skin on skin. One of Nico's legs was slotted between Jadon's, and he was painfully aware of how their bodies lined up, of the slight tremors in Nico's body that made it feel like he was vibrating against Jadon.

"I hate feeling like this," he mumbled into Jadon's shoulder. "I thought I was done feeling like this."

"It's a process." Jadon kept his hand moving across Nico's back. "Ups and downs."

"I hate feeling helpless. I'm not helpless."

"No, you're not."

"I am, actually. I froze."

"You didn't freeze. You ran, and then, when you found help, you improvised a weapon and defended yourself."

"It felt a lot like freezing."

"You didn't freeze." Then, making his voice lighter, Jadon added, "But a little tip for next time: keep running until you're somewhere with a lot of other people."

Nico stilled. And then he laughed softly into Jadon's shoulder and shook his head. He moved like he might pull away. "I'm sorry. God, I'm being ridiculous. You probably think I'm insane."

Before he could think about it too much, Jadon found Nico's hand and clasped it in his own. He brought Nico's fingers to his chest, pressed them against the shirt, and moved them until he felt the familiar ridges of the scars there. Nico's breathing changed.

"I know what it's like to feel helpless," Jadon whispered. "I know what it's like to be hurting and alone and afraid. You don't have to pretend to be okay. You don't have to do anything except be here."

The change in breath against Jadon's neck suggested Nico might speak, but no words came. Just those hot blasts of air, every centimeter of Jadon's skin blazing and awake at the sensation. He released Nico's hand, but Nico kept his fingers where they were, pressed to the scars hidden under Jadon's shirt. Jadon looped his arms around Nico's waist. *Like we're dancing,* Jadon thought, and it felt like a betrayal, but he couldn't ignore it. *This is how he would feel against me.*

"Why don't you change into something more comfortable—" Jadon began.

Nico kissed him.

It wasn't fast. It wasn't sneaky. He turned his head, and their mouths aligned, and then his lips were pressed to Jadon's, and they felt rough and chapped and warm and soft, and they tasted like the beer and like salt and like Nico, the faint hints of him that Jadon had gotten over the last few days. Nico pulled his head back. It was strange how his eyes could be so dark and still be so full of fire.

Almost, Jadon opened his mouth to ask or to tell or to warn or to suggest. And then he remembered the salad, and he didn't. He brought his mouth to Nico's, and he made the next kiss a question. One that Nico answered a moment later when his lips parted, and he let Jadon's tongue into his mouth.

Then they were moving. Nico pulled Jadon toward the bed, shoving on Jadon's jacket to force it off. He unbuttoned Jadon's shirt, stroked his chest, pulled at his waistband. It was like he had a million hands instead of two, and Jadon could only stumble after him. It had been so long, felt like longer, since he'd touched someone, had someone touch him. He'd forgotten how good a kiss could be, how much sensation could carry through the nerves of lips and mouth and tongue. Nico's mouth, for example, was warm and almost unbelievably soft. His kisses alternated between demanding and playful, his tongue teasing Jadon's before he sucked him back in. Jadon was only distantly aware of being turned around—manhandled was the correct term, a part of his brain recognized; Nico is manhandling you—and urged up onto the bed. Nico climbed up to straddle his lap. He'd lost his quarter-zip, and his shirt hung open to expose his flat chest and belly. Then he stopped. Ran his fingers slowly over the scars on Jadon's chest—the lines that marked him there. Jadon opened his mouth with the stupid idea of asking a question, but Nico was there almost immediately, his kisses insistent, crushing.

He pulled his mouth away from Nico's to sit up straighter, and as Nico worked his shirt free from first one arm and then the next, Jadon kissed his way along Nico's jawline. He stopped at Nico's ear, kissing, running his tongue around it, and Nico giggled and moaned and wiggled forward. Jadon grabbed his ass in both hands and hauled him forward the remaining inches. It was a great ass—a cute little bubble butt, surprisingly muscular as Jadon kneaded it with his fingers. Then he had one hand in Nico's hair, pulling his head to the side so he could attack Nico's neck, kissing and sucking and biting. Nico made helpless little noises, one hand coming down to rub Jadon's dick through the wool trousers. Then Nico's hand switched to Jadon's belt and waistband, and he was aware of the zipper being tugged down. He kept his attention on Nico, nipping at his collarbone, kissing hard enough to bruise, sucking. The cocktail of anger and frustration and pent-up horniness frenzied him. The thought that someone had tried to hurt Nico.

"Oh shit," Nico moaned. And then the word drawn out with pleasure, "Jay."

Jadon lowered his head and took Nico's nipple in his mouth and swirled his tongue around the dark bud. He was vaguely aware of Nico's ragged breaths, of his hand fumbling over the length of Jadon's erection, trying to jerk him off through his trunks. He closed his teeth lightly around the nipple, and Nico let out a constrained groan, like he was fighting the noise.

"Up," he rasped. "Up, up, Jadon, lift your hips."

It took some gymnastics, but Jadon managed to raise himself a few inches without spilling Nico onto the floor. Nico yanked Jadon's trousers and trunks down. Cold air met his dick, which jutted up against his belly. Nico fumbled with his own waistband, and a moment later, he was shoving his pants down until his cock sprang free. Like everything else on him, it was beautiful—a nice size, a nice girth, uncut with the hood of foreskin slightly pulled back. His balls were pulled up tightly. He was, of course, groomed.

Nico sounded a little breathless as he squirmed forward on Jadon's lap. It was awkward with his pants around his thighs, and he made a little bleat of distress when Jadon stopped him, forced him to shift his weight to one knee and then the other as Jadon tugged pants down around his ankles. It was easier after that, Nico astride him, pressing in for every inch of contact.

The brush of bare skin against bare skin. Their dicks rubbing together and then sliding apart. Nico's dick rubbing through Jadon's bush, grinding against his belly. Jadon's dick sliding across the smooth toned flatness of Nico's stomach. Mouth on mouth again, Nico demanding more, like he was pulling the breath from Jadon's lungs.

It had been so long. And so much, so fast, was overwhelming. It happened so quickly that Jadon only had time to moan a failed warning — "Nico" — and then the orgasm gripped him, his whole world contracting to the rush of pleasure, the release, the feeling like a part of his mind had blown open onto somewhere else. Nico's hand was tight around him, milking him through the finish. And then Jadon slumped against the wall, every muscle loose and relaxed.

Nico's shaggy hair was a mess. Hickeys covered his shoulders. Jadon had painted himself with his load, and already, it was starting to run down the sides of his chest and stomach onto the mattress.

"I'm sorry," he began.

But Nico shook his head, smiling. He scooped up some of Jadon's load and began to stroke himself. He closed his eyes, thrust into the circle of his fingers. His belly tightened. Jadon had the dreamy image of what Nico would look like when he fucked. Or got fucked.

Nico's face screwed up, and he grunted as he shot — volleying his load onto Jadon's chest. His face relaxed, he let go of his dick, and his eyes opened with a kind of hazy pleasure. He bent forward and kissed Jadon.

Somehow, they stripped the rest of the way and ended up lying together, Jadon spooning Nico as their loads cooled between them, one hand low on Nico's belly, pressing him to him. The possessiveness of it surprised a part of Jadon's mind. But not too much. Not enough to bother him. Their breathing evened out. Jadon kissed Nico's neck, and Nico shivered.

"It's been a long time," Jadon said.

Nico shook his head. "It's fine, Jay. It was wonderful."

"I don't want you to think every time."

Nico's laugh was unexpectedly sweet, and he brought Jadon's hand to his mouth and kissed his fingers. "It's been a while for me too." And then, his voice huskier, he added, "You make me feel safe."

"You make me feel happy," Jadon said, and he hadn't known he was going to say the words until he had. Hadn't known they were true until he'd said them.

Nico didn't say anything, but Jadon could see his mouth curve with pleasure, and he kissed Jadon's fingers again.

"Come to a Halloween party with me," Jadon said.

With a laugh, Nico looked over his shoulder. "What?"

"Tomorrow. Please. I don't want to go, and I have to, and the only way I'm going to make it through the night is if I get to spend it with you."

Nico was silent for several moments. Then he said, "Okay. I've got the closing dinner of the seminar, and then I'm free." In a hesitant voice, he added, "You could come with me."

"Really?"

"Yes." And then, his voice slightly different, "Is it a date?"

"I'd like it to be."

Jadon's heartbeats sounded loud in the silence that followed.

"I'd like that too."

"Then," Jadon said as he leaned in for another kiss, "it's a date."

13

Jadon

That night, Jadon didn't sleep.

At first, it had been the excitement of it all — the two of them alone, that whole floor of the dorm to themselves. They'd padded naked to the bathroom. They'd showered together, and showering had turned into fooling around, and Jadon lasted a slightly more respectable time, but only barely. The whole thing had felt like a crossover between a slumber party and a hookup, with a weird college porn background, and it had been hot and fun and…easy. Maybe that wasn't the right word. But everything had felt right with Nico. There had been no awkwardness. No uncertainty. It helped that Nico had initiated everything, but it also helped that he was so responsive, that he was so eager. It helped that he was Nico, because that was what made it so different from a hookup. It was one thing to find someone cute to fool around with. It was another for it to be someone you — well, Jadon shied away from the feeling, unwilling to look at it too closely, not yet ready to name it.

You make me feel safe.

They'd made a mess of one bed, so they agreed to share the other, even though it was a twin and the logistics meant being a tangle of limbs. As soon as Jadon had turned off the lights and climbed into bed, Nico had turned into an octopus: arms and legs wrapping around Jadon, tangling them together, and then his breath evening out almost immediately into sleep. Jadon had lain still at first. And then, when sleep didn't come, he'd carefully adjusted the single pillow (since Nico was sleeping happily on his chest). And then, when he realized nothing short of a bullhorn would wake Nico, he'd moved around until he was propped up and comfortable. Nico clung on to him and slept through all of it.

Then Jadon had opened his email and started reviewing the footage that campus security had sent to him. He'd wanted every possible approach to Harlow Hall, everything from the last week. Someone was following Nico, someone who had assaulted other young men on campus. It was the same suspect; Jadon was sure of it. And last night, someone had been in the building, waiting. That meant that the suspect had approached Harlow, had entered it, might have even left something behind—a fingerprint, a footprint, something. Jadon knew he wouldn't be able to get anyone out to process the scene; technically, nothing had happened. Worse, the lieutenant didn't believe this was a pattern of assaults. And even if, by some miracle, he got techs out to the dorm, there was no way of knowing what the suspect might have touched, where he might have left a print. Which meant his next best option was reviewing footage from the security cameras around Harlow.

It was difficult on his phone. Part of that was the interface—he would have preferred his laptop and a mouse to make it easier scrub forward in the recordings. And part of it was the size of the screen, which was too small for him to make out fine details. But he didn't have his laptop with him, and even if he had, he didn't think Nico would appreciate having a computer balanced on top of his head. That was another sign, if he were being honest with himself, that things were different. Maybe dangerously so. A hookup had never kept Jadon from doing his job the best he could; he'd turned more than one guy out of his house because he needed to get some sleep or, more frequently, he needed to work. Tonight, though, he was performing as a human pillow for a sleepy octopus, doing half-assed work on his phone.

Because someone has to be here, he told himself. Because someone has to stay the night.

Never mind that he could have let Nico sleep alone. That he could have sat on the floor and worked. Could have asked Cerise to drop off his laptop.

The videos themselves proved frustratingly worthless. Of the ones from that night, only a single video showed the suspect approaching Harlow Hall. He walked up to the main entrance, and the light near the door went out, and after that, it was impossible to tell what had happened. The suspect had gone inside, Jadon knew, but there wasn't anything on the video to prove it. He fast-forwarded through hours of footage from that camera, hoping to catch another glimpse of the suspect. Maybe he had passed the dorm earlier to investigate the light and figure out how to disable it. Maybe he'd gone into the building another time during the day to learn the floor plan. But when the room began to lighten, and Jadon realized with groggy dismay that it was morning, he hadn't found anything to help him.

When Nico's alarm went off, he flopped around with one hand until he found his phone and silenced it. Eyes still closed, he groaned, "How can it be morning?"

Jadon chuckled. He brushed Nico's hair away from his forehead. And, before he could reconsider, he kissed the smooth skin there.

Nico made a discontented noise and pursed his lips.

Jadon kissed him there too.

Nico parted his lips.

"No," Jadon said with a laugh. "Time to wake up."

Eyes opening to slits, Nico stared up at him. "We should shower."

"Unh-uh. I fell for that once already. You shower."

"What if I slip and fall? What if I drop the soap? What if my big, bad stalker is waiting for me in there?"

The words were light, but a hint of a quaver in his voice, the look in his eyes suggested it wasn't entirely a joke.

"Nico," Jadon said.

Nico's lip trembled.

"Oh my God," Jadon said. "We've got to be quick."

Being quick wasn't actually the problem; as soon as they were under the hot water, Nico's mouth roving across Jadon's chest, licking and kissing, like he wanted to devour every inch of him, Jadon was ready. Beyond ready. They ended up pressed against the shower wall, Jadon's weight pinning Nico to the tile as Nico thrust his hips abortively, the tip of his dick barely moving against Jadon's thigh as Jadon bit and suckled at his shoulder again, marking him with more of the dark purple bruises. He got his hands under Nico's thighs and lifted so that Nico was supported in the air, pinned to the wall. Jadon thrust between his legs, his dick sliding along the cleft of his ass. Sliding over Nico's hole. Nico came first that time. Jadon came a moment later, spattering the wall, arms trembling from holding Nico like that.

"What the fuck was that?" Nico asked, eyes wide, his chest and throat and cheeks still mottled with the sex-flush.

Jadon grinned and shrugged.

"We are definitely doing that again," Nico said.

Working the bar of soap for lather, Jadon tilted his head and said, "Come here and I'll get your back."

Sex, it turned out, was better than coffee. At least, in the short run. Jadon felt fine as he dropped Nico off at Eldridge Hall for the last day of the seminar. He was totally alert as he rushed back home and changed. By the time he got back to Chouteau for the symposium, though, the rush of endorphins had faded to a trickle. His head was starting to hurt, and exhaustion made his body heavy, slow, and clumsy. While trying to get to his seat, he knocked over Allison's coffee—which they managed to save, somehow, before it flooded the multipurpose room—and then, a moment later, he kicked Vic's ankle.

"Watch out, motherfucker," Vic snapped.

Before Jadon could respond, Vic pushed out of his seat and clear of the aisle. He hobbled toward the hallway.

"He twisted his ankle last night," Allison said to Jadon's questioning look. "I told him it was stupid to play soccer with twenty-year-olds. What if you break your leg? How are you going to do your job?"

Jadon apologized when Vic came back, but Vic ignored him, and the rest of the morning passed in an uneasy silence among the three of them. As the hours dragged on, Jadon found himself struggling to keep his eyes open. The heat, and the crush of bodies, and the droning voices all conspired to put him on the edge of sleep. His lids drooped, and he clawed his way back from the edge again and again before they broke for lunch.

He waved off Allison's invitation to join her and Vic for a meal in Waverley; he'd had enough student union food to last him a lifetime. Instead, he picked up one of the coffee shop's to-go lunch options—hard-boiled eggs, a handful of almonds, carrot sticks—and ordered himself a twenty-four-ounce Red Eye. Espresso and black coffee might not be a magic potion, but it came close to a prepackaged heart attack, and Jadon thought that might be what he needed to keep him awake through the rest of the afternoon.

Food in hand, he made his way across campus to Eldridge Hall. It was his first time inside the building; waiting for Nico on the bench had already felt like pressing his luck. The building seemed completely empty, which meant Nico and the rest of his group were still breaking for lunch. Jadon found a spot in the main hall and watched the door and paced, eating his eggs and carrot sticks, saving the almonds for last. The Red Eye seemed to be working, but he didn't trust himself to sit down.

A quarter of an hour later, the scruffy rich kid entered, talking loudly with the Harry Potter type. They both gave Jadon long looks. Clark, Jadon remembered. The kid—he certainly acted like a kid—wore a fresh set of scratches amidst all that movie star scruff. Where had those come from, Jadon wondered. Clark's face was a challenge, eyes fixed on Jadon until he stepped into what must have been the seminar room. It wasn't hatred, not exactly. Jadon had seen hatred. He'd seen crazy too, although they'd had sensitivity trainings, and he knew not to call it that. But this wasn't crazy either. It was something else. He remembered it from his playground days. There had always been kids who thought certain toys belonged to them. And they might not have been willing to fight you for them, but they'd watch, and they'd wait, and then, when they had their opportunity, they'd take it back.

Nico entered next, with a handful of other grad students. He wore the corduroy blazer, oxford, and trousers that he'd dressed in that morning, but with a new addition: the fake glasses were back. Walking next to Nico, Maya cut off mid-sentence when she saw Jadon, and Nico followed her gaze. A smile bloomed on his face, and he hurried ahead of the group. Maya was beaming, and when she turned to whisper to the girl next to her, they both broke out into giggles.

"You look handsome," Jadon said, straightening the collar of Nico's oxford.

"You told me that this morning."

"But it's still true. Would it be unprofessional if I gave you a kiss —"

Before Jadon could finish, though, Nico swooped in to peck him on the lips. His smile broadened, and he said, "I feel like I'm going to shit myself."

"Don't do that," Jadon said with a laugh. "You're going to do great."

Nico bounced on his toes and glanced over his shoulder. The other students were filing into the room.

"Do you want to go in?" Jadon asked.

"It's fine. It's okay. We've got a few minutes."

With another laugh, Jadon rubbed his back. "Let's go in."

Jadon took a seat in the back, nodding reassurance to Nico's questioning look, and Nico sat in one of the front rows next to Maya. Maya asked him something in a whisper and glanced back at Jadon. Several of the other grad students were also giving him looks, including Clark. Jadon ignored all of them, and when Nico turned around, Jadon was ready with a smile and a thumbs-up. Then he realized he'd left his coffee in the hall.

At that point, three people who had to be the professors filed in. One was a white man who must have been in his seventies, with a fluff of hair like cotton candy and a round, almost feminine face. The next was a wiry white woman in some sort of robe or dress that looked several sizes too big for her. The third was a white man, and although Jadon pegged him somewhere in his fifties, he'd kept it tight. He was toned, trim, his hair fashionably cut but in a way that didn't look like he was trying to act young. When he went to take off his jacket, he winced. One arm seemed stiff, and it took him several long, clumsy attempts to get free of the jacket. All three of the professors noticed Jadon, but if his presence was a problem, none of them said anything.

The one with the cotton-candy hair spoke first, and Jadon tried to keep up, but it was clear that he'd arrived in the middle of an ongoing discussion. The professor in the baggy robe-dress argued with the first one, and occasionally the third one spoke up. Some of the grad students tried to get into the fray—the Harry Potter type was practically vibrating in his seat, waiting for his opening. And Clark clearly had something he wanted to say. Both of them looked startled when Maya managed to put a word in before them.

Even though the argument itself didn't mean much to Jadon, he recognized the feel of the room. He'd seen plenty of pissing matches before—law enforcement tended to attract the kinds of personalities that enjoyed drawing lines in the sand—and it quickly became obvious to him that, in academia as in so many other parts of the world, the pissing matches were more about ego than about accomplishing anything productive. The seminar might have been designed to help grad students, at least nominally, but the reality was clearly that it was a chance for these professors to get on their soapboxes and showboat and, most importantly, prove they were right.

Watching the students attempt to get involved, Jadon had to admit, was mildly amusing. It reminded him of the dog park. There was always a pack of big dogs running around the enclosure. They were doing their own thing—chasing a ball, or chasing each other. And then you had the little dogs who yipped and sprinted along behind the big ones. A lot of the times, Jadon thought as the Harry Potter type tried to interject yet again, the little dogs didn't even seem to realize there was a size difference.

"Well," the professor with the trendy haircut said, cutting through the argument, "we'd better wrap up this part of the seminar. We have one more student presentation, and then we'll have our closing remarks. Nico, you know the format by now. You'll give your paper, and then one of the professors will respond." He smiled and added, "I'm the lucky guy. After my response, we'll open it up to everyone, and you'll have a chance to answer questions. Sound good?"

Smiling, Nico nodded as he rose from his seat, collected his papers and moved to the lectern. He set the pages in front of him. He adjusted his glasses. His smile faded, and his features reassembled themselves into intense focus. It was a look, Jadon thought, few people had been privileged to see. And then he thought, He's so beautiful. And then, Get rid of the damn glasses.

"'Marry,' Kierkegaard writes, 'and you will regret it; don't marry, you will also regret it; marry or don't marry, you will regret it either way.' It is tempting to read these lines as evidence of Kierkegaard's own ambivalence about marriage, or as more of the contrariness running through much of Kierkegaard's work, or perhaps as the type of angst-producing absurdity produced by the limitations of finite beings in an infinite universe. But a closer examination of Kierkegaard's aesthetics and their intersection with his soteriological construction of ethical love will show that rather than ambivalence, the complexities of choice and regret invite the Christian soul into the same kind of leap of faith Kierkegaard describes as a move beyond reason."

Nico kept speaking, but Jadon quickly lost the thread of the ideas. Nico had done a good job of explaining his argument the night before, but now, hearing it couched in the technical jargon of academia, Jadon found himself unable to follow. Names, terms, references—he tried, at first, looking them up discreetly on his phone, but there were too many, and by the time he'd read a paragraph about Hegel, he realized he was missing Nico's paper. So, he settled back in his seat and listened, enjoying the sound of Nico's voice, the rise and fall of it. A radiator glugged and gurgled behind him, and the air began to warm. Outside, bare branches moved in the breeze. They cast dancing shadows through the leaded-glass windows. It felt like the whole room was moving.

Jadon might have made it if he'd had his coffee. Sleep didn't come all at once. He caught himself the first time his head dipped. He forced himself to sit up straight, to open his eyes. It helped, for a few minutes. But there had been so many sleepless nights. And Jadon couldn't move, couldn't get up and leave, couldn't do anything without interrupting Nico's paper. All he could do was sit there.

The next time he blinked himself awake, it was because the silence woke him. He wiped his mouth—no drool, thank God—and raised his head. Nico still stood at the lectern. A slight hint of color showed in his cheeks, and he was clutching the pages he'd been reading from. Most of the grad students were still facing forward, with the exception of Clark. He had trained his camera on Jadon and was smirking as he recorded him. Sleeping, Jadon thought muzzily. The little shit caught me while I was asleep. The professor in the baggy robe-dress was watching Jadon too, her face unreadable. Nico was so intently not looking at Jadon that Jadon knew, immediately, that Nico had seen him.

Only then did Jadon realize the professor with the trendy haircut was speaking, his voice well-modulated and calm, his gaze moving from his notes to Nico as he added, "—be happy to help you find some of those articles I mentioned, of course, if you'd like to follow up with me after the seminar."

Nico's hands tightened around his papers. "Thank you, Dr. Meza. That's helpful. I didn't know—" He stopped and after a long beat managed, "I didn't know about that body of work."

Meza—the professor with the stylish hair—sat back, nodding.

"We'll open the discussion now to the seminar," the man with the cotton-candy hair said. "But first, I'd like to point out several inconsistencies in how you use the term subjectivity."

After that, it was a bloodbath. Everyone was polite, of course. But Jadon knew what was happening. Long criticisms only barely disguised as questions. Or the questions that were flat-out interrogations. Or not even an attempt at questions—the Harry Potter kid went on for almost fifteen minutes, and from what Jadon could tell, he was reading from his own research.

Nico bore up pretty well under all of it. He answered questions. He took notes. He nodded and said, "Thank you." That look of intense focus had faded, and in its place was a perfectly polished mask. He even smiled when someone made a joke. Jadon imagined this was the Nico who had posed for photoshoots. The blank, unexpressive perfection of his face. Like the real Nico had gone away somewhere.

And then, somehow, it was over. The cotton-candy professor made some final remarks, and then people were gathering up their stuff, exchanging goodbyes. The Harry Potter type rushed the professors, talking rapidly, hand outstretched. Maya hugged the other girl. Clark slipped out of his seat and headed for the doors. He paused when he reached Nico and said something too low for Nico to hear. Nico gave a one-shouldered shrug, and Clark said something else. Then he kept going, and a moment later, he was gone. The professors filed out, trailed by a few of the more persistent grad students. Maya lingered for a moment, looking at Nico and then at Jadon. She left too. And then it was the two of them, and Jadon's steps sounded loud as he made his way down the tiers.

Nico was packing up when Jadon reached him. He looked up and offered a too-bright smile. "Sorry about that. It must have been super boring."

"No, I'm sorry. I can't believe I did that."

Nico slid his laptop into his bag.

"I'm sorry, Nico. That was so rude, and—God, I'm so mad at myself. I was so excited you invited me, and I screwed this up."

"It's okay," Nico said, and he gave a little laugh. "You were tired. You've been working so hard."

"It's not okay. I am so sorry."

"Jay, stop. It's fine."

Jadon watched Nico sling the backpack over one shoulder. He was still smiling. His eyes were bright.

"How did it go?" Jadon asked. "I'm not an expert on these things, but—"

"Great," Nico said and walked out of the room.

When Jadon caught up with him, he finally came up with "It sounded like people had a lot of good feedback."

"Sure, that's how it always goes."

Nico shouldered open the door and stepped out of Eldridge. The fresh air was good; Jadon felt too hot, a vague nausea rising with his redoubled headache, and the cool day was like a fever breaking. It had rained, and the brick pathways were dark and wet, but the sun was out again, and drops of water glistened on the edges of branches. Nico took off at a fast walk, and Jadon practically had to jog to keep up.

"I know you're upset with me," Jadon said as Nico turned toward Harlow, "and you should be upset, but I want you to know how sorry I am—"

"Stop apologizing." A moment later, Nico rubbed his mouth and let out a breath. In a normal voice, he said, "It's fine, Jay. Dr. Meza said he'd publish the paper with a few revisions. I'm going to meet up with him in a couple of weeks; he's got this vacation home in Vermont, and he said I could finish the paper there."

Jadon thought about how the professor had smiled. About how he'd said, *I'm the lucky guy.*

Nico met Jadon's gaze, coal-fire eyes burning, and somehow, Jadon managed not to say anything.

They walked the rest of the way to Harlow in a silence that wasn't a silence at all. The wet leaves made sticking noises under Jadon's soles. The breeze whistled between the buildings. A crow landed heavily on a branch, and it creaked as it rocked under the bird's weight. Their steps rang out in the dorm's tiny stairwell. Nico kept one hand on the rail, and it made a soft ringing noise under his touch. He's got this vacation home in Vermont. That smile. He said I could finish the paper there. That fucking smile. I'm the lucky guy.

There had to be rules about that kind of thing. Professional ethics. There had to be laws. He couldn't ask him like that, invite him to the middle of nowhere in Vermont, and—what? A kaleidoscope of images: Meza passing Nico a glass of wine; a fire flickering on the hearth, throwing shadows in the hollow of Nico's throat; the way Nico's cheeks reddened in the cold; the professor's mouth on Nico's neck.

Jadon was so caught up in the torture of thoughts that he didn't notice Nico had stopped walking until he collided with him. Nico rocked forward under the impact, but he didn't cry out. He's mad, Jadon thought. He's angry because you fell asleep and, now you have to show him—

But whatever the rest of that thought would have been, shock cut it off. The door to Nico's bedroom stood open, and the room was in shambles. Nico's suitcases had been emptied onto the floor and thrown into the corner. More clothes had been taken from the closet and lay on the floor. The bedding was rumpled, even though Jadon had made the beds himself, the sheets and blankets neat and tight the way his moms had taught him. Because someone had lain there, he thought. And then, more clearly, He was here. He was in here, and he laid on the beds, and he touched Nico's clothes, and he didn't care that it was the middle of the fucking day.

Nico let out a laugh. The sound was hollow, disbelieving, and raw. He stepped into the room, shaking off Jadon's touch when Jadon tried to stop him, and toed through the clothes on the floor. "My underwear is gone." His breathing accelerated. His voice was higher than usual, tight, the sound of a man hanging on. "He was in here, wasn't he? He was in here, and he took my fucking underwear."

14

Nico

In the campus security office, Nico stared at Detective Cao—Cerise, he thought numbly; Jadon called her Cerise—and said, again, "I don't know who did it."

It was a small room, spartan, with filing cabinets and a desk and a computer and, lying next to the phone like it had been forgotten, a pencil eraser shaped like a cat's paw. He only vaguely remembered the walk across campus, with Jadon's hand wrapped around his arm, and then the murmur of voices, the banks of fluorescent lights, until they put him in here. The room smelled closed up, and the computer looked ancient, and Nico had the sense this place didn't get used much. Only when police needed to interview a hysterical victim, maybe. Or maybe only if the victim had special status because he'd jerked off with a cop the night before.

"I understand that," Cerise said. "And I also understand that you're upset right now. But I want you to start thinking about anyone you might have noticed, anyone who seemed even slightly unusual, from the last few days. Just think about it. Keep thinking about it. Something might come to you."

Even through the haze of shock, Nico could hear the request for what it was: last-gasp desperation. They had no leads. No idea who was doing this. They had nothing.

The discovery in his room had changed everything for Nico. Until then, the situation had evolved from a seeming overreaction on Jadon's part into a mild concern—even the strange encounter in the darkened dorm, when he thought about it in the light of day, could have been bad luck. A burglary gone wrong. But finding that his room had been searched, his clothing pawed through, his underwear stolen—that meant something different. Someone was following Nico. Someone was—well, the word *obsessed* came to mind, but that sounded dramatic, like something off TV. It sounded impossible.

Cerise asked a few more questions, asked if Nico needed anything, and left. The door clicked softly when it shut in its frame, and then he was alone. Muffled voices from the next room suggested a conference. I'm going home tomorrow, Nico wanted to tell them. It's not a big deal. And then, without any warning, he was fighting back tears as he dragged out his phone.

Emery answered on the first ring. "What's wrong?"

"Don't do that," Nico said, although the words lost some of their force because he sounded so phlegmy. And then the story spilled out of him — the man who had followed him, the darkened dorm building and the running footsteps, his room.

"I can be there in five hours," Emery said. "I'll stay on the phone with you until you get to a police station. The closest one is either headquarters or central patrol; one sec, and I'll have an Uber headed your way."

"No, Em—"

"Then I want you to wait there for me."

"I don't want—"

"Five hours. Don't hang up."

"Emery Hazard!"

"What?"

"I don't want you to do that! And I'm trying to tell you, and you're steamrolling me!"

More of that silence.

"Oh my God," Nico moaned.

Emery's laughter was barely more than a breath.

"I'm sorry," Nico said.

"No, I should have listened. Although, to be fair, if I see this fucking chiropractor fuck one more woman upside down, I'm going to lose my fucking mind, so I might have been a bit motivated to call it quits on this job."

"What do you mean 'upside down'?"

"Is there more than one meaning?"

"But, I mean, how—" Nico managed to stop. He wiped his eyes. "This one's insurance fraud, right?"

"Yeah, he can't work, he can't walk his dog, he can't take his trash cans down to the road. But he can plow at a hundred and eighty degrees without any complications."

"I still have zero idea what that means. And why did he have to go to Chicago? Can't he find somebody closer?"

"I don't know, Nico. Should I ask him? Maybe there's a special zero-g brothel here."

"Goodbye, Emery. I'll see you tomorrow."

"Why don't you want me to come get you right now?"

"Because you're working. And I'm fine." And, Nico thought, that would be the icing on the cake, having my ex show up a day early to take me home while everybody else in the seminar goes out for the closing dinner. Because I was being stalked. The definition of professionalism. "I'll see you tomorrow, around noon. If you come early, I'm going to be mad."

"Colt would make one of those awful 'That's what she said' jokes."

"It's not a joke. It's something people say."

"Or John. He wouldn't have missed that."

"I'm hanging up now."

"I want you to call North and Shaw."

140

Nico had one horrifying moment when he allowed himself to imagine North and Shaw "helping" him, and in the process, running into Jadon. North would probably say something like *Medical science might be able to save the stump of Jadon's atrophied dick*, and Shaw would probably perform a dogs-only wedding ceremony that was somehow legally binding. "Pass," he said.

Emery laughed quietly. "I'm serious. They're good at what they do, and I trust them."

"That's a remarkable statement since the last time North was going to stop by the office you told me to hide all the good pens, and when I—"

"Because he always takes one with him."

"And," Nico continued a little more firmly, "when I asked you which ones were the good pens, you said all of them."

"Obviously. We don't buy cheap pens, Nico; that's bad office management. You end up spending more in the long run—" Somehow, he reined himself in. "If you don't call them, I will."

"Em!"

"I'm serious. And I want you to stay at their house—"

"No, pass, a million passes. Last time you made me drop something off, I met Jadon, and look how that turned out."

The muffled voices in the next room sounded louder now. Angrier.

"What does that mean?" Emery asked.

"Nothing." When Emery didn't say anything, Nico added in a rush, "I shouldn't have called you. I'll be fine."

"I want you to stay in a hotel tonight."

"Emery."

"I'll pay. Use one of the business credit cards." His voice turned dry. "The one you conveniently forget, on a regular basis, to put back in the safe."

"Because I have to take it out every day, and the door on that safe is fucking heavy!"

"Arm days, Nico. You're not going to be a twink forever."

"I'm hanging up now."

"Text me the name of the hotel."

"Goodbye, Em. I love you."

"And how much it costs. I love you too. In a platonic—"

Nico disconnected the call.

The door opened, and Jadon stuck his head into the room. His body was stiff, and his mouth was a hard slash. He jerked his head, and Nico followed him.

Outside Waverley, the day's chill had hardened into cold. A steady breeze swept clouds across the sky, and a sudden shower of rain fell and then was gone—and then another came in its wake, and that one was gone too. The air smelled like damp soil and wet wood, and even though it was only late afternoon, the day was gloomy, almost dark.

"I'm sorry about that," Jadon said as they started across campus.

"You don't have to be sorry. I'm sorry; I shouldn't have freaked out."

Jaw clenched, Jadon didn't answer.

They walked in silence. A troupe of college-aged boys, ones who had stayed during fall break for some reason, emerged from one of the buildings ahead. They were already dressed for Halloween: slutty cowboy, slutty firefighter, slutty football player, slutty Where's Waldo guy. Waldo, presumably. They were talking excitedly over each other, the words drunk-loud, which meant they'd been pregaming. As Nico watched, the slutty football player pointed toward the quad and shouted, "Bruh, I could totally beat that squirrel in a race." And then he took off at a surprisingly good clip until he tried to hurdle one of the low brick walls, flipped, and landed hard on his back. His bruhs laughed uncontrollably as they made their way to where he lay.

"Do you think we should check on him?" Nico asked.

Jadon shot a flat look over at the guys. Then a tiny smile softened his mouth. "It looks like he's going to survive."

Already, the football player was back on his feet. Honestly, Nico thought the fresh mud on the jersey—and the bare skin and muscle underneath—was going to work wonders for him in the Halloween hookup division.

"I'm sorry they're being such assholes," Jadon said, and as he spoke, heat smoldered in his voice again. "I'm sorry they can't see there's a serious problem happening on campus. I mean, for fuck's sake, they might as well be helping this guy. It's like they don't want him to get caught. And the department—yeah, I know it's a fucking break-in. I know there's always a string of those on campus during the scheduled breaks. I know. I fucking know. And I'm telling you, that's not what this is. It's like they think I've got no fucking idea what I'm talking about."

The bros were moving again, their conversations splintering now that the squirrel race was over. One of them, earnestness carrying even through his slurred speech, said consolingly to another, "I mean, your intentions were good. You were just trying to nut."

Nico worked hard to keep his face straight.

In an underbreath, Jadon said, "You have got to be kidding."

"He makes a good point," Nico said. "The best of intentions."

"Sometimes I think between eighteen and twenty-two, they aren't even real people."

"Try fourteen and twenty-two," Nico said. "Let me introduce you to Colt. I swear to Christ, I've never bought so many bulky, baggy sweaters since he started living with Emery and John-Henry. I practically have to wear a potato sack every time I go over there."

A laugh burst out of Jadon, erasing some of the lines in his face. He took Nico's hand without any apparent hesitation—just reached out and slid their fingers together. His hand was warm and large, fitting nicely around Nico's.

"I'm sorry. Again. I shouldn't lose my temper."

"I'll admit I've never heard you say so many fucks. It's kind of reassuring, actually. I feel like I get a daily ration from Emery, and I've been running short the last few days."

Jadon's mouth quirked, but he didn't answer.

"You can be upset." Nico tugged on his hand until he got another smile. "You can swear as much as you want. It won't faze me."

For a heartbeat, it seemed like Jadon wouldn't speak, but then the words poured out of him. "It's—I mean, yes, I'm angry that they're not taking this seriously. I'm not joking when I tell you that I think the university is being criminally negligent, and ultimately, they're going to be found liable for it. And my department is being just as bad—willfully blind because it's easier for them, in the short run, to believe all these incidents are isolated and unimportant. But what gets me is that—is that it's all about fucking Barr."

He was silent for a long time. They'd lost the drunken college boys, and in the campus's quiet, the only sounds were branches creaking in the wind, and the occasional wet leaf smacking the pavement, and the distant hum of traffic.

Nico didn't need him to explain about Barr—not the basics, anyway. Some of it, in bits and pieces, Jadon had told him in the midnight hours. And some of it Nico had learned through google-fu. Barr had been Jadon's partner, a detective with the Metropolitan police. He'd also been a serial killer, and he'd operated for years without being caught.

"They think I'm an embarrassment to the department, and they're not wrong."

"Jay—"

"But what's worse is they don't take me seriously. I mean, I didn't know my own partner was out there butchering people. What kind of a detective does that make me?" He breathed out slowly, the wind ripping the white vapor to shreds. "Maybe they're not wrong. Maybe I should leave."

"Jadon—" Nico had to stop.

"Peregrin," he said helpfully, because he was Jadon.

"Jadon Peregrin Reck—wait,? Like the falcon?"

"Yes, but also, way, way worse."

Nico laughed in spite of himself. "Now you have to tell me."

"They couldn't agree on a middle name. They wanted something natural, you know. Something related to nature."

"Like a peregrine falcon."

"Uh huh," Jadon said with a trace of amusement. "But one of my moms was into *The Lord of the Rings*, and one of the hobbits is named Peregrin Took."

They walked another yard before Nico said, "You have got to be shitting me."

"They tried calling me Pip and Pippin, but I put a stop to that in middle school."

"Oh. My. God." And after that, there was only one pertinent question: "Does Shaw know?"

Jadon burst out laughing. "No, thank goodness. I was going to lie if he ever asked; thank God it never came to that. I think I was going to tell him it was Michael."

Nico leaned into him, smelling the wool of his suit, the heat of his body, the sweetness of the world washed clean by rain. "I like it. Jadon Peregrin Reck. My little hobbit."

This time, Jadon laughed more quietly.

"He lied to everyone," Nico said. "And everyone fell for it. Not you."

"Not everyone was his partner."

"But he'd killed those guys years before you were partners, Jay. You can't blame yourself. And if anyone else blames you, they're idiots."

Jadon didn't answer.

After another few yards, when he still hadn't said anything, Nico said, "Emery thinks I should call North and Shaw."

"What? Why?"

"Just, you know, for some help. Until he can pick me up tomorrow."

Something flickered across Jadon's face, and then his expression was as smooth as glass. "Do you want to call them?"

Nico opened his mouth to say no, but what came out was "I don't know."

They walked a few more paces. Jadon let go of Nico's hand.

"If you want to call them," Jadon said, "then you should."

"It's, you know, they're good at what they do."

Jadon nodded. "So, call them."

"Emery suggested it. You know, like an option."

"Right."

Nico didn't know what to say. The conversation's rhythm felt off. Jadon's face told him nothing. His hand felt cold, and he thought about reaching for Jadon's. He had the strange sense he needed to apologize.

But before he could do anything, Jadon said, "Because it's not like you're with anybody who can, you know, make sure you're safe."

"Jay—"

"It's not like I haven't been trying for the last three days."

"Hold on—"

"No," Jadon said, "your ex was right. You did the right thing, calling them."

The way he said your ex was like a gust of red-hot air blowing through Nico's head, and for the next few paces, he couldn't speak. When he finally got control of his voice, he said, "I didn't call them, Jadon. I told you that's what he suggested. If you think it's a bad idea, I won't call them."

But Jadon didn't respond.

Harlow Hall rose ahead of them, hulking gray limestone in the shrouding gloom. Nico wanted to take out his phone and check the clock; how long had he been in the security office? What time was it? But he could see how that would go, taking his phone out of his pocket, the way Jadon's mind would jump immediately to the worst possible conclusion.

"I'm sorry," Jadon finally said. His voice was low and rough, and he kept his gaze locked on the building. "Of course you should do whatever makes you feel safe."

"I don't understand what's going on. Can you talk to me, please?"

"Nothing's going on." His mouth slanted, the expression too tired and jaded to be a smile. "I'll call them if you want. Shaw will be thrilled. Actually, North will be thrilled too, if only because it gives him a chance to get a dig in."

"I don't want you to call them for me. I don't want you to do anything for me, Jadon. Believe it or not, I'm a big boy. I want you to tell me what's going on." Jadon's sandy-dark eyes met Nico's for a moment, and Nico thought, No wonder he's losing his mind. The hollows were deeper, the smudges, more noticeable, so bad that, at a casual glance, they could have passed for bruises. It sounded more accusatory than he intended when he said, "You didn't sleep last night."

"I slept." He rolled his eyes at whatever he saw on Nico's face and added, "Some. I've got a lot of work to do."

You're only one person, Nico wanted to say. You have to sleep and eat and take care of yourself, or you're not going to be able to help anyone, let alone keep me safe. You can't keep pushing and pushing. Not forever. You need someone to make you take care of yourself, you big dummy, because obviously you're not doing it on your own.

But what he said was "What if we skip the party tonight? I'll get a hotel, and you can have a staycation. We'll lock the door and have a nice, quiet night." Jadon's eyes brightened, and Nico laughed. "Sleeping."

"God, you know it's bad when sleep almost sounds better than sex."

"Almost?" Nico asked.

Jadon smirked. He hooked Nico's pinky with his own and gave a tug.

"Nico." Dr. Meza's voice boomed with friendliness that sounded a little off key. "There you are!"

Nico slid his hand free of Jadon's. Meza was coming toward them along one of the brick footpaths. He was still dressed in a suit, and he still looked...well, good. He smiled when he caught Nico's eye, and then his gaze moved up and down him quickly before returning to Nico's face. His smile broadened. Nico was suddenly aware of Jadon next to him, of how big Jadon was, and how Jadon made himself bigger by putting his hands on his hips, his shoulders broad, his stance tall and strong.

Oh my God, Nico thought, and the giggle in his throat felt near hysterical. What if he fights him?

"I was hoping I'd run into you before dinner," Meza said, flicking a dismissive glance at Jadon before his attention came back to Nico. He stood close enough that Nico caught a whiff of expensive cologne —lavender, and something citrusy, and something else, darker, smokier. "I wanted to talk about your paper."

"The dinner," Nico said. Because he'd already forgotten.

"You're coming, aren't you? You'd better. It's going to be a snooze if you don't; Bill goes on and on, and he's even worse after a glass of wine."

"I don't know." Nico fought the urge to look at Jadon; out of the corner of his eye, he saw that Jadon was reading something on his phone, his face dark. Was he upset about a message, maybe? Or politely pretending, Nico considered, not to be enraged by the conversation? "It's been a crazy afternoon."

"Nico." Meza lowered his voice, making a wall of his body to wall Jadon out of the conversation. Jadon didn't actually growl, not out loud, but Nico thought he could hear it in his head. "You're making a mistake. This is a big deal. I want to ask Anne to write you a letter, and tonight is your chance to chat with her, make an impression." He smiled again, his voice even more intimate as he caught the lapel of Nico's blazer and rolled the corduroy between two fingers. "And we can have a productive conversation about getting your paper published in the meantime."

"Nico's too polite to say it," Jadon said, and his voice had the brisk professionalism that coded as cop and was about as subtle as a slap, "but he's dealing with some personal issues right now. He's going to have to take a raincheck."

For the first time, Meza looked at Jadon. He was shorter than the detective, but he managed to give the impression that he was looking down on him, his refined features alight with amusement. "And who are you? The boyfriend?"

"No. I'm a detective with the Metropolitan Police. And get your fucking hand off him."

"Jadon!" Nico barked.

Meza opened his hand and released the jacket, the gesture expansive and demonstrative, the message clear: *I'm not the one being unreasonable.*

"Clearly I've interrupted something —"

"You have," Jadon said. "Move along, sir."

Meza stood a little straighter. His cheek creased when he smiled, and it made him look older, exposing the lines in his face. "This is a free country, Detective. Believe it or not. And we're having a conversation in public. And I have every right to be here and to have this conversation."

Jadon opened his mouth, but Nico managed to say first, more sharply, "Jadon."

After several deep breaths, Jadon wrenched his gaze away from Meza. To Nico, in a low voice, he said, "We're going."

"Good God, Nico," Meza said with a little laugh, "do you let your boyfriend talk to you like this?"

Nico's gaze moved from Meza to Jadon and back to Meza. "I'm sorry, Dr. Meza. Today has been stressful, and neither of us is putting our best foot forward."

"Let me guess." Meza did that looking-down thing again, considering Jadon the way someone might have looked at a bug under a microscope. "Big, butch, aggressive. A closet case, I imagine. I think you can do better than that."

This time, Jadon did make a sound — not a growl, but a harsh exhalation that sounded like a period at the end of a sentence. He turned, squaring up with Meza. His fists balled at his side.

"No, no, no—" Nico tried, grabbing Jadon's wrist.

"Is there a problem here?"

The words came from a familiar voice, but Nico couldn't place it until the security guard stepped into his line of sight. Heeley, the one with the hard mouth and the tawny eyes, still looking like he'd been poured into his uniform. He gave Jadon a long, assessing look. Then Meza. And last Nico.

"No," Jadon said, and he gave a little shake, like he was loosening up tight muscles. "No problem."

"Actually, I think there is," Meza said. "This man claims to be a police officer, but I haven't seen any proof. From what I could tell, he was coercing this young man into going to another location with him. It made me uncomfortable, and when I tried to intervene, this man threatened me."

"It was a misunderstanding," Nico said. He gave a broken-mirror smile to Meza and then to Heeley. "It's all a big misunderstanding. There's no problem here."

"Sir," Heeley said, "I'd like to see your ID."

Jadon drew out his badge holder and showed the badge to Heeley. As he did, Nico noticed two more figures approaching out of the corner of his eye. One was a woman, with a bob of wavy, blond hair. The other was a man who looked familiar, the wide face and the strong features. It took only another moment before Nico placed him as the guy from the coffee line, the one who had been flirting with him. Vic.

"What's going on here?" the woman asked.

Vic laughed before anyone could answer, staring at Nico, and then said, "Holy shit, this is the underwear model?"

Meza didn't do anything so gauche as gasp or clutch his pearls or even widen his eyes. But Nico was looking at him when the words landed, and he saw the shock run through Meza. The professor's expression closed, and he put his hands in his pockets, his head turned away from Nico now.

"For fuck's sake, Vic," the woman said, but she was examining Nico too.

"Are we done here?" Jadon asked Heeley.

Heeley opened his mouth to answer, but Meza was the one who spoke. "I am." And he turned on his heel and hurried off down the path.

"Not trying to cause a problem," Heeley muttered. "It's my job, you know."

Jadon made a sound that could have meant anything, and Heeley retreated.

"So, this is why you're looking so bushed," Vic said with another laugh. His gaze skipped from Nico to Jadon, and he grinned. "Work all day, play all night."

"Vic," the woman said. "Fuck off. What was that all about?"

"A misunderstanding—" Jadon began.

Nico started walking, and when Jadon called his name, he didn't look back. Quick steps. Almost running. He pushed into the darkened lobby of the dorm and climbed the stairs. Behind him, he heard the door swing open again, but he refused to look back.

He got into his room, shut the door, and locked it. He stared at the mess of clothes. He grabbed one of the suitcases and opened it and began tossing things inside.

The doorknob turned, and the door rattled in the frame. A moment later, a knock came.

Nico shoved more clothes into the suitcase. He closed it, started on the zipper, and it caught immediately.

"Nico," Jadon said. "Will you please open the door?"

"No." Nico yanked on the zipper again. It wouldn't budge. He got a better grip and tried again, hauling on it this time. For an instant, it wouldn't budge. And then it came free completely. Nico fell back, hard, still holding the zipper in one hand. His head hit the metal bed frame. The pain made tears come to his eyes, but it all felt distant. He threw away the broken zipper and got to his feet.

Jadon was still hammering on the door. "What happened? Are you okay? What—"

Nico threw open the door. Jadon stood there, his gaze automatically flicking past Nico, as though checking for a threat.

"Go. Away."

"I'm sorry for how that went down—"

"Go away, Jadon. Go the fuck away. Are you hearing me?"

Jadon's mouth tightened. "I'm sorry I embarrassed you—"

"Embarrassed me? You think I care about being embarrassed? I've had people talk about whether they want to pluck my crack right in front of me. I've had people tell me my balls are weird and ask if I can't tuck them for the shoot. For fuck's sake, one time, Emery got us kicked out of a movie theater because he insisted on seeing the ingredients label for the artificial butter. You tanked me, Jadon. That was it, right there. My career is over."

It was strange, seeing it firsthand. How Jadon's face relaxed. How his whole body said, without using a single word, *Oh, that's all?*

When he spoke, his voice was more measured. "I'll apologize to that professor, and I'm sorry, but Nico, there's no way your career—"

"He knows I used to model!" The words came out more like a scream than a sentence, and Nico barely managed to wrestle his voice down again. "He knows, you stupid, selfish fuck. Because you had to go bragging to your fucking buddies about how you were fucking an underwear model."

Jadon looked like Nico had slapped him. "I never—"

"And you know what's worse than having your fucking cop buddies show up and blab in front of Dr. Meza? You know what's even more humiliating? The fact that you stood there and talked for me, like I was some fucking braindead piece of meat, like I'm not capable of making my own decisions. How fucking dare you?"

"I was trying to—"

"I know what you were trying to do. You were trying to mark your territory. You didn't like that he was looking at me—"

Jadon's normally composed face was ruddled with emotion. "No, I—"

"—and so you decided to do your fucking alpha-male routine and ruin my fucking career, even after I told you how important this seminar was."

"Nico, why in the world would your career be over? I was trying to keep you safe."

"That's my choice! I get to decide what I'm going to do!"

Something in Jadon seemed to snap. His expression hardened. "No, you don't! Because the fact that you think drinking wine and talking about old books and giving fuck-me eyes to a bunch of old men is a good idea right now tells me you have zero fucking sense of self-preservation!"

The silence between them had the sensation of falling.

Finally, in a trembling voice, Nico said, "Get out of my room."

"No."

"Get out!"

"No. Pack your bags. We're going to a hotel—"

"I want you to leave."

"—and we're going to stay there until Emery can pick you up."

"I can take care of—"

Jadon slapped the door. It was old, solid wood, and the clap sounded enormous. It startled Nico, and pins and needles ran through him. "You can take care of yourself? Be serious, Nico! You talk this big game about how independent you are, how important your career is. Fine. But this isn't your career. This is someone hunting you like it's a fucking game! I thought you understood that! You can't take care of yourself, you're—"

Jadon stopped himself, but Nico had heard the unspoken remainder of the sentence. "What?"

"A civilian."

Nico shook his head. "I'm a what?"

Jadon didn't answer. His chest rose and fell like he'd been running.

"I'm a grad student. No, that doesn't sound right. I'm a kid. Except—" It was strange how easy it was to smile. "—I'm older than you. I'm a model.

I'm a dumb underwear model. How did you put it? Giving fuck-me eyes to a bunch of old men."

It only took a moment before Jadon seemed to find his footing again. "What do you want me to say? The way he looks at you, the smiles, the touching. He's not talking about publishing your paper because he thinks you're a breakout scholar, Nico. He thinks you're pretty and you'll do whatever he wants you to do as long as he can promise to help you."

Nico laughed, and that felt easy too. "Fuck you, Jadon."

"You want to be taken seriously as a scholar, right? That's what you keep saying. But it's hard to take you seriously when your big professional breakthrough comes because you gave an old creep what he wanted."

"That's life, okay? That's how life is. People want things from you, and you can either play the game or not. It won't be the first time I sucked a cock to get what I wanted, Jay. But then, I'm not perfect like you. I'm not Jadon Reck. I'm not Superman. I can't run a million miles every morning and eat vegan power bowls and solve every case that lands on my desk by working twenty-two hours a day."

"Pack your bag."

"You know what's sad? You're a good guy, Jay. Or, most of the time. When you're not being such a complete asshole."

"Pack your bag, or I'll pack it for you."

"I'm going to do you a favor because you've tried hard to help me this week, and I appreciate that. I'm going to tell you the truth. The truth is, everybody who spends more than five minutes around you can see what you're doing. How hard you work. The hours you keep. No sleep. Minimal food. Constant exercise. Everybody looks at you, and even though you think you're doing a good job hiding it, they can tell you're falling apart. You're as bad as an alcoholic—you picked work as your drug of choice. And that's sad, because I think for the most part, you're a good guy, and you deserve to be happy. But you're so scared of making the same mistake again that you're killing yourself. You're like a little kid who's so afraid of the dark that you'll burn the house down while you're still in it just to have some light."

Jadon wavered on his feet. One hand moved, barely more than a twitch, but in Nico's mind it was like Jadon had reached for the jamb, like he was afraid he might fall. His lips moved, but it didn't sound like his voice when he said, "Maybe you're right. But at least I know who I am. I'm not so desperate for other people's approval that I'll be their little rent boy to feel like I belong."

Drunken, Halloween laughter rose outside, muffled by the glass.

Nico shut the door slowly and thumbed the lock, and he listened until the sound of Jadon's footsteps faded.

15

Nico

Nico sat on the floor of the dorm room for a long time. The building was never truly silent, so he listened to the sounds: the wind raking the roof; the plonk of rain drops against the glass; the ping and clang of the old boilers. His face felt hot. His eyes were dry. He made lists in his head: pack, find a hotel, call an Uber. Then he'd start over, amending the list: find a hotel first, then pack. Find a hotel that you can afford. Get an Uber.

Instead, he changed into running shorts and a tank. He grabbed a hoodie and realized, too late, it was Jadon's, so he left it. He left his phone too, and his last thought, as he pulled the door shut, was, Fuck it.

His run took him into Forest Park again. He made sure not to follow the same route that Jadon had taken him on. That was part of the reason, he was sure, why the park felt so different. And the fact that it was late afternoon, moving into evening—that was part of it too. The sun was a small, hard ember in the west, the sky brushed in broad purple strokes, and dark hung in the branches, thickening. He passed two women fighting, shouting as they shoved each other until one of them misjudged a curb and fell, screaming. He passed an old man laying out a piece of cardboard on a bench, the tarp on the ground next to him suggesting he planned to spend the night. One of the tiny creeks he crossed was choked with foam go-cups and single-use plastic bags and what he thought, in the gloom, might have been a dead possum. The sound of his steps on the pavement seemed too loud, echoing out into the vast darkness, and even though his body warmed and loosened as he ran, he felt cold the whole time. He caught himself thinking, occasionally, treacherously, of the hoodie. And then he'd have to remind himself that it was Jadon's. The pain was like something lodged under his breastbone. In his mind, it was the tip of a knife.

When his legs were shaking and he couldn't run anymore—could barely walk—he dragged himself back to campus. Full dark had settled. The campus lights popped on in little white spheres that didn't do much to push back the night. A group of grad students—math, he guessed, or engineering—passed him; they were dressed in normal clothes, but they wore headbands printed with equations and formulae, and they were laughing and talking excitedly. One of them (the only one Nico recognized, the Pythagorean theorem) shoved his friend as he laughed, and then shouted, "We are all totally going to make love tonight!"

Make love, Nico thought, and he waited for the giggle. Instead, tears stung his eyes, and he had to grapple with the wave of emotion that threatened to crush him.

Harlow Hall was roasting after the chill October evening, and the heat was half-welcome to Nico and half-suffocating. He dried his face with the tank as he pushed into the stairwell. A startled squawk made him freeze. And then he stared.

On the other side of the door, Gio was rubbing his shoulder and glaring—first at the door, and then at Nico. Next to him stood Dr. Meza, who had changed into a marled sweater and looked elegantly casual. They were holding hands.

Gio reacted first, dropping Meza's hand as color rushed into his face. Meza considered Nico, but his expression remained cool and unperturbed. He caught the door, met Nico's eyes, and said, "Evening, Nico. I guess you're not joining us for dinner."

How long had it been? An hour? Two? Nico tried to work out the sequence of events. At most, two hours had passed since that awful encounter on the quad. And in that time, Meza had already moved on. What had it been, Nico wondered. A blow job in the dorm room? Or maybe they were saving that for a more romantical evening, and today, in a hurry, it had been making out, maybe a quick fiver? It must have been a rush for Meza, hooking Gio so quickly. Or maybe he'd been working on him all week, the way he'd been doing with Nico.

Now, to Nico's surprise, the giggles came. He shook his head, fighting another wave of laughter as he said, "No, Dr. Meza. I won't be joining you."

Annoyance tightened Meza's features. Gio still looked scared out of his mind.

"But I hope you have a lovely evening," Nico said as he slid past them. "Oh, and Gio, remember that old people's skin is delicate, so, you know: watch your teeth."

Meza let out a sharp breath. Gio murmured something. Nico didn't look back, and a moment later, the door at the bottom of the stairwell closed.

He showered until the shaking in his legs stopped. Then he padded to his room. No towel, mostly because he'd forgotten one. But also because he couldn't bring himself to care. If Dr. Chapman spotted him, the old man was going to get an eyeful.

Jadon had been right, he thought as he stood in the tiny room, considering the clothes laid out on the bed. Right about the pretense. Right about Nico's desperation. Right about the ridiculousness of the whole situation. Quarter-zips and button-ups and cardigans. So many goddamn chinos. Nico hadn't even brought his best tanks—just athletic ones in neutral colors. Who the fuck was I kidding, he thought, and a wave of tears came again. Self-pity, mostly. But also frustration. And anger at himself, for having believed so much bullshit. For having wanted so badly to believe it.

He slipped into Jadon's hoodie. It was warm, light, soft. His underwear was gone, so he found a pair of joggers and pulled them on. He'd made a mess, shoving everything into one suitcase, so now he went to work packing things the way he should have. Like an adult, Emery would have said. That made him smile, but it also made him want to cry.

It had been an overreaction, which was classic Nico. Letting his temper slip. His emotions getting the best of him. Pretty on the outside, one of his exes had told him once, and an ugly little fucker on the inside. And wasn't that the truth? Because Jadon hadn't been trying to ruin Nico's career—Nico had blown the whole thing out of proportion. Hell, even saying he had a career was blowing things out of proportion. What had actually happened? Jadon had been worried for him. Jadon had been...protective. And, yes, a little jealous, which Nico could admit that he liked. The memory flashed of a kiss in the Pretty Pretty, of the untapped well of Emery's rage, and his face heated with embarrassment. So, maybe Jadon had been out of line, first in speaking for Nico when he answered Dr. Meza's question, and then when he had insisted he knew what was best. But the ugly stuff, the hurtful things, those hadn't started until Nico had struck first—until he'd ramped everything up, higher and higher, the way he always did. His face got hot as he remembered how easily Jadon had identified Nico's hypocrisy.

With a sound of disgust, he gave up on folding the clothes neatly, shoved the rest of them in the second roller bag, and decided that was good enough. He was fairly sure Emery wasn't going to inspect his luggage— fairly sure was about as good as it got with Emery, who might, at any point, decide that Nico's packing required his supervision. He'd order takeout, hole up in the dorm room, and yes, unashamedly barricade the door with the spare bed. And tomorrow, Emery would be here, and he'd go home, and this would all be over.

A knock at the door sent a flush of startlement prickling through him. He stared at the door, trying to tell if he'd engaged the thumb lock. Then another knock came and, "Nico? It's Maya."

She looked fantastic—a wrap dress with a chunky cardigan, gold bangles of varying sizes on one arm, a heavy gold necklace that managed to look both old-fashioned and stylish at the same time. She looked at him, looked past him, and then asked, "Are you okay?"

"Yeah, I'm all right. I guess."

She gave him another appraising look. "And you're not going to dinner? Don't let that asshole win, Nico. There's still time, and you deserve to celebrate—Dr. Young practically fell out of her chair telling you how much she liked your paper."

"No, she said—she said I made some good points. And anyway, it's not—" He caught himself about to tell her that Jadon wasn't an asshole, and that it wasn't about winning. But he changed it to: "I think I'm going to stay in tonight."

"Want to talk about it?"

They ended up on the bed (the clean one), and Nico told her about all of it—the stalker, Jadon, the weird half-argument about North and Shaw that had escalated into something uglier when they'd run into Dr. Meza, and then the fight in the dorm room.

"That slimy piece of shit," Maya said.

"Honestly, Maya, Jadon's a good guy. I think it was a lot of bad stuff happening at once, and I didn't make it any better."

"No, that's obviously at least fifty percent your fault. I'm talking about Meza. I thought he might be a scumbag—he's too smooth, you know? But I didn't think he'd proposition a grad student at a seminar in exchange for publication."

"Yeah, well, that offer is off the table." Maya's thick eyebrows knitted together, and Nico added, "I think he and Gio already had round one. I caught them in the stairwell."

"What a sleaze."

"Who cares? It's over."

"I care. Assholes like him get away with this kind of behavior—" With an obvious effort, she stopped herself. "I won't go on my rant."

"Rant away."

"No, you already know how I feel."

"But you'll feel better if you tell me again."

She thought about it. And then she said, "In the first place, the only reason he gets away with this is because he's a white man in an institution dominated by white men, and he uses marginalized people's vulnerabilities against them."

It went on for a bit after that.

"Feel better?" Nico asked.

"No," she snapped. "Now what are you going to do about Jadon?"

"What am I going to do? Nothing."

Maya gave him a disgusted look.

"There's nothing I can do, Maya. I said some pretty shitty things to him. About the shittiest, actually."

"Which you didn't mean."

"Obviously I didn't mean that stuff. I mean, not all of it. I got carried away."

"No, you overreacted. You get that, right?"

"Yes, thank you." Nico couldn't keep the waspish tone out of the words. "I did manage to figure out that much on my own."

"So, you tell him you overreacted. And you tell him you're sorry. That's basically how an apology goes."

"He doesn't want to talk to me. He definitely doesn't want anything to do with me, not now."

"How about you let him make that decision?"

Nico chose to ignore that. "And anyway, even if I did apologize, he's in this weird place right now, and I don't think he'd let himself, you know, see what could happen with us. Maybe he'd try. For a while. But things would get bad at work, or he'd feel like he wasn't doing enough, and eventually he'd cut me off."

A little too loudly, a little too forcefully, and definitely a little patronizingly, Maya said, "Oh."

"You can leave now."

"I didn't realize that the prerequisite for any relationship is that it be perfect and have an ironclad guarantee that it'll last forever."

"You realize nobody else sees you be this bitchy. They all think you're sweet and polite and professional all the time."

"That's their loss. Nico, you've got your head up your butt. I'm saying that sweetly and politely and professionally, because what I want to tell you is that you've got your head so far up your ass, you could use your throat as a periscope."

"Seems a bit labored."

"Nico!"

"I don't know what you want me to say!"

Maya took a breath. She smoothed her dress over her leg. Then, to Nico's surprise, she took his hand. "How about this? Let's start with why you're scared of going out with Jadon." Nico opened his mouth, but before he could speak, she said, "And don't tell me you're not scared. He's gorgeous. He's kind. He's clearly got the patience of a saint. And if the last few days don't tell you how much he's willing to sacrifice for you, then you've been walking around with your eyes closed. But you don't want to even see if there's a possibility with him. It's easier to sit here and tell me he's gone and it's over and that's too bad, but life will go on. And that's bullshit."

Nico shook his head. Tears started in his eyes, and he blinked them away. "Okay, well, I don't know why everyone acts like I'm crazy because I want to be taken seriously as a scholar and hooking up at a seminar—oh my God, I think your nails are literally inside my hand!"

With a saccharine smile, Maya relaxed her grip. She patted Nico's leg with her free hand. "You were saying?"

"I—" But for the first time in a long time, Nico was too tired to put up with his own bullshit. He drew his legs up, pulled his knees to his chest, found a more comfortable spot against the wall. Maya sat with him, her talons—thank God—mercifully withdrawn. "Before you and I were friends, I was dating this guy, Chendo."

Maya seemed to consider what to say. "I heard a little about him."

"How he got murdered?"

"That."

"He was…well, I mean, it feels so weird to say this out loud, but he was abusive. Not physically, but pretty much every other way you can imagine. He'd send me texts about how he was cheating on me. He'd say the most horrible things. About how I was worthless in pretty much every way. About how that's why he cheated, because I couldn't give him what he wanted. And I put up with it for a long time. I don't know why." His throat was dry, and he heard himself say again. "I don't know why."

Maya rubbed his arm.

"And then he was dead, and I couldn't—I mean I couldn't even process that, couldn't make sense of it. I never got to tell that fucker off. I never got to stand up for myself. He was gone. And I'd eaten his shit for so long. And then I met Emery, and—"

"I know," Maya said. "I remember."

"It wasn't the breakup, Maya. I'm happy for him and John-Henry." His laugh caught in his throat. "Well, most days. But while Emery and I were dating—God, it was torture. I still had all this insecurity about Chendo. I was angry at him. I was sad. I was angry that I felt sad, that I was sad even the tiniest bit. I was angry that he was gone and I'd never get to tell him to fuck off. And meanwhile, Emery and John-Henry were falling in love. Emery's not perfect, but he's a great guy, and I had to stand on the sidelines and watch as he fell in love with somebody else. And every time I tried to talk to him about it, every time I wanted to do something about it, he'd pretend it wasn't happening, or that he didn't know what I was talking about."

"He was gaslighting you."

"I don't know. That's harsh, and honestly, that's not Emery. I think he didn't know. Or didn't want to believe it. And we did talk about it, eventually. But the bottom line is that, for the second relationship in a row, I felt like I was going crazy. I'd meet these guys. I'd feel a connection. And then the whole world would turn inside out because no matter how much they liked how I look, they didn't like me. Not as a person. And I—I'm tired of that. I don't want that. I want the next guy to be someone who loves me for who I am."

"And it'd be nice if you had some scholarly credentials," Maya said with a hint of a smile, "to prove how good and worthy and valuable you are on the inside."

"Okay, first of all, you don't have to be such a bitch."

Maya broke up laughing, and after a moment, Nico smiled too.

"How do you know he doesn't like who you are on the inside?" Maya asked. "Jadon, I mean."

Nico shrugged.

"That's not good enough."

"Oh my God. I don't know, Maya. He bragged to his buddies about hooking up with an underwear model. I mean, I didn't lure him into bed by talking about Christian existentialism."

"So, you did hook up with him?"

Nico gave her a flat look.

"It wasn't this bed, was it?"

"Thank you for your help, Dr. Freud. I'm fine now. You can go."

"I'm serious. What makes you say he doesn't value who you are as a person? Did he do something one of your exes did? Did he say something?"

"I told you about that conversation with Dr. Meza. It's like I wasn't even there; Jadon took over."

Maya stared at him long enough to communicate what Nico took to be total disbelief in how stupid he was. "He's a guy."

"Right, but—"

"And a cop—"

"Okay, yes—"

"Of course he's going to get all bristly and protective. And he definitely didn't like that Dr. Meza was being such a creep."

"He said it was stupid, arguing about old books. That I was wasting my time."

"After you riled him up."

Nico opened his mouth, but nothing came out.

"Look," Maya said, "I don't know the guy. Maybe he's a superficial jerk, like you say. But I haven't heard anything that sounds like that's the case."

Shutting his mouth slowly, Nico tried to think. Yes, in the argument, Jadon had been dismissive of Nico's work. But had that been true more generally? He thought about Jadon's insistence that Nico finish his paper. How Jadon had snuck food into the library so Nico could keep working. How Jadon had asked about Kierkegaard and kept asking, wanting to know. And how he had listened. How he had remembered. He thought about how Jadon had changed the location of their first meal because he'd noticed Nico was interested in the Walk of Fame, how he'd wanted to give Nico another piece of history.

Maya was looking annoyingly smug.

"I don't like you," Nico told her.

She smirked. "Of course you don't. You love me. Now get dressed. We're going to dinner, the two of us."

On the verge of saying yes, Nico stopped himself. "Actually," he said slowly, "I think I've already got plans. A Halloween party."

"With a certain detective?"

"Maybe. I don't know." Even to him, Nico's grin felt sheepish. "I hope so."

"God, this is adorable."

"No, it's not."

"And pathetic."

"No, it's not."

"You're practically glowing. Where's the dark, angsty bitch I fell in love with?"

"I'm still angsty," Nico said. "I'm still a bitch."

Maya hopped off the bed and kissed his cheek. "Come on. Let's figure out a costume."

"What about the closing dinner for the seminar?"

She scoffed and waved a hand.

"Oh no," Nico said. "You're going. You've got to go. Otherwise, Gio is going to take over the conversation, and Kaylee and Ridson are literally going to die from overexposure."

"They'll be fine—"

"Besides, Dr. Chapman wanted to talk to you about that summer fellowship—"

"I can email him."

"—and if you don't go, I'm going to stop being your friend and cut all ties."

Maya didn't look particularly frightened by that threat.

"Go," Nico said, nudging her toward the door. "I'll be fine. I'll get my costume, and I'll call Jadon, and I'll keep you updated in case I'm wrong and he hates my guts and I have to go eat myself to death in a Ben and Jerry's."

"Text me every five minutes."

"Absolutely not."

"Every ten minutes."

"I'm closing the door now." As it swung shut, Nico sang out, "I love you."

Maya laughed as her steps moved away down the hall.

Nico considered his options. Almost all the clothes he'd brought were professional and responsible and would have satisfied any straight guy shopping for outfits at Target. He could do something with that—like a hot nerd, maybe, which wasn't a costume idea so much as a way to get in Jadon's pants again. The fake glasses, maybe. Jadon had gotten a kick out of those. The real shame was that Halloween was in the fall because what Nico wanted Jadon to see was the tiny swim shorts—

Oh, Nico thought. Lifeguard. Easy.

He changed into a pair of tiny red shorts—technically, they were for running, not for swimming, but they had white trim that was cute and retro, and they made his legs look amazing. And, if Nico were being honest with himself, his junk too. He kept Jadon's hoodie on for now; in a pinch, he'd wear it to complete the costume, but he had the thought that if he hurried, he could still get into the school store and find a windbreaker—something that a lifeguard might wear on a windy California beach. Something that he could leave hanging open, so his chest and belly were on display.

He stepped into a pair of slides and gave himself a once over in the mirror. A whistle. They'd probably have one of those as well in the school store—self-defense. And then one more idea hit him, and he dug through his toiletry bag until he found what he wanted: a moisturizing lotion with sunscreen. Daily skin care routine, obvs. But even more importantly, tonight he'd lay a thick white stripe of zinc down his nose. Lifeguard to the rescue. He tucked the bottle into a pocket of the tiny shorts (it fit, which was amazing all on its own).

Phone in one hand, keys in the other, he headed out of the dorm. Darkness had settled over everything, but light pollution made the sky seem low and flat. Oppressive, Nico thought. Like a steel lid. The air still smelled woody and wet, and even as Nico wondered about the rain, a fresh spritz caught him. He thought he heard footsteps, but when he turned, all he saw were new-fallen leaves tumbling and scraping across the pavement. He was wound too tight; too many days of looking over his shoulder (figuratively and literally). The party would be a step in the right direction. And making things right with Jadon, that too.

Unlocking his phone as he crossed the quad, he bobbed in and out of pools of darkness. He tapped Jadon's name and put the phone to his ear. The call rang. Leaves spun and fell, and when they whispered against the brick footpaths, Nico thought again that they sounded like the scuff of soles. And then the sound was louder, unmistakably footfalls. Nico started to turn—

The blow connected with the side of his head, and his world went white. He didn't lose consciousness, but for several moments, the connection between his brain and body lagged, and all he could do was stumble. A hand caught Jadon's hoodie and yanked, and somehow, Nico kept his balance and managed to slip free, leaving the hoodie behind. He tried to catch himself, and then he fell as the weight of another body bore him down to the ground. Fingers forced something hard and rubbery between his teeth, stifling his cry for help before he could fully form it. His arms were forced up between his shoulder blades until he screamed against the gag. Then rope tightened around his wrists, and he could feel the change in the other body: the slackening of muscles, the physical relief. Because, a part of Nico knew, the hard part was done. It was over.

16

Jadon

Jadon drove home on autopilot. His brain was dark except for the occasional misfire of neurons, and then fragments of the fight would glow in hypersaturated colors: Nico framed in the doorway, Nico flinching when Jadon slapped the door, Nico saying, *You're so scared of making the same mistake again that you're killing yourself.*

He let himself into the south city bungalow. The lights were off, the air stale. Over the last few days, he'd barely been here, but it was more than that. It had the empty, closed-up feel of an abandoned place. Somewhere nobody lived.

Turning on the lights—

You're like a little kid who's so afraid of the dark that you'll burn the house down while you're still in it just to have some light.

—seemed like too much work, so he made his way through the gloom. He kicked off his shoes in the bedroom. He lay on the bed. He caught a musty whiff; the sheets needed changing. Above him, the ceiling was faintly luminous, the glimmer of white plaster a long way off in the dark. From the neighbor's house next door came the barely audible thump of a bass line.

He'd lost his temper; Jadon could admit that. He'd been trying to stay calm, trying to stay reasonable, trying to master his own mingling frustration and fear so that Nico, in turn, would also stay calm. Then, like the two most annoying fucking jack-in-the-boxes in the world, North and Shaw had popped up. Again. Like they always did. And then the professor had appeared, coming toward them like a homing missile, and the way he'd looked at Nico, the way he'd smiled.

Giving fuck-me eyes to a bunch of old men.

Jadon pressed his fists against his eyes. Yeah, that hadn't been good. But he might have held it together, might have managed not to say what he was thinking—something along the lines of, *Keep it in your pants, or I'll cut it off*—if he hadn't gotten that text. The one from a patrol officer telling him that, the night before, another young man had been assaulted on campus.

He dug out his phone and called Cerise.

"No," she said. In the background, Dhan's familiar voice rumbled, and Cerise sounded like she was speaking away from the phone when she said, "I'll take care of the pumpkins. Go change." Then, her voice moving back to the phone, she said, "No. You are not allowed to cancel. You are not allowed to have an excuse. You are coming to this party. Dhan's worked hard to make everything perfect." Her voice cut away again, a kind of vexed love: "I said I'd do the pumpkins. Get into your costume!"

"What are you going to be?" Jadon asked.

"Alice and the Hatter."

"Eh."

"Thanks for the feedback. What are you going to be?"

"There was another attack."

"Jesus Christ, Jadon. What is wrong with you?" Her silence vibrated for a second across the line, and then, in a slightly softer tone, she said, "I'm sorry. How bad?"

"Shaffer and Carney got it. He put the kid in the hospital. He's getting bolder, Cerise. Escalating." He managed not to say the rest, what he didn't even want to think after he'd seen the pictures: *He looks like Lang. Like Nico.*

"He. You say that like you know who did it."

Jadon didn't say anything to that.

Cerise broke first. "Are we going over there?"

"No. I wanted you to know. I asked some of the patrol guys to call me if anything like this came in; that's the only reason I heard about it." He couldn't keep the bitterness out of his voice when he said, "Of course, the department will insist there's no connection."

"Are you going over there?"

"No."

"Are you lying to me?"

Jadon laughed. "Not this time. They've got him sedated. I'll see if I can get Shaffer and Carney to let me have a chat with him tomorrow."

"And let me guess: you're not coming to the party."

You're killing yourself.

"I'm worn out."

"Jay, this is what we talked about."

You'll burn the house down just to have some light.

"I'll think about it. Maybe a quick power nap."

"You know, this isn't about the captain. Not really."

"What?"

In the wake of the words, the thud of the bass from next door seemed louder. Probably was louder. It had a way of doing that as the night went on, and Halloween was a night for parties.

"I meant what I said earlier: I think you need to pull yourself together. I think you need to make sure you're not giving them anything they can use against you. But mostly, Jay, who the fuck cares what they think? I'm worried about you. We all are."

"Thanks." In the darkness, in the stillness, Jadon felt like he was floating. He wasn't sure how many seconds passed before he said, "I'll try to come."

Cerise's answer was a sigh. Then the call disconnected.

For what felt like a long time, Jadon lay there, staring up at the moon-glimmer of the ceiling. And then he got out of bed. He could add this to the list: socializing, finding time for recreation, setting firmer boundaries on his work hours. If he took cases home, if he worked them from his living room instead of his office, he could get almost as much done, but the captain wouldn't see. He'd make sure he attended happy hours, department events. It could be one more thing he'd do. Perfectly. The voice sounded like Nico's. Perfect Jadon Reck.

You're killing yourself.

He showered. He even turned on the lights. The costume was ironic in that fork-twisting-in-your-intestines way, although Nico couldn't have known: a red-and-blue top, Superman's S replaced with the letter G. Supergay, of course. And then a navy suit, the white shirt unbuttoned so that the spandex top was showing. Fake glasses. He went back and forth on those—would they set Nico off? And then he remembered that didn't matter, and he liked them, and he liked that they made him think of Nico, even if it was that fork-in-the-guts kind of way. He checked himself in the mirror. Perfect Jadon Reck, he thought, who couldn't keep his temper, who didn't know how to keep his mouth shut.

When he started driving, it took him a few minutes to realize he wasn't going to Cerise's. Instead, he ended up outside a gingerbread house. The lights were on in the windows. An inflatable Frankenstein bobbed on the lawn, the drone of the motor audible when Jadon killed his engine. The sidewalks were empty; in Jadon's neighborhood, the kids all went elsewhere for trick-or-treating. It looked like the same thing might be true here.

He knocked, and the door opened a moment later. North McKinney was big, blond, and usually trying a little too hard for butch, with the Red Wings and the Carhartt clothes and the nonstop shit-talking. It was hard to keep that in focus, though, when he was dressed as a cartoon tiger—an orange and black-striped onesie, fuzzy tiger paws on his feet, and, of course, a furry hood with cat ears pulled up over his mess of blond hair. He was holding a bucket full of candy, and he was beaming. At his feet, the puppy (no longer a puppy) barked and pranced until North scooped him up.

The smile soured into a glare when he saw Jadon and said, "Fuck me."

"Cute costume."

"Are you fucking kidding me? The first fucking trick-or-treater of the evening, and it's Supergonorrhea."

"Hi, North."

North gave him a second dose of the glare and then bellowed, "Shaw!"

Shaw appeared a moment later as North retreated into the house with the dog. He was slender, and although he wasn't classically handsome, the sharp features of his face were compelling. Enough time had passed since their breakup that Jadon no longer felt a pang. It helped that, tonight, Shaw wore a ridiculous blond wig and a red-and-black striped T-shirt.

"Supergoop! No, wait. Superguy!"

"Calvin and Hobbes? I thought Hobbes was supposed to be smaller."

"I fucking told you!" North shouted from deeper in the house.

"And wouldn't it have made more sense for North to be Calvin since he's already blond?"

"See?" North appeared behind Shaw. "See? I told you!"

"He begged to be Hobbes," Shaw stage-whispered.

"Like fuck! Now give Jadon a box of raisins and tell him to fuck off and quit wanking all over our stoop."

Opening the storm door, Shaw said, "Come in."

"Jesus Christ," North said as he stomped away. It was less effective in the tiger slippers. "What did I just say?"

When North came back, he had a pumpkin ale from Schlafly, and a second bottle for Jadon. The bottle was cold enough to make the bones of Jadon's hand ache pleasantly, and when he tried a sip, he was surprised he liked it—cinnamon and ginger and caramel, but not too sweet.

"We're checking all the candy for razor blades," Shaw said as he plopped on the sofa next to North. "North knew a kid one time who ate a razor blade, and it cut open his asshole when it, um, came out."

Jadon looked at North.

"Hand to fucking God," North said. "He had to wear diapers."

"There's no way that's true," Jadon said.

"I'm sorry we're not all ass experts like you, you big poof."

"You're gay too!"

"But I'm not Supergay."

"I knew it!" Jadon stabbed a finger at him. "I knew you knew what my costume was!"

North scowled and took a long pull of his beer. Then he flipped Jadon off.

"And we're watching a scary movie," Shaw announced as he opened a vanilla Tootsie Roll. A pile of wrappers suggested he was picking them out of the bucket. "*Jung Frankensteins*."

"*Young Frankenstein*," North snapped. "And it's a comedy, fuckwit." Then he looked at Jadon over his beer and said, "What the fuck is wrong with you? You look like shit."

For a moment, the world had almost felt normal again: the shit-talking, the general upside-down sensation of being around these two, the rhythm and routine of their friendship. North's question popped that bubble. Jadon's mouth felt grainy with the sweetness of the beer, the taste of cloves overpowering now. He set the bottle on the coffee table and wiped his mouth.

"Hey," Shaw asked, his voice quickening. He even abandoned a Tootsie Roll mid-wrap to grab Jadon's hand. "What's wrong?"

Jadon was surprised to find himself squeezing Shaw's hand, as though he were holding on. A wave of emotion crashed over him, and he struggled not to go under, to keep his breathing slow and deep. "I, uh—I fucked up."

He waited for the zinger from North, but all the blond man did was sit forward, both hands around the brown glass bottle, and watch. Shaw scooted closer and rubbed Jadon's knee with his free hand.

"He's not here, is he? I thought maybe—I mean, I guess you would have said something if he was."

"Who?" Shaw asked.

"Nico."

North shook his head.

"I didn't even know Nico was in town," Shaw said. "What's going on? What happened?"

Jadon tried to start at the beginning, but he botched that too. He started with the fight, and then he had to jump back, and then he got sidetracked to the assaults on campus, and then he found himself talking about, of all things, Chuck Berry. North and Shaw mostly listened, although at one point, North left for a while, and when he came back, he had a couple of burritos on a plate and a glass of water. He handed all of it to Jadon. He had wrapped a napkin around the fork, and for some reason that little detail made Jadon almost start crying again, and he had to hold himself together as his voice tried to dissolve.

"Do you think he's in danger right now?" Shaw asked with a glance at North.

North rose again. "I'll call Emery."

"I don't know," Jadon said. He cut one of the burritos with the side of the fork, and the smell of carnitas, smoky and sweet with cumin and orange juice and a million other delicious things, rose to meet him. His stomach rumbled, and he tried a bite. It was amazing—the blend of flavors, the meat and tortilla falling apart in his mouth. He ate several more bites. It seemed impossible that he could be eating, but then, it seemed impossible that he could be here, having this conversation, that anything from the last few days could have happened. Through another mouthful of food, he said, "I don't even know where he is. That's the worst part."

Shaw made a soothing noise and rubbed Jadon's knee some more. "It's going to be okay. He's upset, and you're upset, and you're going to work it out. Emery will call him, and then we'll know more. He's probably at a hotel, like you talked about. He's probably hoping you'll call him."

"He's not. He's furious at me. And he's right to be furious. I said — God, I said some awful things."

North, leaning in the doorway to the kitchen, said, "Give me a break."

"North," Shaw said.

"What? He's being dramatic." To Jadon, he repeated, "You're being dramatic."

"He feels guilty."

"What'd he do? Tell Nico he was having a bad hair day?"

"You heard him. He said awful things. Really awful things. Like, monstrously awful. Like we wouldn't even recognize Jadon, we wouldn't even know who he was, if we'd heard the things he said."

"I mean, they weren't that bad," Jadon tried.

"Bullshit," North said over him. "Look, Jadon's pretty —"

"Thank you," Shaw said. "Finally."

With a glower, North continued, " —but he's got no substance, no fire. He's like one of those American Girl dolls you beheaded."

Some of the carnitas got stuck in Jadon's throat.

"He probably said a four-letter word and immediately felt guilty and then apologized with, I don't know, an Elizabethan sonnet."

"Cunt," Shaw proclaimed.

Jadon choked again.

"That was probably the word," Shaw said.

"Well?" North asked, staring down at him with a mixture of disgust and pity. "What's your hangup?"

"I don't have a hangup," Jadon said.

North snorted.

"I don't! I lost my temper, and I said things I shouldn't have, and now he hates me." Memory ignited again, and he groaned. "Jesus, I called him their little rent boy."

With a laugh, North dropped back into his seat. Shaw grinned and, when he noticed Jadon looking at him, tried to hide the smile.

"What?" Jadon asked.

"You've got it bad," North said.

"No, I don't."

Shaw nodded. He was trying to look grave, but that smile kept poking out.

"I don't," Jadon said. "And even if I did, it doesn't matter anymore, because I blew it."

"Jay," North said, his voice surprisingly kind, "bud, it's okay. You're a pathetic loser who's as bad at dating as he is at solving cases, and you're an ugly little toadfucker to boot. It's not your fault."

Jadon opened his mouth to volley something back, and instead, laughter came out. He tried to stop it, but it kept coming. North laughed too, a quiet rumble, and Shaw giggled into a pillow. The laughter rolled through Jadon like something had broken inside him. He reached for the water, hoping that taking a sip would help him calm down, but a fresh wave of laughter made him fall back on the couch, wiping his eyes.

When he finally calmed down, he felt better. Not good. But some of the tension that had been winding his body like a clock for the last couple of years had eased. His body felt looser, relaxed. His headache, which he hadn't noticed until now, had faded.

"I think I'm in love with him," he said. And he hadn't realized it until the words were out of his mouth. "Or I'm falling in love with him. Or something."

Shaw made a noise like that was the most adorable thing he'd ever heard.

"It's not cute," Jadon said. "It's a disaster. I don't know what to do. I've screwed everything up."

North heaved himself out of his seat. "I'm going to try Emery again, since the miserable fuck couldn't be bothered to answer last time." He hesitated, as though considering something, and said, "You're a good man, Jay." Then he scrubbed a hand through Jadon's hair—nearly wrenching his head off his neck and messing up Jadon's careful styling in the process—and added, "Don't fuck this up."

Then he stepped into the kitchen. Shaw looked at Jadon with a familiar curiosity—intense, yes, but also bewilderingly innocent and open. After a moment, Jadon had trouble meeting his eyes.

"Want to talk about it?"

Jadon laughed. He found the beer again and drank. "We were always good at that, weren't we? Talking, I mean."

Shaw smiled, but he didn't answer.

"I don't know, Shaw. I don't know what's going on. Honestly, he's probably better off without me; I'm such a mess."

"A little less self-pity," Shaw said, but his smile crooked to take the sting out of the words, "and a little more self-discovery. Oh! Maybe we should meditate together!"

Jadon rolled his eyes as he turned the bottle in his hands, but the words slackened the tension in the air. In some ways, this was why he and Shaw had worked so well together—all the things that people found weird (or that North rejoiced in as reasons for further bullying) had felt, for Jadon, familiar. Homey. Meditation, sage sticks, smudging, crystals. His moms had loved that stuff, and while Jadon's life had taken him away from those things, they still had a place and a power that he recognized.

"I might—might—have started to lose my cool when Emery told him to call you and North."

Shaw was practically quivering. "Emery told him to—"

But the horse was out of the barn now, and the words galloped out of Jadon. "And that's such bullshit. I mean, here I am, not sleeping, not eating, staking out that goddamn dorm, and it's like I don't even exist. North and Shaw will take care of it. The way they always do."

"Damn straight," North called from the kitchen.

Shaw rolled his eyes. "Jadon."

"What? Every case I touch, I hit a dead end, and then you and North swoop in and solve it."

"Not every case."

"Every single case."

"No! You arrested those horny thieves."

A laugh slipped out of Jadon, and he took another sip of the beer. "They were kind of hard to miss, fucking in the bed of the house they'd broken into."

"But you still caught them! And you caught that guy who was, um, violating those goats."

"A goatfucker," North shouted. "Great job on that one." And then, like he was speaking to someone else, "No, not you, you big goatfucker."

Jadon took a longer drink.

"And," Shaw said like someone who was worried he might be losing the argument, "every time North and I have solved a case, it's because you've helped us."

"Like fucking hell" came from the kitchen.

"Yeah, that's definitely not true," Jadon said.

"You're a great detective." Shaw scooted closer. "You're a wonderful detective."

The smile cut across Jadon's mouth. It felt like the edge of a razor.

"Jay," Shaw said softly.

"Except for Barr."

Shaw shook his head. Tears brightened his eyes.

"You're thinking it." Jadon shrugged. "I'm thinking it. North is thinking it."

"I'm thinking about how I'm trying to have a fucking phone call while you two fuckwits go down on each other verbally."

"How do you go down on someone verbally?" Shaw asked.

"No, don't ask—" Jadon tried.

Glugging noises came from the kitchen, and then, "Not you, fuckwit! How many times do I have to tell you?"

Shaw looked at Jadon. It was hard to separate out the mixture of what Jadon saw on his face there. Compassion, certainly, because Shaw was one of the most compassionate people Jadon knew. And pain, because the West End Slasher was one of Shaw's scars—literally and figuratively. And something else, more complex. Shaw took Jadon's beer and set it on the table. Then he took Jadon's hands in his.

"Jadon, what Barr did—it was before you were his partner. Before you were even a detective. You can't keep carrying that around forever. And before you say something silly like 'I should have known,' let me remind you that I was face to face with him, that I was as close to him as you and I are right now, and when I met him again, years later, I didn't know." Jadon opened his mouth, but Shaw spoke over him. "You are a good detective. When Taylor and Waggener came after you, tried to scare you—" Shaw's eyes slid to Jadon's chest, to where the scars were hidden by his shirt. "—you didn't give up. You went looking for them. And you found the money. And you found the evidence that led back to them."

"And they tortured the shit out of me. They grabbed me in the middle of the night and—" His throat closed: the cigarette burns, the cuts, the kicks and punches, the piece of pipe they'd used as a club, the broken ribs. The bag over his face like a caul, every time he tried to take a breath, the plastic sealing around his mouth and nose.

"And you got away," Shaw whispered. He was clutching Jadon's hands so tightly that they hurt, but the pain was stabilizing. Jadon's next breath was easier. "And you survived. And you didn't give up that fucking money to those murderous fucking monsters. And we got them because of you, Jay. Because you left us a trail. Because you were careful and smart and an amazing detective."

Jadon shook his head, but the rush of tears was real, and for a moment, all he could do was battle the tide of emotion. He wrested his hands from Shaw and wiped his face. Snot made it hard to breathe through his nose, so he sucked in air through his open mouth. The only clear thought he had was that he was not going to cry in front of North McKinney.

As though summoned by the thought: "Jesus Christ," North said from the doorway. "What did you do to him?"

"I didn't do anything!" And then, without missing a beat, "I gave him a motivational speech."

"Oh, because that went so well for you last time." To Jadon—and without any visible regard for what he must have seen of Jadon's distress— North added, "He gave a forty-five minute 'inspirational speech'—" He drew the air quotes with his fingers. "—to this lady at the courthouse."

"She was so nice to me! She kept saying I had beautiful skin!"

"Because she makes dresses out of people, shit-for-brains! The handcuffs might have been a fucking clue! He kept saying, 'You can do anything you set your mind to' and 'I believe in you' and 'If I can help you, I'll do whatever I can.' Thank God I was there when he tried to give her a business card with our home address written on the back."

"Her name was Suzette," Shaw told Jadon proudly. "She had pointy teeth."

North made a noise of disgust and then looked at Jadon. "He already told you you're a good detective, and I'm sure as fuck not going to say it again. So, what the fuck is the real problem?"

The lunacy was enough to help Jadon master the worst of the storm of emotions. He dried his face one last time, killed his beer, and was surprised at how easy it was to say, "My captain is trying to get rid of me. Not fit for duty, that kind of thing." And then it all came spilling out: Cerise's warning, the symposium, the cutting accuracy of Nico's final comments about all the ways he'd avoided dealing with what mattered in his life. "I mean, is he right? Am I that fucked up?"

"No," Shaw said.

"Yes," North said.

"North!"

"What? He is. You are." North adjusted his Hobbes hood. Then he said, "Look, Jay, you're in a bad place. That's not your fault; you've been through a lot. But you need to get some help."

"You're not fucked up," Shaw said. "You're hurt, and you're healing. I think you've done a good job finding healthy ways to cope with what happened to you. But I think Nico might be right that now those mechanisms are starting to be not so healthy. And that means you need to keep adapting, learning new strategies, checking your priorities." Shaw flashed a grin. "Plus North is jealous that you have abs."

"I have abs, motherfucker," North shouted. "Every fucking one of you harping on the same fucking thing. It's called muscle. Muscle is denser than fat. That's science." Rounding on Jadon, he added, "And eating lentils every day and working out and then having a gym bro tsunami of diarrhea in the locker room, that isn't healthy. You need to eat a balanced diet."

"Eight servings of cheese isn't balanced," Shaw said in an underbreath.

"Excuse me?"

"Nothing," Shaw said sweetly.

"I feel like I have to point out that I never said anything about diarrhea," Jadon said.

"Yeah," North said, "we read between the lines."

"The point is," Shaw said, "that it's not fair that your captain is gunning for you. But that might not be the most important thing. The most important thing is, are you happy? Honestly, Jadon, the way you're living right now — are you happy?"

A wet nose touched Jadon's hand, and he flinched. The puppy—no longer a puppy—looked up at him, and Jadon smiled and scooped the dog up into his lap. After a few turns, the dog settled down, his head on Jadon's thigh. Jadon stroked the soft fur, felt the warmth of another living body. He thought of all the nights he'd slept in a chair or in a car or in an empty bed. About what it had felt like, that one night (which felt like a million years ago) when Nico had pillowed his head on Jadon's chest.

"I'm fine," Jadon said, which he knew wasn't an answer—and, in its own way, was. "I know there's—there's stuff I'm missing out on. But right now, that's okay. I've got a job to do. It's an important job. And yeah, I know, I'm replaceable, all that stuff. But it's my job. And I want to do it well. I want to do it the best that I can, because I've let myself get distracted before, and it cost me."

A quicksilver glimmer of pain crossed Shaw's face and then was gone.

"That's not what I meant," Jadon said.

"I know what you meant."

Jadon stumbled into the silence that came after, not sure what he was saying, only sure that it was better than the hurt he had seen on Shaw's face. "It's—I want a normal life. I want a balanced, happy, fulfilling life. I want a partner. Someone to come home to. But—but it needs to be the right person, and the right time. Someone who will understand I'm giving my best self at work because the job is important. And someone who will understand that it doesn't mean I love them any less, even if I have to work late, even if I have to work weekends, even if I'm gone a lot. And I don't know—I don't know about Nico. He deserves someone who puts him at the center of their life. And even if I—" He almost said, again, *love him*. "—feel something for him, I don't know that I can give him that."

"Fuck doll," North said.

For maybe the first time since Jadon had known him, Shaw choked on his spit.

"What?" Jadon asked.

Slapping Shaw on the back, North said, "You want a fuck doll. A sex doll. That's great, Jay. That's easy. You can get good ones in Japan, we'll find you one."

"I don't—"

"Yeah, you do. Doesn't bother you. Doesn't complain. Stays home and is available whenever you need him. Doesn't mind being second in your life. That's a fuck doll, buddy. You get that and a maid service, and you're set."

By that point, Shaw had recovered enough to say, "North!"

"Tell me I'm wrong."

"You're—" Shaw grimaced. "Well, actually, he might be right."

Jadon transferred the puppy to Shaw's lap and stood. "Okay, I remember why I never come to you for advice."

Shaw squawked—it was hard to tell, because Jadon only saw it out of the corner of his eye, but it looked like the puppy had bitten him and, for only an instant, appeared immensely proud of itself—and stood, dislodging the puppy onto the sofa. North immediately bent to check on the dog, saying, "Be careful with him!" The look on Shaw's face made Jadon think of the lady who made dresses out of skin. Pointy teeth, indeed.

Cradling the dog to his chest, North gave Shaw a passing glare and then said to Jadon, "Life is a bitch, Jay. It's not fair. It's miserable. And relationships are hard as fuck, especially when one of you is a grown-ass man who gets jealous of a puppy."

"He bit me! Jadon, you saw him!"

"I'm not saying I'm the expert, but I'll tell you one thing: there's no such thing as a complication-free relationship. You're never going to find a person who's going to take a back seat and give you all the benefits without any of the emotional commitment, without the compromises, without the sacrifices. If that's what you want, then, yeah, I guess you should let Nico go, because it wouldn't be fair to him. But if you're tired of being the Million Dollar Man or a cyborg or whatever the fuck you are living off almond butter and oat groats, if you want an actual human life with an actual human

man and an actual fucking chance at happiness, then nut up, buddy, and go tell him you're sorry."

Jadon stared at him. "That has got to be the worst motivational speech I've ever heard. That's got to be worse than the one Shaw gave that cannibal."

"It got better at the end," Shaw reassured North, "when you got to the part about 'nut up.'"

"Fuck you," North said, "and fuck you. Fuck the pair of you, you old pocket wangs."

Jadon rubbed his eyes. He wasn't sure how to put it into words, the way when he thought of Nico, he could feel the emotions building, feel the static charge that made the hairs on his arms stand up, feel himself rushing toward—something. And then a part of him balked, and he knew what that was: fear. *A kid who's so afraid of the dark.* "Oh my God," he said, unable to help the dismay in his voice. "I have to talk to him."

North snorted.

At the door, Shaw kissed his cheek.

"Do not fuck this up," North said.

"You're going to do great," Shaw said. "Call us and tell us how it goes."

"I'm not going to do that," Jadon said.

"Thank God," North said and started to close the door.

As Jadon made his way down the walk, Shaw said, "You realize that I slept with Jadon, and Jadon slept with Nico, and Nico slept with Emery, which means by the transitive property, Emery and I are lovers."

"By the transitive property," North said, "that means you've fucked a goat."

"Always a pleasure," Jadon called over his shoulder.

The door slammed shut.

It was going to be an easy murder to solve, Jadon thought. Honestly, the judge and jury might even find North's actions justified.

17

Jadon

Jadon was parking on the edge of campus when the call came. Nico's name appeared on the car's display. For a moment, all he could do was stare. Then he reached to accept the call. Before he could, though, it ended. He thought it couldn't have rung more than once.

He sat there, counting the seconds. After a full minute, he placed a call to Nico. It rang until it went to voicemail. Jadon counted two full minutes next time. The counting was helpful; it let him focus on breathing, keeping everything even and regular. He tried to center his thoughts. I'm sorry. That would be a good way to start. I'm sorry for how I acted and what I said. I was out of line. I'm sorry. I'm sorry, Nico. I'm so sorry.

When he placed the call again, it went to voicemail.

"Hi. I saw you called, and I'd like to talk to you." Jadon had to stop. He felt it again, that part of him rushing forward, the sudden stop as he balked. "I'm sorry, Nico. I acted inappropriately, and I was out of line. I'd like to apologize in person and see if we can find a way to—" Again, that surge of emotion, and then the hard stop. He felt like he had something stuck in his throat. "—to figure this out."

He disconnected. And he thought, That, ladies and gentlemen, is how a coward does it.

The phone stayed dark. A minute. Then three. Then five.

I can go home, Jadon thought. I can go home, and I can pretend that was it—he called, and I called, and that was our chance. And that would be easy and safe and it would hurt like hell, but in a few days, Jadon knew he'd be back in his routine, and the pain would get a little easier every day.

He got out of the car and headed for Harlow Hall.

The dorm lights were on tonight, making it a limestone island that dissolved into the low, hard sky of clouds. Inside, it had an emptiness that Jadon didn't remember—the white noise of silence, the rebounding echoes in the stairwell, the way you could tell, sometimes, that you were the only one in a building. Nico's door was locked, and the strip underneath was dark. When Jadon knocked, no one answered.

"Nico?"

Nothing.

It was a dorm room in an old building. The lock might as well have been make-believe. Jadon loided it with a credit card, and when the door popped open, he braced himself for—

Shouts. Outrage. Worse: Nico lying there, still and unresponsive.

But the beds were empty, and Nico's luggage still lay in the middle of the room, surrounded by clothes. He hadn't finished packing. He hadn't gone to a hotel.

Jadon did a quick walkthrough, checking for anything that looked out of place. Nothing. He let himself out of the room, pulling the door shut behind him. His heart was beating a little faster as he made his way out of the dorm. Nico had called him only a few minutes ago. That meant, at the minimum, he was still thinking about Jadon. Wanted to talk to him. He might have felt conflicted about a conversation—that could explain why he hadn't answered when Jadon called back—but a part of him wanted to talk. His bags were still here. He couldn't have gone far. He was probably somewhere on campus still—

Dr. Meza's face floated in Jadon's vision. The way he had smiled. The way his pale fingers had rolled the corduroy of Nico's lapel back and forth.

The dinner, Jadon thought. The closing dinner for the seminar. That made the most sense—Nico had decided to go after all, maybe to patch things up with Meza, maybe simply to round out his time at the seminar. Jadon started across the quad at a jog. He knew, from previous visits to campus, that the college had a private club for the professors. Then he realized he didn't know if any of the professors from the seminar were actually faculty at Chouteau; they might have gone somewhere else. The Central West End had lots of great restaurants, the kind of upscale places that a group of academics might go for wine and overly priced tapas, for example. He placed another call to Nico as he passed through a clump of trees, the shadows deeper under the shroud of bare branches.

If it hadn't been so dark, he wouldn't have seen the light. Jadon noticed it, lying off to the side among the trees, and he almost kept going. Then his brain recognized the familiar shape—a phone screen, lighting up as a call came in. His own phone, still pressed against his ear, continued to ring. He stopped jogging.

He ended the call to Nico. A moment later, the phone on the ground went dark.

Jadon turned on the flashlight on his phone. He directed it at the grassy stretch next to the path, took one step, and then another, sweeping the light left and right. He stopped again. To his left, a few yards back in the direction he'd come, muddy depressions and torn grass showed where something heavy had fallen and then slid. Not something, his brain corrected. Someone. Where someone had fallen.

It was luck, a part of him recognized numbly. If the ground hadn't been so soft from the steady drizzle, there wouldn't have been any sign at all. Luck and carelessness. Because he'd left the phone.

He took Nico.

It was a jump in logic—the rational part of Jadon knew that. But he also knew it was true. He used the phone's weak flashlight to check the ground as best he could, and then he took a looping route toward where he'd seen the fallen phone. Finally, balancing on an old tree root to keep from disturbing the marks and prints left on the ground, Jadon snagged the phone. He knew this was reckless, knew he should have waited for an evidence team, knew, at the least, he should have been wearing gloves. But it didn't matter. It was Nico's phone; he recognized the case, the corner of the molded plastic where Nico, lost in thought, had chewed on it. And something else, too—a dark, wet clump of fabric. His hoodie, the one he had loaned Nico on that morning run.

For a moment, Jadon couldn't do anything. Then, holding the phone and hoodie, he retraced his steps to the brick path. He needed to call Cerise. No, she wasn't on duty, and this wouldn't be her case. He needed to call this in, get a patrol unit out here. Only it was Halloween, one of the busiest nights of the year for the Metropolitan PD. They'd be spread thin, and Jadon wasn't sure that pulling rank would help him. If the captain caught wind of it and shut him down—he could hear her now: *He dropped his phone while walking across campus. Believe it or not, it's happened before, especially after someone's had something to drink. Do you think that might be a possibility on Halloween on a college campus?*

He placed a call to the campus security office instead. The voice that answered was male, older, gruff. After identifying himself, Jadon said, "I've got an active crime scene that I'm trying to secure, and a possible assault currently in progress. I need as many people as you can spare to search the campus—anywhere you wouldn't be able to see on a camera."

"That's a lot of campus, Detective. And we've kind of got our hands full with a fraternity party—"

"Really? Does that seem like your priority? What do you think your supervisor, or the dean, or the chancellor, or whoever the hell I have to get on the phone, is going to think when I tell him that a sworn officer of the law requested help to prevent a sexual assault in progress, and you decided that a bunch of toga-wearing assholes breaking the campus alcohol policy was a bigger deal?"

Silence. Then, in a stiff voice, "I'll send some people over." There was a pause, and the next words were even starchier: "Do you still want me to call that detective?"

"That's me," Jadon said and disconnected.

Some people, whatever that meant, wouldn't be enough. Someone had Nico. Right then, at that moment. Jadon was sure of it. And whoever it was, he'd been planning things, trying to get Nico for days. He could see, in his mind's eye, Dalary Lang's bruised and battered face, the tamped-down horror in his eyes. Dark eyes. And dark hair. And a slender, almost waifish build. Not quite like Nico, who was more lean muscle. But the same dark, shaggy hair. Jadon remembered what it was like to be helpless. To be unable to move. To be unable to fight back. Unable to make them stop. He remembered when he lost control of his breathing, and he tried to gulp air, and the bag sealed its plastic around his mouth and nose again.

For a heartbeat, it was like something physical lodged in Jadon's throat; he couldn't breathe. Then he forced himself to calm. Whatever had happened, whatever was happening, he couldn't do anything to help Nico if he didn't keep his head.

In the meantime, all he could do was try. He placed a call to dispatch and requested a patrol car and a detective on duty. Then he stood there, his fingers growing numb from the cold, his face and clothes wet with the misty rain, listening to the drumbeat inside his head.

"Nico!" he shouted. He kept his distance from the disturbed ground where the attack had happened and began to move outward in a spiral. "Nico! If you can hear me, make some noise!"

A girl in a Wonder Woman costume stared at him and then hurried away. Jadon kept moving and calling out. As he did, he tried to be logical, tried to make sense out of what had happened. Someone had been following Nico. Someone had made attempts. That suggested a pattern, a fixation. Again, in his memory, the vision played of Dr. Meza rolling the wale of corduroy between his fingers. But Jadon could also admit to himself that it was a stretch. The assaults had been happening for weeks, and for all Jadon knew, Meza was a tenured professor at some institution on the coast. The same was true for the next person in Jadon's lineup — Clark clearly had an interest in Nico, perhaps even an unhealthy one, and he certainly hadn't been pleased that Nico had chosen to spend time with Jadon. But again, the assaults had been happening for weeks. Unless Clark was a grad student in the area, then he was out too.

Of course, there were other explanations. The attacker might have simply recognized the pattern of assaults on campus and realized it would make perfect cover for his own actions — kind of like a copycat. Even that felt weak to Jadon; the physical similarities between Nico and the previous victims were too great. If someone was simply taking advantage of the situation, then the odds of that similarity would have to be astronomical. Then Jadon remembered the strange security guard, the one who had been there when he and Nico had run into each other (literally). The guard who had appeared, as if by magic, when Meza and Jadon had started going at it. Had Jadon seen him other places? Maybe; he had a vague recollection of spotting a familiar face on campus. But then, Chouteau was a small college, so it didn't seem unusual that he'd might run into the security guard by accident. Maybe the best thing would be to call the security office again and see if that guard was on duty tonight. Or if he could be located. A home address, maybe. If Jadon had thought of it earlier —

And that stopped him. Because the man in the security office had said, *Do you still want me to call that detective?* And Jadon, in a hurry, had dismissed the words. But Jadon hadn't asked campus security to contact him about an assault. Jadon had asked some guys in patrol, ones he was friendly with.

Do you still want me to call that detective?

It was like pieces of the puzzle lining up. Vic saying, *Reck, that kid is some grade-A pussy.* Vic saying, *Holy shit, this is the underwear model?* But Jadon had been careful never to bring that up because he knew how sensitive Nico was about it. So, how could Vic have known —

Unless he'd learned it himself.

Vic, who was always walking a fine line of homophobia. Vic, with that harassment complaint hanging over his head. Vic, always insisting it was just a misunderstanding.

A young Black woman in a security guard uniform was approaching, flashlight in hand. "Sir?"

"Don't let anyone touch that crime scene until the patrol officers get here," he said, pointing at the disturbed section of grass. Then, still clutching the hoodie and phone, he sprinted toward where he'd parked his car.

18

Nico

The inside of the hood smelled like vinyl, and the hot air of Nico's breath, and the fragrance of his hair product. His attacker had pulled it over Nico's head shortly after he'd been tackled on the quad, and he'd worn it during the walk across campus, then the car ride (which he'd spent in the trunk), and then as he'd been forced into a building and down a flight of steps. His initial hope that someone would see him, would save him, had guttered and died—it was Halloween, so what was strange about a couple of guys with their BDSM gear on?

Strangely, his panic had leveled out—still panic, yes, but even with his heart going a mile a minute, even with him gulping to try to get enough air, he could force himself to think. He had to think. Or else he was pretty sure he was going to die. If you see his face, a small voice inside his head told him, he's going to kill you. Nico had been around enough cops, seen enough cop shows, to know that.

Now, tied to a chair, he tried to think. First, he took inventory of himself. He was wet, his shoulder throbbing from the fall he'd taken, and covered in mud and grass. The cold made him shiver, and his toes had gone numb. A ball gag filled his mouth, and his jaw ached from being forced open for so long. He'd lost Jadon's hoodie and, more importantly, his phone. He had no weapons, no tools, nothing. He thought of what Emery would do.

Emery would probably have a multitool up his ass. The thought made a giggle rise in Nico's chest. He sensed the hysteria behind the laughter and clamped down on it; if he started laughing, he wasn't sure he'd ever stop.

Next, he tried to make sense of where he was. A basement, yes. The air was cool. He'd lost his slides when he'd been tackled, and underfoot, he felt tile. When he moved, the acoustics of the room suggested that it was big and empty. A basement, he thought again. In a home, he guessed. When they'd come inside, the basement stairs had been directly in front of them. That was good. If he could get to the stairs, it would be a straight shot to get out of the house.

He tested the ropes. The ones around his wrist had already chafed the skin raw, and every movement burned. Another rope ran from his wrists to his ankles, passing under the chair to keep Nico from standing. Nico pulled as hard as he could, but all he managed to do was draw the rope tight. It was too strong for him to break, and all he succeeded in doing was making his wrists burn.

The edge of his panic sharpened again. He remembered another time, another place—being cold, in the dark, alone. His breaths came more quickly. It was the hood; he couldn't get enough air. He felt like his head was on fire, like—

A quiet laugh made him jolt upright. Adrenaline rushed through him, like pins and needles on every inch of exposed skin. He tried to determine where the sound had come from, but all he could tell was that it had not been close. Then one of the treads creaked, and footsteps came down the stairs. They crossed the room, and then a familiar sound: the rustle of clothing as someone lowered himself to the floor.

Hands touched Nico's bare feet, and he flinched. The laugh came again. Nico kicked, or tried to. He couldn't move his feet, since they were tied to the legs of the chair, but he tried anyway. The man kept laughing. He curled his fingers under Nico's feet, stroking his bare soles, rubbing his thumbs over Nico's toes. Everything felt slow, almost affectionate. He's taking his time; the thought rose in Nico like a bubble of panic. He's taking his time because he doesn't have to hurry.

Hands wrapped Nico's ankles again, squeezing — *too fat, practically cankles* and *don't be ridiculous, his ankles are fine; it's his calves that are the problem* and the look on Jadon's face when Nico had told him — and then stroking upward, the fingertips now, teasing the hairs on Nico's legs. When the hands settled on his knees, the man applied light pressure, a nonverbal cue for Nico to spread them. Instead, Nico drew his knees together. The man made an annoyed noise and let go of Nico's knees. Then he punched Nico in the solar plexus.

The blow drove the air from Nico's lungs. He sagged in the chair, the pain compounded by his body's automatic panic *can't breathe can't breathe can't breathe.* He was only distantly aware of the man easing his legs apart, of the hands continuing their journey up his thighs. Slowly, as his body relaxed, Nico was able to suck in a breath. A tear ran to the tip of his nose and hung there. More stung his eyes, and he tried to blink them away.

If the man noticed, or if he cared, he gave no sign of it. His hands paused at the tiny red running shorts. He slid the bottle of lotion out of the pockets, and he laughed again. The sound of plastic hitting tile suggested he'd tossed the bottle to the floor. His hands continued up, and then he pressed against Nico's dick with his thumb — soft at first, and then harder, until Nico tried to shift away. He laughed again.

He stroked Nico's belly, tracing the definition there. Then up again to tease Nico's nipples. He leaned in and sniffed Nico's pits. In the chill of the basement, his body heat radiated against Nico. A long finger followed the line of his collarbone. And then a hand wrapped around his neck, thumb pressing against Nico's throat, hard enough that Nico fought the urge to gag, and then harder still. With the rubber ball still in his mouth, it was already hard to convince himself he was getting enough air. Now, for a moment, Nico couldn't get any. He fought again, trying to kick, wrenching his body in an effort to get away. The man laughed longer this time, a rolling chuckle.

The hood was ripped away—and, with it, some of Nico's hair. He blinked, partly to adjust to the light, and partly from the fresh tears. He tried to breathe through his nose, but the tears had made him snotty, and it was harder than ever. He felt dizzy. The basement tilted. Nico tried to focus on the man.

Vic. His name was Vic. He had wanted—Nico wasn't sure. Something about coffee. They'd been in the coffee shop.

Vic stared back at him. The veneer of flirtation and good humor that Nico remembered from their first meeting was gone; now, his eyes were hungry. He was smiling, and it widened as he took Nico in. He still hadn't said anything yet. Say something, Nico wanted to shout. He bit into the gag, and the dull pain in his jaw spread into his teeth. Say something!

But Vic only stared. His hands came back to Nico's thighs, and again he pressed his thumb against the thin fabric of the running shorts. What had seemed, earlier, to be part of the costume's appeal—the knowledge this body was almost completely on display, that Jadon would be looking, wouldn't be able not to look—now made Nico shout into the gag, trying to draw his knees together. Vic moved his thumb slowly but insistently. Nico screamed again. With Vic between his legs, though, there was nothing he could do, nowhere he could go. Vic bent and kissed him through the shorts, and then his thumb came back again. Groping. Mashing. Determined, Nico thought with a kind of bewilderment that straddled horror and a kind of manic hilarity. Determined to get me hard.

Finally, Vic sat back on his heels. His smile had flattened out into a blank-faced fury. Then he slapped Nico, and Nico felt his lip split under the blow. His head jerked sideways. Droplets of blood sprayed the tile. More drops landed on his thigh, hot. It was hot on his chin too. Hot dripping onto his chest.

Vic's own chest was rising and falling, but his face still had that terrible blankness. He hit Nico again. And then again. For a while, pain and the physical disorientation of the blows rendered the basement for Nico in snapshots: the fluorescent light fixture overhead; exposed drywall painted with something that looked like liquid rubber; the red of his blood like pomegranate seeds on the small, white rectangles of porcelain. The final blow rocked Nico sideways, and the chair went with him. He fell hard, his injured shoulder ablaze with pain as he landed on it again. The tile felt cool against his cheek. The smell of bleach and mildew met him, mixing with the taste of blood, like he had a mouthful of loose change. The world continued to spin, and Nico closed his eyes. I can fall asleep, he thought dizzily. I'll go to sleep.

But when Vic moved, Nico opened his eyes. From where Nico lay, still tied to the chair, Vic looked enormous. His face had relaxed again, the wide mouth hinting at a smile. Little drops of blood flecked the back of his hands. Some of them had tails curled like commas. A pause in the sentence, a dull voice said in Nico's head, before we start again.

Maybe Vic noticed his gaze. Or maybe the movement was reflexive. He turned his arm and wiped the blood on the back of his jeans. His erection bulged in front. He took deep breaths, but even deep and measured, they still sounded excited.

Upstairs, a doorbell rang. Nico flinched. A glower crossed Vic's face. The bell rang again and again. It kept ringing. Nico could imagine a child's hand pressing the button. Or teenagers trying to stir up shit. Vic made a disgruntled noise and went upstairs. He didn't look back.

Adrenaline and fear had kept the worst of the pain at bay, but Nico could feel it waiting for him, ready to rush in the moment he started to lag. A part of him wanted to close his eyes again, lean into the cool tile, and stop. But that way lay death. If he lets you see his face, he's going to kill you. The thought came back with the quality of a struck bell. He's going to kill you.

As awful as the campus assaults must have been, Nico knew, this was worse. Because he'd been escalating. Either he was learning what he enjoyed and trying to get more of it—more of the hurting, more of the control. Or his usual tricks were starting to wear thin, and he had to work harder and harder to get the high he was chasing. And he'd been planning for this: the rubberized paint on the walls. The tile. His eyes fell on a drain at the center of the floor. When it was over, Vic would bleach every available surface and wash away any sign that Nico had ever been here.

Nico strained at the ropes again, but he still got nowhere. The ropes around his wrist had a tiny amount of slippage, which was why they'd chafed the skin there so badly. And if he twisted and pulled, he could get the loop to the heel of his hand. But then, no matter how he compressed his hand, he was stuck. There simply wasn't enough room to slide his hand free.

He squirmed in the chair, hoping the fall had loosened the construction. Wood squeaked and protested, but no matter what Nico did, the chair refused to give.

Upstairs, Vic was yelling.

It wasn't fair. The surge of outrage and indignation only lasted a moment, but it left Nico on the brink of tears. It wasn't fair. He hadn't done anything wrong. It was like the last time—he'd gotten caught in the crossfire through no fault of his own. And this time, Emery wasn't going to save him, and Jadon—he could hear Jadon's furious shout: *You can't take care of yourself.*

No, Nico thought. I guess not. But the memory of Jadon, of how hard he'd tried to keep this from happening, of what this would do to him —

Destroy him, it's going to destroy him.

—was enough for Nico to make an effort again. The rope around his wrist seemed to be the weakest link. If the ropes had a little more give, or if he had something to ease the passage of his hand. Blood, maybe. If he could get his wrist to bleed, maybe that would—

And then his eyes fell on the bottle of lotion. The one Vic had taken from his shorts. The one he'd dropped on the floor. For my zinc stripe, Nico thought, and another giggle washed through him. He fought it off and began to squirm around, rocking his body back and forth. The chair moved with him, inching forward and back as wood screeched against tile.

The sound seemed tremendous, but Vic didn't come running. After what felt like an eternity, Nico had to stop, the muscles in his back and abdomen screaming. He listened, and from upstairs came a strange thump-thump noise he didn't recognize. A gun? Was Vic shooting someone? But then Vic's shouts picked up again, sounding even more distant, and Nico realized he was wasting a golden opportunity. He rocked and wiggled and squirmed. And slowly, he spun the chair around until, searching blindly behind him, he closed one hand around the bottle of lotion.

It took a fumbling moment before he got the lid open. Then he squeezed the bottle again and again, emptying the lotion over his hands. It stung when it made contact with his scrapes, but Nico barely felt it. He turned his arms. The lotion was slippery and ran along bare skin. He could feel it soaking into the ropes. When he felt like he'd coated his wrist as best he could, he pulled his arm up, bringing his hand to the loop enclosing it. He could feel his hand sliding, sliding, sliding—

And then stop.

Tears sprang to Nico's eyes. He huffed around the ball gag.

Jadon sleeping in his car. Jadon waiting in the hall with two coffees. Jadon, and the run through Forest Park. The prism of the Jewel Box opening in the autumn morning.

Tears turned to rage, and Nico began to yank. Control was gone. Planning. Reason. He was an animal with his leg caught in a trap, and he went wild. The lotion made his arm slip back and forth within the circle of rope, his hand jamming against the opening each time he tried to draw it free, pain building as he brought all his strength to bear, trying to force his hand through the opening.

And then his hand slid free.

Disbelief froze Nico. Then he fumbled with the rope around his other hand. His fingers were slick. The rope was slippery. But he found the knot and undid it. When he brought his arms around in front of him, he was shocked by the blood—it coated his arms up to the elbows, mixed with the pearly streaks of lotion. Pain blazed to life in his shoulders and elbows, which felt locked solid after being immobilized for so long. But he fought through the pain, loosening the knots around his ankles. The ball gag went next, his jaw on fire. And then he was free. He got to his feet, slipped on the tile, and caught himself. His hips and knees protested too. His next step was slow, uncertain, shortened like an old man's. And the next. But then his body limbered up, and by the time he reached the stairs, he took them two at a time.

The door at the top of the steps was open, and beyond it lay a small landing with another door, clearly some sort of transitional space between the upstairs, the downstairs, and the outside. Nico reached the landing and wobbled as a wave of dizziness rushed over him. Black spots ate away at the edges of his vision. Blood pressure, maybe. He'd been still for so long, and now—

He had to grab the door jamb to keep himself upright. He glimpsed a kitchen to his right: walnut cabinets, an old trestle table, mustard-colored laminate counters with matching wallpaper. Then he felt steadier, and he flipped the deadbolt and let himself out into a darkened carport. An old Buick was pulled all the way up under the aluminum awning, old, close to twenty feet of chrome and fins. An Impala was parked behind it. Beyond that was the sloping driveway, the street, the dusty glow of a streetlight, a yellow-brick house with a vinyl decal in its front window of a witch riding a broomstick and the words WE KNOW HOW TO HAVE A GOOD TIME in spooky script.

I have to get to the house, Nico told himself. The concrete pad was rough under his bare feet as he took his first hobbling step.

Arms closed around him. Vic's breath whispered against his ear, loud and rasping. Nico screamed, and this time, without the gag to stop him, he gave full voice to his fear and rage. Vic grunted, his arms tightening, and lifted Nico's feet from the ground—no easy feat, considering Nico was taller and had been eating way too many carbs under Jadon's influence. Staggering slightly under Nico's weight, Vic took a step back.

Their reverse journey flashed through Nico's mind: the vestibule, the stairs, the bleachy tile and the rubber paint on the walls. He screamed louder.

And then he remembered Jadon in the park, his arms around Nico.

If someone grabs you from behind, there are a few simple ways to escape.

Nico couldn't drop to the ground—it was too late for that, with Vic already holding him in the air.

But.

Nico planted his feet on the side of the Buick. He kicked off, and the unexpected force sent Vic off balance. Combined with Nico's weight, it sent him reeling backwards, trying to catch his balance. Then his foot caught on something—the doorstep, Nico guessed, and they went down.

Beneath Nico, Vic took the worst of the fall. Nico heard his head crack against the concrete. Vic's arms loosened, and when Nico elbowed him in the ribs, Vic let out a gasp, and his arms loosened. Nico broke his hold and scrambled upright. He couldn't seem to catch his balance, so he leaned against the Buick, dragging himself down one retro fin.

A gargling noise behind him made him turn. Somehow, Vic was on his hands and knees, spitting blood onto the concrete. His head came up. Blood made a mask across his face. He planted a hand against the side of the Buick and tried to push himself up, but his hand slid, leaving a bloody smear behind it. He tried again, grabbing one of the Buick's rotting tires, and this time, he got to his feet.

"Get back here, you fucking faggot!" Vic screamed. "You're mine!"

"You have got to be shitting me," Nico said and tried to go faster.

He released the Buick and forced himself into a jog. Beyond the carport, the wide expanse of the street waited. All he had to do was —

A shadow moved in front of him, blocking his path. Instead of panic, outraged disbelief rolled through Nico. Not here. Not this close. Not now. He ducked his head, jogged faster, and braced himself for what was going to be the worst tackle in the history of the world.

"Nico?"

It was Jadon's voice.

And then, "Vic, show me your—Nico, down!"

Nico dropped.

A gun barked. A flash of light. The hot expelled gas. The smell of gunpowder.

Silence came roaring in. Nico kept his face to the rough concrete. Whatever reserves of energy he'd had, they were gone now.

Footsteps moved past him. And then a familiar ratcheting sound — handcuffs.

Warm hands settled on Nico's shoulders, and a moment later, Jadon was helping him sit up. Jadon's darkly sandy eyes roved Nico's face, and Nico opened his mouth to say something. Instead, he noticed that Jadon was dressed like Superman. The white dress shirt, the suit, and underneath it all, the spandex costume. Only not Superman. A G. Super Gay. And he remembered that stupid jab about being Superman. The stupidity of all of it. He touched the G, felt the warmth and solidity of Jadon's body beneath it. He started to laugh, and Jadon cupped the side of his face. And then he started to cry.

19

Jadon

When they finally let him see Nico, it had been hours. Hours of answering questions. Hours of repeating himself. Hours of trying to explain.

And now here, this: the semiprivate hospital room, the dark, the fading astringency of a cleaning product. At first, he could only put together fragments. The privacy curtain closing off the other patient's area. The lamp next to Nico's bed. The window that looked out on the swells and troughs of more darkness. Like an ocean, he thought. And all the lights bobbing out there, everyone lost at sea.

Nico wore a gown, and it swallowed him up, making him look frail and small. Bruises covered one side of his face. His lip was split. Jadon couldn't see it from where he stood, but some of that dark, shaggy hair had been ripped out. His hands started to shake, and he pressed them against his legs.

Maybe the movement drew his attention; Nico looked up, uncertainty creasing his face, and then a smile. Air whispered in the ducts. Then it stopped.

"Do you want to sit down?" Nico asked.

Jadon sat with his back to the dark ocean. The lamp lit the side of Nico's face. It threaded coils of gold through his hair. It made a blaze of the long expanse of his slender neck. Where the gown exposed part of his shoulder, it gleamed on the coppery skin there.

"I look that bad, huh?"

After a moment, Jadon realized it had been a question. He shook his head.

Something changed in Nico's face. His expression didn't close, not exactly. It wasn't even wariness. A kind of reserve, maybe. Or hesitation.

"Nobody will talk to me about Vic."

"He's alive. I winged him, that's all."

"What's going to happen to him?"

"He'll go to prison. We've got him for—" Jadon barely stumbled over the words at all. "—for what he did to you. He still had your underwear in his house. We'll get DNA. Bring in previous victims. He's never going to hurt anyone again."

Nico nodded. It seemed like there should be more, but Jadon couldn't think of anything. He wanted to say, *You were so brave.* He wanted to say, *I'm sorry.* The inside of his mouth felt like glue.

"I talked to him in the line for coffee," Nico said, and he sounded on the verge of tears. "I didn't do anything."

"It's not like that. It's not logical. It's a fixation, an obsession. He had a type, Nico, and you had the bad luck to cross his path. You didn't do anything wrong."

Nico wiped his face on his shoulder. "It feels like I did."

"You didn't. This isn't your fault."

Neither of them said anything. A machine beeped. Steps moved out in the hall.

"So," Nico said, "thank you. I was too busy being hysterical to say that before." Then a tired smile gleamed in the darkness. "They've got me on something good now. I solemnly swear I will not lose my shit."

Jadon could hear it now in his voice—the honey-thickness of whatever they'd given him slowing his speech. "You can lose your shit."

Nico smiled again. He squirmed around in the bed, little blips of pain crossing his face, until he lay on his side facing Jadon. "And I'm sorry."

"You're sorry?"

"For not listening to you. You were trying to keep me safe, and I was...I was such an asshole to you." The waver on the last words was followed by a fresh shine in Nico's eyes. He turned into the pillow for what felt like a long time, and when he lifted his head again, his face was dry. "You were right. About everything. And I should have listened."

"Nico—"

"No, please. Because whatever this stuff is, it's good, and I want to say this while it's easy."

But then he didn't say anything. He lay there, looking at Jadon. Or maybe looking past him. Out into the great dark. Jadon thought about closing the blinds. And then he thought no. Because he'd looked into the dark too. We carry it with us, he wanted to say. We carry it around inside us. So, you can close your eyes. You can rest for a while. You don't have to keep looking, not right now.

"I thought I'd grown out of it," Nico said, and the words had a dreamy slowness to it. "I kept telling myself I'd grown up, gotten over it. That I was an adult now." He laughed, and it sounded dry and croaky.

Jadon reached for the cup and pitcher next to the bed. His hands were still shaking. He had to lean against the little table, one arm pressed against it, so he could pour the water without spilling. When he passed the cup to Nico, he could see the ripples on the surface. It made him think of *Jurassic Park*. Of something huge coming. The heavy weight of its steps shaking everything as it approached. And you can't run. You can't get away. Because it's coming right for you.

Nico accepted the cup. He took a slow drink, and his Adam's apple bobbed when he swallowed. When he passed the cup back, his fingers brushed Jadon's, and Jadon followed the fine-boned hand up to the wrist, where bandages hid skin torn raw. Nico seemed to sense his gaze. He slipped his arm under the thin hospital blanket.

"I definitely," he whispered, "shouldn't have shat on you for pointing it out."

His eyes were banked coals, alive with heat shimmer. Tears, Jadon corrected himself. He thought maybe he was getting loopy. He thought maybe he needed to sleep.

Nico was still looking at him.

"It's okay," Jadon said, even though he had no idea what they were talking about. "It's all okay. You need to rest now."

"In Argentina, we were never in one place long enough for me to fit in," Nico said. "And then, when I went to boarding school, I was brown when everybody else was white, and on top of that, I was gayer than God. Maybe I would have fit in at Columbia—it's big enough, mixed enough, that I could have, I think. But then I was trying to model, and school fell apart. And then, at a shoot, I'd look around, and I'd realize I was all alone. There was only so much I could say to the other guys. And the girls wanted to talk about the guys. Even when I was dating someone, I was alone. Because they liked what they saw on the outside, but they didn't like me." He swallowed. "Always alone."

You're not alone, Jadon thought. The words were so loud inside his head that his heart skipped, and he thought he'd said them out loud.

"When I started grad school, I was determined to be done with that. Done with never fitting in. Done with never being...right. I was going to be the perfect grad student. Only—only I kept taking jobs, and I'd fly back to the city. And I'd tell people. And then I'd hear them talking about it, about how school was a game for me, and—and what I'm trying to say is you were right. I'm a hypocrite. I talk this big game about wanting people to take me seriously, and then I turn around and make a big deal about a job I booked, or I wear fake glasses, or..." He trailed off with a shrug.

"Or brag about sucking dick?" Jadon said. The words popped out before he could stop them, and horror rushed in behind them.

But Nico burst out laughing, the sound bright and electrically alive. "Oh my God. I still can't believe I said that."

To his own surprise, Jadon laughed too—a real laugh, albeit a short one.

When silence fell again between them, Nico rubbed his eyes. Then he lay still again, staring out at Jadon, through him. When he spoke, his voice had become syrupy again. "I'm going to drop out of grad school."

Jadon tried to say nothing. Then it slipped out of him: "Nico."

"I am. My mom's been after me for years to come back home. She wants me to be in a telenovela—do you know what that is?"

Jadon nodded.

"So, maybe I'll do that. My brother does some directing. It could be a family thing."

Jadon's head throbbed. He tried to find a more comfortable position in the chair.

"What?" Nico's voice sharpened.

"Okay."

"What does that mean? You don't approve?"

"I didn't say that."

"No, you didn't say anything."

"What do you want me to say? It's not my life."

"So, you don't approve."

"Like I said, it's not my life."

Instead of whatever Jadon was expecting—shouting was at the top of the list—Nico started to cry. Little tears only, but a steady stream of them. He turned into the pillow again and held himself still. Finally, he lifted his face. It was wet, the tear tracks glistening the color of salt. "I think I want to go to sleep now."

Maybe it was the late night. Maybe it was the way Jadon's bones felt hollowed out by exhaustion and fear and adrenaline. He wrapped his hands around the arms of the chair to steady them. "I don't know what you want me to say. I don't want you to go to Argentina. I don't want you to go back to Wahredua. I want you to stay here. And I know that's not realistic. I know how hard you've worked for the career you have. I know you need to move and start the best doctoral program you can get into. And I want that for you." His voice started to unravel. "But how am I supposed to sit here and listen to you tell me how you're going to throw it all away because, what, you realized you're a human being, and you're complicated, and maybe you want more than one thing at the same time? I mean, Jesus Christ, Nico, that's the stupidest thing I've ever heard. You're gorgeous; of course you're going to enjoy the fact that people like how attractive you are. Of course you should be proud that you've done modeling work. That doesn't change anything about your work, about how smart you are, about the insights you're bringing to the scholarship." He tried to stop there, but the rest burst out of him. "I mean, a telenovela?"

Nico stared at him, his dark eyes wide. Then, slowly, a huge smile cracked his face.

"Oh my God," Jadon said under his breath.

Covering his smile, Nico continued to stare at him.

"I'm sorry," Jadon said. "It's been a long night, and—" He started to rise. "I'm sorry. I'll go."

Nico caught his wrist. His grip was surprisingly strong. For what felt like a long time, they were chained together like that, Nico still trying to cover that stupid smile. Slowly, Jadon sank back down into his seat.

"I'm sorry," he said again.

Nico shook his head. "No, you're right. I'm embarrassed, that's all. It's—it's so superficial. So vain. I mean, according to all my ex-boyfriends and TikTok, I might need validation. Scratch that, I definitely need validation. But I don't like that about myself. And I don't like...I don't like how it makes me act."

"Believe it or not," Jadon said drily, "there's a middle ground between dressing like a suburban dad and blowing your professor for a publication credit."

"Jadon Reck!"

Jadon shrugged.

"Come over here."

"Uh, pass."

"That was the bitchiest thing I've ever heard you say."

"I—"

"I loved it. I want to pull your hair out."

"Lots of mixed messages tonight."

Nico's smile was cockeyed. One of those fine-boned hands curled around the bedrail. The bandage cuffing his wrist rustled when it brushed the hospital blanket. He was aware, again, of Nico's sleepy breaths. Of how little distance separated them.

"I'm not a good person," Nico whispered. "I thought you liked me when we were texting, and then you didn't, and then we met in person and I was even worse, and you're—you're so wonderful. And I'm such a mess."

"I think maybe you're being a little hard on yourself," Jadon said, his voice so thick he thought it might crack. "I'm a mess myself. What would Kierkegaard say about all this?"

"Kierkegaard definitely wouldn't be in favor of quid-pro-quo BJs."

Jadon gave him a look.

That cockeyed grin widened and then, after a moment, faded again. "Kierkegaard wasn't a big fan of the aesthetic."

"That's not the part I'm talking about. I'm talking about the other stuff."

Nico rolled his eyes. And he managed to put enough spin on it to make a middle-schooler proud. But after a few huffing breaths, he said, "Do you not know that there comes a midnight hour when everyone has to throw off his mask?"

The words sent a frisson down Jadon's spine. The hairs on his arms stood up. The midnight hours. All those midnight texts.

"Do you believe," Nico continued in that same voice like he was reciting something, "that life will always let itself be mocked?" He stopped and swallowed. "In every man, there is something which to a certain degree prevents him from becoming perfectly transparent to himself, but he who cannot reveal himself cannot love, and he who cannot love is the most unhappy man of all."

The chill that had run through Jadon's body felt like an iron band around his chest. He couldn't breathe. Couldn't even talk. He thought about all the things he'd said to Nico, all the things he'd never told anyone else. The things he hadn't even known about himself until he'd put them into words. And the way Nico had told him what no one else would. Had helped him see himself, even if it hurt.

"I'm tired of not being who I am," Nico said in that slow-thick voice again. "I'm tired of caring what people think. I'm tired of trying to convince myself if I can be smart enough, if I can be good enough, if I can find the right part and play it perfectly, someone will actually want to be with me. With me, Jay. And that's so stupid, because how can anyone be with the real me when I'm trying so hard to be someone else? I want to wear super slutty clothes if I want to wear them. I never in my entire fucking life want to wear a quarter-zip again. I mean, my God, they're like the Emery Hazard of clothing. And I am tired of not being honest about how I feel. I like you, Jadon." Nico stopped. His Adam's apple moved again, and he gave a weak laugh that sounded mostly like despair. "Actually, I think I love you, which is your cue to run as fast as humanly possible. I love the guy I got to know over all those texts. I love the guy right here, right now, who's so much better than words on a screen. I love that you listen to me, and more importantly, that you pay attention to me. You care about the things I care about. I love how resolved you are, how disciplined, how much you give of yourself to do what you think is right. And that goddamn picnic in the library." Nico's voice broke. "I mean, how the hell am I supposed to do anything after that?" He was quiet again, and when he spoke, his voice softened to a whisper. "So, there it is. I love you. And for the record, being vulnerable is not cute."

The last part he said as though it were a joke, but Jadon didn't laugh. That length of iron still felt like it was wrapped around his chest. He felt dizzy, and a part of him recognized that it was because he wasn't getting enough air. Finally, though, he managed to say, "You were right when you told me I was afraid. I've been afraid for a long time. Afraid of meeting someone I would…would care about, I guess. Afraid of what that would mean. And I told myself it was because I didn't want to get distracted. That was the truth, but only partly. I'm having a…" The laugh tore out of him. "I guess you could call it a hard time. I'm having a hard time letting go of some stuff. What happened to me with Barr, you know about that. And it was more than—more than what they did. The injuries, I mean. It's what they took from me. Who I thought I was. Strong, tough. The stupid idea that I knew how to handle myself, let alone how to handle everything else. They took that from me. And so I've been on this fucking—this fucking treadmill, running as fast as I can and no matter how hard I try, I'm always falling behind."

Nico's breathing sounded slow and deep, almost like he was sleeping, but the coal-fires of his eyes glittered back at Jadon.

"But that's part of it," Jadon said and gave a ragged laugh. "The other part is, I think I knew once I met someone, I couldn't—I couldn't do this anymore. Keep juggling everything. I knew once I met someone I cared about, I'd have to deal with it. And I'm scared—" He had to stop; his throat closed. Finally, in a tight voice, he said, "I'm fucking terrified of dealing with it."

"Jay," Nico whispered, and his hand shifted on the rail like he might reach out.

"So, you deserve to know that. There's a lot going on in my life right now. And I'm not handling any of it well. And I told North and Shaw, and they said I wanted you to be my fuck doll—"

"Excuse me?" Nico murmured.

"—and that's not what I want, and I keep feeling like I'm banging my head against the wall."

The smile on Nico's face had faded slowly as Jadon spoke. Now, his expression unreadable, he watched Jadon for a long moment. Then he wiggled his fingers. When Jadon didn't do anything, he made a vexed noise and wiggled them again. "Scoot, Jay. I want to hold your hand."

So, Jadon scooted. He wrapped Nico's hand in his own. A moment later, Nico threaded their fingers together.

"You don't have to do anything," Nico whispered. "You don't have to say anything. You don't have to be anything. I shouldn't have told you that tonight. We're both in a weird place, and I know I put you on the spot. I wanted you to know that I care about you, and I'm happy I know you. Kind of doubly so, I guess, since you also saved my life tonight. But I'm not asking for anything, Jay. I promise."

This time, Jadon did laugh. It was another one of those sounds that felt ripped out of him, and he shook his head. "No, that's not—I love you."

"Jay, you don't have to—"

"Please." Nico didn't say anything, but Jadon shook his head anyway. "I do. I love you, and I didn't think—I don't know. I guess I didn't think I'd ever feel this way again. I had all these reasons. All these lists. All the explanations and justifications and arguments. And then we started talking, and—and I fell in love with you. And I could tell you it's because you're so sensitive, and you understand me, and you make dumb jokes, and you have great taste in movies. And it is those things. But it's also—I don't know how to say it. It happened, Nico. It happened, and everything was different. I was in your dorm room, and your head was on my chest, and it fucking happened. It was like that leap of faith you were talking about. I was on the other side of it, and I realized none of those stupid reasons mattered. None of them made any difference at all. I love you, and I have no idea what to do about it."

When he looked over, Nico's eyes were wet.

Jadon heard what he'd said. "Okay, I understand that didn't sound romantic—"

"I don't want romantic," Nico said, his voice rough. "I want you."

Jadon squeezed his hand.

"Well," Nico said with a note of impatience. "Kiss me, dummy."

Jadon kissed him. The roughness of his split lip was new, but the shape of Nico's mouth was familiar, the taste of him, the way he relaxed and let Jadon's tongue in. Only a little, because they were in a hospital after all.

When he pulled back, fresh tears had spilled and left silvery tracks on Nico's cheeks. "I love you," he whispered.

"I love you too." Jadon kissed Nico's knuckles. "Although I didn't think this was how tonight was going to end."

"You thought you were going to get some booty."

"I thought I'd invite you back to my place to watch a scary movie." Then Jadon grinned. "Netflix and chill."

"No," Nico said, trying to pull his hand free. "I take it all back. I can't. You're disgusting."

Jadon laughed and held on, and Nico settled back onto the bed.

"Do you want me to bring anything? I know it's a pain, staying overnight."

Nico shook his head. "What a waste of a Halloween. I shouldn't even be staying overnight, only they said I couldn't go home unless I had someone who could check on me while I was sleeping."

Jadon gave him a long look.

"Oh." Nico offered a lopsided smile. "Right."

20

Nico

They stopped at Chouteau long enough to collect Nico's bags, and by the
time they got to Jadon's house, it was near two in the morning. It was hard
to make out much of the house in the dark—a ranch, brick, bars on the
windows. Jadon carried the bags to the porch and let Nico inside. He led
Nico through the living room and kitchen, where all the signs of bachelor
living were on full display: the massive TV, the obligatory leather sectional,
the black-and-white prints in black frames. A few throw pillows, Nico
thought. And next time, he'd bring something with some color. Something
for the coffee table, maybe.

"Let me change the sheets," Jadon said as they moved into the
bedroom, "and you can sleep here. I'll make up the sofa—"

Nico pulled his hair hard enough to get Jadon's attention, and then he
kissed him. Jadon was a good kisser—responsive, intense, demanding.

Then Jadon pulled back, breathing a little more quickly, and said, "You
need to rest."

Nico started unbuttoning Jadon's shirt.

"Nico." Jadon wrapped his hand around Nico's. "Tonight—"

Nico met his eyes, and Jadon released his hand.

He undid the buttons carefully, parted the shirt, and ran his hand over
the spandex Super Gay suit. Jadon's body was so warm it almost felt hot.

The muscle beneath the thin layer of fabric was dense and firm. He pulled the spandex up and over Jadon's head, exposing his chest. Wide, dark nipples. enough chest hair that he looked like a man and not a boy. And so much muscle—broad, hard-packed muscle. Nico kissed Jadon's collarbone. He mouthed downward and took a nipple in his mouth, and Jadon let out a breathy, satisfied noise. His split lip still hurt, and his jaw ached from the gag. Jadon slid his fingers into Nico's hair, half-holding him in place, half-caressing.

Kissing his way down Jadon's belly, Nico got to his knees. He undid Jadon's belt and the button on his waistband and lowered his pants. He untied Jadon's shoes.

"Let me—" Jadon said.

Nico shushed him and helped him out of shoes, socks, and pants. Jadon's dick was hard. Nico leaned forward and rubbed his cheek against the head. He breathed in the musk, the slight sourness of Jadon's body and a day's sweat. Slowly, he slid his hands up and down Jadon's quads. Then he leaned in further, burying his nose in Jadon's bush. Jadon's hand found his hair again, tighter this time, gripping. Nico's tongue darted out to lick the root of his cock, and Jadon let out another of those pleased breaths.

He took Jadon's balls into his mouth one at a time, and then, for a while, he played around, trying to fit them both in his mouth. Jadon liked that; he made noises, and his dick got, if anything, harder, occasionally slapping Nico's face. One hand was still firmly tangled in Nico's hair. The other petted Nico's shoulder, careful of the bruises even while, at the same time, he tried to be an attentive partner. Nico wanted to tell him he didn't care, not right then. Right then, he wanted a dick. Specifically, Jadon's dick.

So, he took it. Jadon moaned as Nico wrapped his lips around his dick, as he ran his tongue along the underside. He tried to take more, gagged, backed off, and tried again. It took him a few more attempts to get Jadon into his throat, and then Jadon grunted, and his hand knotted in Nico's hair until it hurt.

"Shit," Jadon gasped. "You are so fucking tight."

Nico settled in and went to work. He used his tongue. He used his lips. He stroked the base of Jadon's cock with one hand sometimes, and then he took him into his throat again. The beauty was that there wasn't any rush. Even with his lip throbbing and his jaw aching, Nico loved every second of it. Part of it was the pleasure of giving a good blow job—knowing he was making Jadon happy, enjoying the taste and smell and feel of a dick in his mouth, even the forcefulness when Jadon couldn't control himself anymore and started to rut, driving his dick toward Nico's throat, his hand pulling at Nico's hair again. Jadon's dick hardened more, until Nico could feel every vein outlined against the skin, the head ballooning in Nico's throat.

"Stop," Jadon said hoarsely, and he made a weak effort to draw Nico off him. "I'm going to come."

Nico sucked harder, and a moment later, Jadon groaned—the sound part pleasure, part surrender—and shot, his hips bucking wildly. Nico looked up the length of his body, past all the hard muscle to the sculpted beauty of his face. Jadon's eyes were half-closed, and his lashes were dewy.

"Oh my God," Jadon said, his hand sliding to cup Nico's nape as Nico pulled off. "Oh my fucking God."

Chuckling, Nico nudged him toward the bed.

"I think my knees locked up," Jadon said as he sat heavily. He flexed one knee in demonstration. "I think you broke me."

Nico maneuvered him onto a pillow. Jadon caught his arm and drew him down so they were lying next to each other. Nico's hard dick was trapped between their bodies. Jadon's erection had only partially subsided, and it was wet, still leaking against Nico's thigh. Jadon kissed him, his tongue demanding again. One hand followed the curve of Nico's ass before settling at the small of his back. His kisses moved to Nico's ear, and Nico made a weak little noise of pleasure. Jadon doubled down on his attack, using teeth and tongues, until Nico was whimpering, sliding his dick against Jadon's belly.

With a smirk, Jadon pulled back. He bit Nico's neck. Then his shoulder. And Nico realized, with a start that sent a flush through his body, that Jadon was finding all the spots he'd marked the last time, marking him again. He arched his back, his head falling back, leaving him more exposed. A day's worth of stubble scratched and burned against sensitive skin, followed by the wet heat of Jadon's mouth—which soothed at first, and then made him writhe in a different way.

When Jadon got onto his knees and began to move down the bed, Nico caught his wrist.

"I want to make you feel good," Jadon said.

But Nico shook his head. Vic pressing his thumb against the softness of Nico's dick. Vic pushing and poking and manipulating.

Maybe Jadon saw it in his face. He lay down again, the length of his body pressed against Nico's. He ran a hand down Nico's flank. Then he rubbed Nico's belly in slow circles. He took Nico in his hand, and Nico caught his wrist again.

"Okay," Jadon murmured, releasing him. "That's okay. What can I do for you?"

Another time, another place, another Nico—he would have turned it into a fight. But his heart was thumping wildly in his chest, and those waves of heat kept rolling through his body, and Nico was closer to the brink of crying than shouting. And hard. He was still hard.

Jadon made a quieting noise and took Nico in his arms. He kissed him again, tightening the embrace, adjusting their bodies until they were pressed together. Nico's dick brushed Jadon's belly, and then it pressed more firmly there as Jadon drew them even closer together. Jadon was hard again too, his cock sliding along the crease of Nico's thigh. He kissed Nico again, kissed Nico's jaw, kissed the side of his throat. He attacked his ear, but slowly and steadily, and Nico whimpered. He rutted against Jadon's belly. The need was incredible, but every time Nico thought he was getting close,

Vic flashed into his mind, and his hips stuttered, and he fell back from the brink.

Jadon shushed him again, and then he moved back to look Nico in the eye.

"I think it's not going to happen tonight," Nico mumbled, glancing down.

Strong fingers carded the hair above Nico's ear. "That's all right. If it doesn't happen, it doesn't happen." Then those same fingers moved to Nico's chin, tilting his head back. "Will you try something else, though? One more thing."

"I don't—"

But surprisingly, Jadon's fingers tightened on his jaw—not enough to hurt, but the message was clear. Jadon's darkly sandy eyes met Nico's, held him, and the silence was a second message that Nico couldn't mistake. Then Jadon said, "Suck my cock."

Nico let out a ragged little breath.

"Did you hear me?"

Nico nodded.

"What?"

Wetting his lips, Nico gave a little bob of his head. "Yes. Yeah, okay."

Jadon propped himself up with pillows, hands behind his head, biceps swelling. His cock lay heavy and hard against his belly. Nico took him into his mouth again. His lip was still throbbing from the kisses and the first time he'd sucked Jadon off, but he ignored it, focusing on the sound of Jadon's breath when he took Jadon into his mouth. Jadon took him by the hair, and this time, there was no mistaking the suggestion of control. But Jadon didn't face-fuck him. He didn't thrust at all. He made Nico work, and for some reason, that only made it hotter. Nico's sore jaw made it harder to get the perfect seal he wanted. Drool ran down Jadon's shaft, glistening in thick strands in the dark hair at the root.

"Look at me," Jadon said.

It was hard, with a cock halfway down his throat, but Nico did. Jadon didn't look angry. He didn't look mean. He looked like Jadon, but…more intense: the set of his brows, the line of his mouth. This was the guy who ate vegan power bowls and ran every morning and did Brazilian jiu-jitsu for fun. The guy who, when he chose to exercise it, had a will like iron. Jadon's fingers tightened as a reminder, and Nico moaned around him.

"Rub off on my leg while you get me off."

Nico crawled to straddle Jadon's thigh. It changed the angle of the blow job, and he found himself gagging more, struggling to take Jadon as deeply. If the tightness of Jadon's grip was any indicator, he liked it more that way. Dividing his attention between taking Jadon and rutting against his thigh meant that, for a few minutes, Nico wasn't doing either well. Then he found his rhythm, his hips bucking as his dick scraped across Jadon's hairy quad, his head pumping up and down, the taste of Jadon filling his mouth. To his own surprise, Nico suddenly realized he was close, and he started to whine.

"Look at me," Jadon said again.

Nico met those darkly sandy eyes, the smooth firmness of Jadon's expression. The orgasm seemed to start by inches, rising in him. And then Nico made a low, helpless noise as he came. It felt like something bearing him up. It felt like something pulling him apart by the arms and legs. Somehow, he kept Jadon's dick in his mouth as his world imploded. When his brain kicked on again, he was vaguely aware of the head of Jadon's dick between his lips, Jadon's fist twisting beneath him, and then Jadon's grunt as he sprayed his load.

Nico ended up draped across Jadon. One of Jadon's hands tickled his back, running lightly back and forth. Nico already felt himself sinking under the weight of exhaustion and trauma and excellent sex.

He mumbled, "Well, that was embarrassing."

"That wasn't embarrassing." Jadon laughed. His hand slid slowly back and forth. "That was hot."

Nico put a hand over his eyes.

Another laugh. A surprisingly long one. Jadon shifted them around until they were under the covers, and Nico realized he was about to fall asleep.

He did, however, manage to murmur, "Twice, Jay?"

The last sound he heard before he crashed was more of that gentle laughter.

21

Nico

They started the day slowly. Nico lingered in bed while Jadon made coffee, and then both of them moved out into the kitchen so Jadon could make breakfast—some kind of omelet, if you could call it that when it was made out of egg whites and tofu and an ungodly amount of kale. Nico entertained himself by snooping through the junk mail on Jadon's table: a lot of boutique clothing mailers, which wasn't exactly a surprise considering the clothes Jadon wore; the weekly circulars; an invitation to the Metropolitan PD's annual holiday party.

"I'm going to clean that up today," Jadon said. The embarrassment was audible in his voice. "I'm going to clean the house, actually. I'm sorry, again; I've kind of let things get away from me."

"Literally not a problem at all. It makes my snooping much easier." Nico's phone buzzed, and he checked it and was surprised to see a message from Maya. And then another. And then another. He started laughing as he read them. "Oh my God."

The beaten eggs sizzled as Jadon poured them into the frying pan. "What?"

"Apparently Chapman ripped strips off Gio's ass last night at dinner. Clark said something about Gio and Meza hooking up, and Chapman lost his mind."

"I don't suppose anybody took strips off Clark's ass."

Nico grinned. "Do I hear a tone?"

"You do, as a matter of fact."

"Clark gets away with everything, that's—oh shit." He stared at the next message that had come through.

"What? What happened?"

"Dr. Young asked Maya why I wasn't at dinner. She wanted to talk to me about applying to the doctoral program at Wash U."

Jadon brought the omelets to the table and touched Nico's cheek. "That sounds like good news."

"It is. I don't know. I mean, I guess it is."

"It's good news."

Nico opened his mouth to reply but his phone vibrated again. This time, he groaned.

"This is a roller coaster of emotions," Jadon said with a laugh.

"We have to go on a date before I leave," Nico said and took a bite of the omelet—and he had to admit, it was surprisingly good. "Maya's orders. A real one, not eating dinner together and pretending we're friends. Otherwise, she will actually kill me. That's literally what the text says."

Jadon dropped into the chair opposite Nico. He wore joggers and a hoodie that said DRINK TEA–RUN–BE HAPPY, and he had bedhead because he hadn't fixed his hair yet, and he tucked one foot under his other leg to keep it warm. It was so adorable that the universe was probably on cuteness overload. And then Nico heard his own thoughts with a kind of distant horror and wondered if he was legally obligated to turn in his bitch card now.

Without appearing to notice any of Nico's internal dilemma, Jadon checked his phone. "Emery's supposed to be here in about three hours."

"Which means he'll be here in two and a half."

Jadon looked a question at him.

"Don't ask," Nico said. "It's too much. This is still the honeymoon phase."

That made Jadon laugh, but all he said was "A date, huh?"

"At least one."

"A real one."

"It has to be a real one. We can't eat barbeque and jerk each other off."

"I kind of liked that one, but yeah, it might be a little early in the morning for barbeque."

One of the bits of tofu was the perfect size, and it hit Jadon in the cheek.

Laughing, he wiped his face. "All right, here we go."

"Let me change."

"Nope, no changing."

"Jadon, it's a date. I have to change."

"You told me twice this morning that you're looking forward to not getting out of your pajamas—what did you say? 'Ever again in this lifetime'?"

"That was before I knew you were taking me to one of the city's fanciest restaurants."

"Nice try."

"Tickets to a sold-out musical that's been sweeping the country."

Jadon got out of the chair, took Nico's hands, and pulled him to his feet.

"I meant on a riverboat cruise," Nico said.

"Yes, Nico, I'm taking you on a riverboat cruise this morning."

"I changed my mind. I don't want to go on a real date."

It was lucky for Jadon that Nico's pajamas, that morning, consisted of Wroxall sweatpants and a tank that said nothing but I LOVE and then had a silhouette of a rooster. Sneakers and a jacket completed the outfit, at least temporarily, and he let Jadon chivvy him out to the car.

They drove in comfortable silence. Jadon put on music, and after a couple of songs by Bob Vylan and Better than Bullets, a familiar song came on.

"Is this Kumbia Queers?"

Jadon shrugged. "You said you liked them. I thought I'd give them a try. I like them."

Nico settled back into his seat. A few minutes later, he realized he was still smiling.

Then Green Day came on, and he had to take away all of Jadon's points.

The sky was blue and clear, and it made Nico think of how glass could look blue sometimes. The rain had moved out, and in its place, the sun shone down, warming the November day. They drove along the Mississippi, and the river was muddy and riffled with light. Ahead of them, the Arch caught the sun and became incandescent.

"The Arch?" Nico asked when Jadon exited the highway and headed toward the structure. "Really?"

"Have you ever been?"

"No."

Jadon laughed. "But?"

"I don't know."

"Do you want to do something else?"

"No."

Jadon glanced over at him.

"I don't want to do something else," Nico said. "I'm excited. I'm officially excited."

For some reason, that made Jadon laugh again.

They parked and hurried across the landscaped grounds. The breeze off the water was stiff and chilly, and even with the sun, Nico was glad to follow the ramp down below the Arch and enter the museum. For a while, they wandered around, looking at exhibits, learning about steamboats and Manifest Destiny and the building of the Arch. Not once, Nico noticed, did Jadon point out a historical inaccuracy, or an anachronism, or try to debate (with Nico, of all people) Jeffersonian democracy. He held Nico's hand, and he let Nico lead, and when Nico pointed something out, he nodded, or he leaned closer to read the text, or he said something simple and usually thoughtful.

When it came time to take the tram to the top of the Arch, they got in line and were loaded into the tiny cars. Poor Jadon was so big that his knees bumped the man across from him, but the guy laughed and waved it off, and the woman next to him smiled at Nico and took out an issue of *Country Living* like they were going to be there for a few hours.

At the top, they reversed the process, unloading into a stream of people moving onto the observation deck. The windows looking out were small and a little cloudy—either from age or the weather or both—but Nico could see, on one side, the industrial build-up on the Illinois shore, and then the grit of East St. Louis, and miles and miles of farmland quilted together beyond. On the other side of the Arch, he looked down on St. Louis: the Old Courthouse, Busch Stadium, the skyscrapers of downtown. It was disorienting, looking down from that height. Maybe Jadon knew, because he put his hand at the small of Nico's back. Or maybe he did it because he wanted to touch Nico. Either way, Nico didn't mind.

And then it hit him, for the first time all morning, that he was going home.

"What are you doing for Thanksgiving?" he asked.

"Some years, I go back to Iowa. Some years, I stay here." He shrugged. "This year, I'm staying here. What are you doing for Thanksgiving?"

"Going to Emery's."

"If you change your mind—"

"Perfect. I'm coming here."

Jadon grinned. "Are you visiting your parents for Christmas?"

"God, no. I'm spending it with you. You've now been officially informed."

The grin spread. "I'm supposed to visit my moms."

"Perfect. They're going to love me."

"Yes," he said, "they will."

"And that's it? Are those the only two times I'm going to see you?"

Jadon nudged him toward the other side of the observation deck, where the tram would take them down. "Shocker, I've got a lot of PTO I've accumulated. I could come down for a long weekend if that's not cramping your style."

"We can trade weekends," Nico said. "My schedule is pretty flexible."

"Is it?" Jadon said, and he looked annoyingly smug until Nico elbowed him.

As they waited in line for the tram, a family ahead of them looked like they were nearing meltdown. A manic blond boy was zipping back and forth, clearly in need of one of those parental leashes—or a parental straitjacket. A girl who must have been his sister was screaming, her head thrown back as she spun in a circle, windmilling her arms and clearly trying to clobber anyone who got within reach. The dad had a donut of thinning black hair, and a carpet of more black hair on the back of his neck. The mom was a wrung-out dishrag of a woman who was trying to placate both children with candy.

"Do you want kids?" Nico asked.

Jadon laughed—literally—until they got on the tram.

"Don't forget," he said as they started down. "You're supposed to turn in the revised copy of your paper before Thanksgiving, or they won't consider it for the edited collection."

Nico turned a startled look on him.

"I wasn't asleep the whole time," Jadon said, a smile slanting across his face. "And I'm going to text you every day to make sure you're working on it."

"Oh my God."

"I might even tell Emery."

"Jadon, I know you think you're joking, but I need you to understand that you cannot do that."

That slanting smile widened.

"Please," Nico said, and it felt dangerously close to begging. "One time, I let him see my bibliography, and he made me cry. And that was when he was trying to be nice."

They were almost to the bottom when Nico remembered something he'd seen on Jadon's table. "Speaking of responsibilities, you know you have to go to that party, right?"

"What party?"

Nico made a despairing noise. "The work one." Still nothing. "The department holiday party. You've got the invitation on the table."

"Oh."

"Unh-uh, Jadon. You have to go."

Jadon made a face.

"That's part of showing these assholes they've got nothing on you. You're not going to give them a single reason to force you out."

"I think the stuff with Vic will help, actually. They won't be able to get rid of me for at least six months."

"I know you think it's cute to joke about this, but I'm serious: you're going to the party."

Hands raised in surrender, Jadon said, "Okay, okay."

Nico watched him to be sure he'd made his point.

"We can bring a plus one," Jadon said tentatively.

"Obviously I'm going," Nico said as the tram rocked to a stop. "Otherwise you'd sneak out in the middle of it to stop a bank robbery or something."

They filed out of the tram, shuffling toward the exit with the rest of the throng. Long weekends, Nico thought. And holidays. But if things went well, he'd be graduating in the spring, and—

"Stop worrying about it," Jadon said, his voice brushing Nico's ear. "We'll figure it out."

Nico looked over his shoulder.

"Yes, I know you're going to have to move for your doctoral program," Jadon said. "I told you: we'll make it work."

"You know this is a public setting. It would be a great location for our first fight."

"Watch your step."

The worst part was that Nico stumbled on the ramp anyway. He didn't mind, though; it was kind of nice to have someone catch your arm.

Outside, the wind whipped his hair, and he blinked against the sunlight. They walked together, the Arch gleaming in a silver band above them. A few yards ahead, the family from the observation deck had officially begun their meltdown.

"That was so stupid," the boy was screaming. "I hated it! Give me your phone!"

The dad eagerly produced his phone, and the boy sulked off with it.

"I noticed you didn't answer me about kids," Nico said.

Jadon bumped him. "Subjectivity is truth. Who knows? Maybe those parents are having a great time."

Nico doubted it; the mom was crying into what appeared to be a burrito wrapper while the dad shielded himself from a barrage of blows from the daughter.

Instead of heading to the car, he and Jadon walked to look out over the river. He found himself thinking about the museum, about the catenary curve of the Arch, the white-hot band of it like something out of a book or a movie—a portal to another world. And that's what it was meant to represent, after all. A gateway to a vast unknown. And then Nico corrected himself. Not another world. More of it. Whatever came next.

The sound of vast waters, the toot from a barge, the cry of a gull. The wind shifted into his face, and his eyes stung. Light splintered on the water, and he thought of the morning he had seen the Jewel Box, how it had become a prism, breaking everything and making it more beautiful. Subjectivity is truth; he had said that, and Jadon had remembered. They had talked about Kierkegaard. And about love. About what it meant to love someone, truly love them. Responsibility. Commitment. Choice.

Jadon's arms slipped around him, and in the lee of his body, he was warm. Jadon kissed his hair. And he must have been remembering too (or, much scarier, reading Nico's thoughts).

"I choose you," Jadon whispered. "I'll always choose you."

Nico turned his head for a kiss. "I choose you too." And then horror struck: "Oh my God. I'm going to have to introduce you to Emery."

The Kiss Principle

Keep reading for a sneak preview of *The Kiss Principle*, the next book in Hazardverse: Sidetracks.

1

"Keep it simple, stupid."

Augustus sounded like he was trying not to laugh. "That is a terrible name for a life plan."

"It's not a life plan, sugar-tits." It took me a moment to come up with: "It's a life philosophy."

"It's terrible either way."

"Sorry, Augustus. Not all of us had the opportunity to enroll at Dong Knockers University."

"I have no idea what that means, but I'm going to take it as a compliment."

"It's not. It's a dig about you being a dong knocker."

On the other end of the call, Augustus sighed. Then his voice changed, and he said, "I'm talking to your Uncle Fer."

"Is that Lana? Put her on the phone."

"You want to say hi?" Augustus said, still speaking to Lana. "I don't know, sweetheart. He's pretty busy."

"Give her the phone, monkey balls!"

"All right, here you go."

Fumbling and scraping noises came, and then Lana said, "Hi, Uncle Fer." Her voice was flat, but even the diminished affect couldn't hide her excitement. It made me smile. "Papi's taking me snorkeling."

"Swimming," Augustus said in the background, and I could hear the smile in his voice.

Lana then launched into a convoluted explanation of...something. It had to do with the pool and with another girl and I thought maybe there was something in there about *Finding Nemo*. Finally, Augustus's voice came closer as he said, "Okay, let me talk to Uncle Fer now."

"Bye, Uncle Fer!"

"Bye, princess."

"You never had a cute nickname for me," Augustus said.

"What's a cute nickname for a crotch fungus you can't get rid of?"

In the background, Theo said, "Did I hear 'crotch fungus'?"

"Fer," Augustus said.

Theo made an understanding noise.

"Tell him to shut the fuck up," I said.

"He says he loves you," Augustus said.

"No, I didn't, dick-snot."

"Hi, Fer," Theo said. "I love you too."

"Tell him he's an infected ulcer." Genius struck. "An ass ulcer."

"He's got a new life plan," Augustus said. "He's going to keep his life simple."

Theo laughed way too long about that.

"I am going to keep my life simple, fuckwad."

"You should hear him," Augustus said, still talking to Theo. "It's adorable."

"You know what's not going to be adorable? When you and Theo send out Christmas cards of you swinging on an ass hook in your sex dungeon."

"You're talking about our asses a lot today."

"That's because that's prime real estate for you two butt pirates."

"Do you think about our asses a lot?"

"This is what I'm talking about. This is the kind of shit I'm not going to have to deal with anymore."

"Oh Fer."

I chose to ignore that. "You're off my hands now because you're officially the responsibility of the senior living center you call a home."

"That wasn't one of your best ones."

"And Mom's getting married at the end of the year."

"God, I hope not."

"He's barely older than a cumstain, but he seems like he's serious, and that means she'll be out of my hair too." Augustus's silence was unhappy, so I hurried past that part. "Chuy is doing his usual fuck-all, but he's clean, and that means he's officially not my problem either."

"I don't think you're supposed to say clean. I think you're supposed to say he's not using drugs."

"And now that I actually have a chance to live my own life, I'm going to keep it simple. I'm going to smoke a lot of weed. I'm going to watch whatever I want on TV. And I'm finally going to be done with fucking pharma sales." I didn't want to sound like an enormous geek like Augustus, but I couldn't keep myself from adding, "I've got a fucking fantastic chance at a new job."

"What? Fer, that's amazing. What job? Where?"

"Do you remember Lou?"

Augustus groaned.

"Knock it off," I told him.

"Are you serious?"

"She's got one of the biggest grows in the county. Business is fucking booming."

"I'm not worried about her business."

"She's my friend."

"She gave me panties for my sixteenth birthday. In front of all my friends. Before I was out."

"That was a compliment. She said you had the ass for them."

"She said my wedding photos would be me getting gangbanged by a crew of roughnecks."

"That was a compliment too. Like, stamina. And a willingness to please."

A (horrified) pause. "What is wrong with you?"

"What's wrong with you, you ungrateful little shit?"

"Why do I ever talk to you? Why do I pick up the phone?"

"It's a great fucking job, Augustus. Head of sales for the entire fucking grow. It'd mean a pay cut at first, but that business is going to keep getting bigger, and I can swing the pay because—"

"You're going to keep your life simple," Augustus said drily.

"Fuckin' A."

"Okay. I guess we'll see how that goes."

"What the fuck does that mean?"

He sounded like he was grinning when he said, "Bye, Fer. See you tomorrow."

Acknowledgments

My deepest thanks go out to the following people (in alphabetical order):

Alyssa, for lending me her typo telescope, for help with continuity, and for that most generous of phrasings "Chouteau spelling throughout."

Antara, for spotting Heely vs. Heeley.

Nichole Reeder, for helping catch even more errors that made it through somehow.

Mark Wallace, for sending along the errors he found, and for his thoughtful analysis of the book—especially chapter sixteen—in addition to his kind words about the story.

And thanks to everyone else who messaged me, commented, or otherwise pointed out a problem! I'm so grateful for the help!

About the Author

For advanced access, exclusive content, limited-time promotions, and insider information, please sign up for my mailing list at **www.gregoryashe.com**.

www.ingramcontent.com/pod-product-compliance
Lightning Source LLC
Chambersburg PA
CBHW022134240626
47153CB00007B/2367